BENEATH THE LOW LIGHT

BENEATH THE LOW LIGHT

Donald Hacker

CHIVERS

THORNDIKE

This Large Print book is published by BBC Audiobooks Ltd, Bath, England and by Thorndike Press®, Waterville, Maine, USA.

Published in 2005 in the U.K. by arrangement with the Author.

Published in 2005 in the U.S. by arrangement with Donald Hacker.

U.K. Hardcover ISBN 1–4056–3441–3 (Chivers Large Print))
U.S. Softcover ISBN 0–7862–8015–8 (British Favorites)

The text of this Large Print edition is unabridged.
Other aspects of the book may vary from the original edition.

Set in 16 pt. New Times Roman.

Printed in Great Britain on acid-free paper.

British Library Cataloguing in Publication Data available

Library of Congress Cataloging-in-Publication Data

Hacker, Donald.
    Beneath the low light / by Donald Hacker.
        p.   cm.
    "Thorndike Press large print British favorites."—T.p. verso.
    ISBN 0–7862–8015–8 (lg. print : sc : alk. paper)
    1. Chemical industry—Fiction. 2. Male friendship—Fiction.
    3. Burnham-on-Sea (England)—Fiction. 4. Large type books.
    I. Title.
PR6108.A325B46 2005
   823'.92—dc22   2005017695

For my daughters, Tracy and Karen

ONE

The sudden ring of the telephone startled the man. Hunched over his desk as he was, his body gave an involuntary jerk as the intruding sound broke his concentration. He reached for the instrument, left-handed, across a desk-top laden with chemical engineering flowsheets and foolscap pages of calculations, while his eyes stayed with the figures before him, and he was so engrossed in his work that he continued to add to a column of the figures while he held the telephone, motionless and impotent, in mid air.

'Hello? Hello?'

Faint, complaining tones piped out at him from the receiver and he hurriedly pressed it to his ear.

'Wallace—'

'Hello, Dave. Dan Pengelly here.' The caller was shouting to make himself heard above a background of clanging metal and hissing steam-traps.

'Yes, Dan?'

'We've run into trouble on Number Four Still—the Iron Lady.'

'More trouble, you mean.'

'More trouble, then, yes! But she's a bitch, Dave; it's no one's fault this time.'

David Wallace pursed his lips as he

contemplated the name plate which sat on the front of his desk. Its lettering read: 'D. Wallace, B.Sc., A. R. I. C. Section Manager. Number Eight Section,' and he thought morosely to himself that he knew every mark, every scratch, every time-faded punctuation mark on the damned thing.

'The pressure is rising fast!' Dan Pengelly's warning chased his wandering thoughts. 'Up to seven, and the mid-still temperature is one hundred and rising. That's ten degrees above normal, for Christ's sake!'

Through the earpiece, Wallace could hear the sounds of running feet on steel-plated platforms and bawling voices in the background, then Pengelly's muted bellow as he turned away from the telephone to yell instructions. The man at the desk knew that the sounds emanated from process workers in the Still House as they scurried frantically around the one-hundred foot high iron monster of a still in their efforts to regain control.

'We can't hold her, Dave!'

Wallace cursed freely with some annoyance. 'Are the instruments giving true readings?' he queried. 'When were they last checked?'

'I had the fitter check all the instruments and they're accurate to within plus or minus one degree. It looks like the Raschig Ring packing has collapsed,' Pengelly said shortly, 'that is, if you want my opinion, of course. I'll have to shut her down, anyway, so you'd better come over?' The Somerset man had fifteen years' experience on that particular type of process plant, and he sounded justifiably peeved that the Section Manager had queried such elementary precautions.

Wallace grinned into the mouthpiece at the caller's discomfiture. He could imagine the language Dan Pengelly would use when he replaced the receiver. 'Yes, Dan, I'll be with you in a few minutes.' He gazed down on the papers which lay before him. 'Dan?' he added quickly, before the other had time to hang up.

'Yes?'

'One tank will do it.'

The telephone remained silent.

'Did you hear?'

'I heard you.'

'It's safe enough.'

There was no reply.

'It'll be all right, I tell you! We need just one tank full; twenty tonnes of liquid gas. I've repeated my calculations.' Wallace leaned over the desk and peered at his figures intently. 'When it vaporizes and expands that will produce a big enough cloud.'

'You are the scientist—you should know. There'll be one hell of a pile of corpses lying about the place if anything goes wrong.'

'Nothing can go wrong. When I come over, can we take a look at the storage tanks?'

'When you come over, the first thing we'll

3

do is get this cursed Iron Lady sorted out.'

The legs of the steel-framed chair scraped long turnings of grime off the floor covering of brown linoleum as David Wallace replaced the telephone on to its cradle and thrust himself away from the desk. He was a big, muscular man, just under six feet in height, with powerful legs and shoulders which denoted a youth much occupied with sport. Now, at twenty-nine years of age, he carried too much weight as a padding of fat which stretched his shirt tight across his back, and as a paunch which indicated too high an intake of alcohol. His brown eyes were quick of movement, like those of a fox. Slight tints of grey prematurely coloured the black thatch of hair that curled above an intelligent face, and he spoke with a marked Welsh accent. The desk filled one corner of the tiny room, the walls of which hung with curling flowsheets, process charts and endless minutiae, all stuck to a coat of yellowing emulsion paint by slivers of Sellotape. An outdated Bristol Omnibus Company's timetable, pinned to the wall above the room's only radiator, flapped rhythmically in currents of rising heat. Uselessly, it proclaimed that operating times between Burnham-on-Sea and Bristol would be as given; that asterisked schedules were liable to suspension without notice. Alongside it a garishly coloured calendar strove to make Smith's Stainless Steel Nuts and Bolts sexually

4

provocative.

Wallace surveyed his dingy surroundings and muttered aloud: 'Not for much longer.' As he became aware of the sound of his own voice he checked himself and thought: 'God! Don't start talking to yourself, you fool.'

He rose to his feet and gathered up the flowsheets which lay open on his desk into a yard-long tube, then he carefully folded the foolscap sheets before locking both into the top drawer of his desk. That done, he rolled down his shirt sleeves and pulled on his coat which had hung from the back of his chair and reached a donkey-jacket down from a plastic knobbed coat-stand which stood alongside the office door. The jacket had been black when new; now it was punctured and pocked with families of small holes scattered over its fabric, holes burned there by the viciously corrosive action of stray droplets of concentrated nitric acid. Finally, he donned a white safety helmet.

From his office he walked to the end of the corridor of the Section Office and peered out through the glass-panelled external door. Droplets of rain pattered on the window as he stared towards the towering bulk of the Still House which loomed three hundred yards distant. He hunched down into the upturned collar of his donkey-jacket and stepped out into a light, driving rain to make his way along a narrow concrete strip of path. As he followed the path, a maze of pipework criss-crossed the sky above his head, like some giant spider's web that held him under its lattice. Through it, in the outside world, he could see rain-clouds gathering to the north-west, over the River Severn; clouds which slanted fronts of sleet on to the rhine-chequered Somerset plain on which Forsters was built.

Forsters! Forsters International Synthetics. A gigantic, sprawling complex of chemical plant which spread out over two square miles of the low-lying, ranging wetlands of North Somerset, ringed by the Mendip Hills to the south and by Bristol to the north-east.

Forsters! Built by the ingenuity of man on this sea-abandoned land. A bustling industrial complex, owned and operated by the powerful chemical combine that was Forsters. From its conglomeration of laboratories and chemical engineering plant, this multi-million pound company spawned an enormous and widely diversified range of products. The company's export account alone ran into several million pounds sterling a year. Management organization at Forsters was similar to that of comparable establishments; a Board of Directors, Production and Accounts Directors, Area Managers and Section Managers, in descending order of hierarchy. Physically, the factory was split into twelve production sections, each with a graduate production chemist or chemical engineer as

Section Manager. Two Area Managers each controlled six Section Managers.

The leader of Number Eight Section hurried along the walkway which led to the Still House. Around him, immense and intricate structures, sculpted from compatible metals into the chemical engineering complex that was Number Eight Section, dwarfed him to insect-like proportions, Whistling puffs of steam and foetid breaths of red-brown nitric acid fume erupted from its innards, like the gasps of some great, slumbering dragon. David Wallace finally shouldered his way through a heat-retaining swing door and stepped inside the Still House. He stood motionless for a moment and gazed upwards through floors of latticed steel as he remembered his very first visits during his student days to large scale plant similar to this, and he realised that he still felt the same sensations of awe, like confronting ogres in a darkened cave. From the ground level where he now paused, the base of Number Four Still, known to all who worked on her as the Iron Lady, rose as a giant column through five floor levels, plated steel floors over which men scurried to serve the iron she-monster with feed stocks of acids and liquors, and to bleed her body of samples and liquids. Successive flights of metal stairways gave access to the top of the totem, high in the roof of the House.

7

Wallace climbed the first two flights and, on reaching the second floor, turned from the stairway and made for a control panel set in a wall at the far end of the room. A man stood there, with his back toward the approaching newcomer, concentrating intently on the instrument console before him and occasionally bending to peer into the face of one of its innumerable dials. Wallace strode across the dimly-lit second floor and stepped out of the gloom into the broad band of fluorescent light which illuminated the panel area. He had to raise his voice to a shout in order to make himself heard above the belching, rumbling noises issuing from the iron belly of the still.

'Trouble, Dan?'

The man who turned in answer to his shout was thirty-seven years old, but looked older and more worldly wise than the average man of that age. He was tall, taller than Wallace by a good two inches, with a lean and rangy muscularity about him that denoted a high level of physical fitness. Among his ancestors were gypsy travellers who roamed the West Country, and the panel lights caught at high, Romany cheekbones and a strong jawline. Wallace knew from past experience that it was a jawline that could clench with quick and fiery rage and that Dan Pengelly's temper was always on a short fuse.

' 'Fraid so. The goddam pressure keeps

rising and the temperatures are all over the place. Do you think the packing has collapsed?' The man's voice rolled with a strong North Somerset accent; his movements had an easy grace. Dan Pengelly, senior process foreman of Section Eight, glanced quickly along the line of instruments on the console as he spoke. Then, since a reply was not immediately forthcoming, he snapped: 'What about it, Dave?'

'Eh?' It was obvious that the mind of the Section Manager was not concentrated on the problem at hand. 'Yes—well, what's the gravity?'

'Fourteen hundred, but it's up and down all the time. We'll be pumping low gravity acid into the make tank if we aren't careful.'

'She's going under suction, Mr. Wallace!' A white-clad process worker wearing protective visor and gloves yelled the warning from his station on the far side of the Iron Lady. 'She's fuming off!' There was urgency in the man's voice as he pointed upwards, high above their heads, to where swathes of red-brown nitric acid fume puffed from seals in the still. He knew what might happen, as they all did, if they allowed the delicate balance of the concentration process to become upset so that the toxic nitric fume filled the building. Breathe too much of that stuff, and oedema of the lungs sets in to drown the victim in his own secretions.

9

'Shut the still down,' Wallace decided, albeit belatedly, 'and let the maintenance fitters start work. When I get back to the office I'll make out the necessary clearance forms for them to strip the Iron Lady down so that we can see where the fault lies.'

The foreman set about issuing instructions to his process workers, while Wallace waited with ill-disguised impatience. He pushed his safety helmet to the back of his head with some irritation and wiped his perspiring brow. He had a meeting arranged which included the tall, senior foreman.

When Pengelly returned, Wallace said: 'Steve and Ian will be in the canteen by now.'

'Should be.'

'I did say ten o'clock.'

Behind them, the Iron Lady gurgled and groaned as men deprived her of her feeds and her heat and her power. Soon she would grow cold and revert to being simply an immobile mass of metal, until the day when her keepers gave her life once more. The footsteps of the two men rang out as they walked across the steel-plated floor. When they reached the top of the flight of steps, Dan Pengelly placed his hand on his companion's shoulder. Wallace stopped.

'Yes, Dan?'

'You be careful with Steve.'

'I will, I promise you.'

'Aye—'

For several long seconds the tall foreman held his grip on the other's shoulder while continuing to gaze into his eyes. Then he released his hold, and turned to lead the way down the metallic steps, only to stop halfway down the flight and look back up at Wallace. 'You realise what it means? This job you've planned will be no picnic. If we are caught they won't let us off lightly.'

'It's all right,' the answer came softly. 'I know what I'm about.'

'I worry about you, sometimes,' the Somerset man said with grim paternalism. 'I do! I worry about you.'

Wallace paused awkwardly, his way blocked. There seemed to be no appropriate answer and he knew better than to make a facetious reply. It was simply the older man's way of reminding him that he must play his part well.

'We can take a look at the ammonia tanks after we collect Steve and Ian,' he said quietly.

As the taller man turned and led the way to the ground floor, Wallace smiled with some affection at the broad back which preceded him. Dan Pengelly had been a sergeant with the Desert Rats in North Africa during the war. He was strong and tough, a real hard man, more than reliable in a tight corner, and Wallace held him in high esteem.

The tiny staff annexe of Section Eight's canteen hung thick with tobacco smoke. Droplets of nicotine had condensed from the

11

heavily contaminated atmosphere on to the insides of the closed windows, and ran down the dirty panes of glass in brown trails. Two men were seated at one of the gaudy, plastic-topped tables which filled the room, and they both looked up from steaming mugs of strongly-brewed tea as the door opened and Wallace and his companion entered.

Steve Williams had not altered appreciably since the war years. Wallace knew this from Williams' personnel file which contained a photograph of his fellow Welshman in sergeant's uniform, submitted when he applied to join the firm. The same source of information also gave details of Williams' return from the battle of Rouen on the Seine with a terrible gunshot wound; of his long recuperation in military hospitals until that wound was healed, at least physically. There was always a restlessness about the little Celt, a hint of rebellious savagery never far below the surface, but no one knew whether these qualities were inherent in the man or whether they were a legacy of wounds which never heal. Of course, physically he had aged since the war-time photograph was taken, that was inevitable over a period of eighteen years, but his only concessions to his thirty-eight years were traces of silver in his black, curly hair, a thickening of his waistline, and a coarsening of his features. He stood about five-feet nine inches in height and his short body was tough and wiry, characteristic of men from the mining valleys of South Wales. His dark eyes glowed with the brooding fires of his ancestry. Here was a man to have as an ally, but never as an enemy, and Wallace knew that he must be on guard against the excesses that erupted from the little man's mercurial nature.

Their home valleys were adjacent amid the high mountains of Wales; Wallace's home had been the village of Maesycwmmer in the Rhymney valley while his compatriot's birthplace had been the mining town of Blaina. Both men had migrated to Somerset, as many Welsh people do, and in fact they now lived at opposite ends of the Esplanade at Burnham-on-Sea. Steve Williams lodged with his younger sister and her husband in one of the tall, Victorian houses overlooking the beach. There was a wife, somewhere, but they had separated and the little man never spoke of her; any attempted conversation on the subject met with a wall of morose hostility, and most men who knew him found it wiser not to probe too deeply into his private life. He was employed at Forsters as a services foreman, which meant that he supervised the supply of services such as water, power and steam, to the process sections, Number Eight Section included. He was known as a capable and efficient foreman, even though he had a curiously mocking attitude to authority which had almost landed him in trouble on several occasions, but then, it was a faceless authority which had sent him out to be cut down by a Schmeisser bullet when little more than a youth.

Ian Myers was one year older than Steve Williams, though, like Pengelly, he looked older than his years. Myers had been a Navy diver and had worked on the Mulberry Harbour during the invasion of France. The only bachelor among the three ex-sergeants, he lived with his widowed mother in a house on the sprawling Highbridge council estate, on the south side of Burnham. He was a big man in the real sense of the word; as tall as Dan Pengelly but without his lean build. His chest was huge and barrel-shaped, his weight was over sixteen stone and, as with many big men, he was quiet to the point of shyness. His hands were enormous, completely hiding the mug of tea held clutched in both fists. Steady, stolid Myers had joined the work force at Forsters at about the same time as Steve Williams, after their war was over and both had been demobilized. Now, eighteen years later, the Somerset-born Myers bossed the gangs of riggers at the plant, though he still worked on a part-time basis for a commercial diving firm based in Falmouth. His Royal Navy training and years of experience made him much in demand for such work and he would often travel away on week-ends to make dives.

The two seated men eyed the newcomers as

they entered the room.

'So, the high command has arrived!' Steve Williams said with a grin, though his eyes did not reflect the smile on his lips. At his side, Ian Myers sat quite still with cup to mouth, and slid a calculating gaze from face to face without speaking.

Wallace seated himself opposite the two veterans as Pengelly ordered and brought two mugs of tea to the table.

'The van is in at eleven-fifteen,' Wallace said to nobody in particular. He sipped at the muddy-looking liquid in his white, china mug.

It was as well for the four grouped men that the room was otherwise unoccupied, for there was an obvious tension between them which was only partly masked by Steve Williams' manner.

'Did you get that information from Barnfield?'

'Yes.'

'He's not suspicious of these questions you ask about the security van?'

'I don't just walk up to him and ask him outright, you know!' There was a snap in Wallace's tone; it was strange how the aggressively mocking approach of his fellow Welshman always managed to rile him, but he smiled quickly, almost too quickly, in an effort to stifle any animosity which might flare between them. He knew that he needed Williams, needed to harness his warrior-like

15

nature and to channel the man's aggression to do his bidding, if the crazy scheme was to have any chance of success.

'That wouldn't surprise me,' Williams muttered in an aside to Myers, though loud enough for all to hear.

Wallace made a placating gesture with his hands. 'Believe me,' he said, 'I've been cultivating Barnfield for months. I guarantee that he won't remember anything out of the ordinary.'

The little, dark Welshman allowed his scowl to relax. 'Okay, okay,' he said abruptly, 'let's go if we're goin', then!'

Pengelly gulped at his mug. 'For God's sake, Taff. Anyway, Dave wants to look at the ammonia stocks before we go to admin. He's got some figurin' to do.'

'Figurin'?' Williams echoed. 'It's a bit late for that, isn't it?' Insolently, he studied Wallace through a skein of smoke that writhed upwards from an unextinguished cigarette end smouldering in the ashtray between them. 'We don't want any last minute changes in the set-up. I thought you had worked out your side of things?'

David Wallace stared blankly at the services foreman. To have months of hard and exacting work dismissed so contemptuously, in so few words, stretched Wallace's tolerance to its limit. He eyed the little man bleakly. 'I simply wanted to check exactly how much

16

liquefied ammonia Dan and I have managed to abstract from the process. We need twenty tonnes of the stuff before we can hit them, and we must be close to that by now. I'm not altering the plan in any way.'

One of the plants under Wallace's control on Section Eight was a Pressure Oxidation Plant which operated by burning gaseous ammonia at a very high temperature as it passed over a platinum and rhodium gauze catalyst. This process produced nitric acid fume, which was in turn condensed and then absorbed in water to make nitric acid. It was a process common to many chemical combines, and in Forsters' case the nitric acid was further concentrated to sixty per cent strength before either being sold as such, or being pumped to Section Five where it was converted to artificial nitrogenous fertilizer. Over the last four or five runs on his Oxidation plant, with the assistance of Dan Pengelly as his senior process foreman, Wallace had 'removed' some twenty tonnes of the liquid gas, and this quantity now lay hidden in one of the reserve ammonia storage tanks, reserve tank 'A', to which only the two men could gain access.

'How do you "lose" that much ammonia?' Myers asked, after Wallace had told them what quantity he expected there to be in 'A' tank.

'Does it matter, for Christ's sake?' Williams interposed.

17

'It's a good point,' said Wallace. 'For the last five runs on the Pressure Oxidation Plant,' he explained, 'I've entered the plant efficiency as being three or four per cent lower than average. We often get "highs" and "lows" in efficiencies for any one of a multitude of reasons, for example, the gauze maybe torn or "poisoned" by impurities, or the condenser tubes may be partly blocked, so nobody worries unduly about that size percentage variation on such a process. So, for several months we have used less ammonia than we claim to have used, and Dan has been pumping the excess liquefied ammonia into storage tank "A" in the reserve bund, the door of which is kept locked by Dan who holds the key. It's foolproof.'

'So was the Titanic,' Williams quipped. He pushed his chair back noisily and stood up. 'Let's go.'

It was Friday the 28th of June. The staff at Forsters were paid on the last Friday of each month and, in many cases, salaries were paid directly into bank accounts. However, a large number of staff, including most of the foremen, still collected their monthly salaries in cash as they had done when they were weekly-paid process workers. In addition, the huge workforce of weekly-paid employees, including a large number of contractors' men, collected their pay every Friday from several branch wages offices dotted about the

18

complex, the total payroll being first delivered by a firm of security specialists to the central cash office in the administration building.

Wallace raised one hand to hold the attention of his companions a moment longer. 'While I speak with Barnfield, you three take a good look around, and particularly look at the items we have discussed. Remember, the bars over the windows and the steel grille above the counter will be our main obstacles. I'll try to prolong my visit so that we all spend as long as possible inside the room. This may be the last time we visit the place together, legally that is, so try to take in every detail that may be of use.' He rose to his feet. 'We can take a quick look at the ammonia tanks, and then we'll collect your pay packets.' He stood to one side to allow the trio to file past him on their way to the door, as he added: 'Though why the hell you don't have your salaries paid into a bank beats me.'

'Bank? Not me!' Steve Williams walked jauntily towards the door and his voice was emphatic. 'I like my money in my hand.'

The rain had stopped by the time the four men left the canteen, and the beginnings of a sea mist had drifted in from the River Severn. They walked in single file along a wet, concrete path towards the Pressure Oxidation Plant, and as he moved along in the silent company of the three veterans, David Wallace felt a sudden sense of apprehension, a first sense of fear at the enormity of the outrage he was to set in motion.

The liquefied ammonia storage compound, which served Section Eight, lay alongside the nitric acid manufacturing Oxidation plant. They walked along the path until, on turning a corner, they were confronted by a fifteen-foot high brick wall which was the bund or retaining wall surrounding the ammonia tanks. Steve Williams peered in through an open door set in the brick wall, though they all knew what lay inside; five ominous-looking, silver-painted cylinders completely filled this main enclosure with their torpedo-like, fifty-foot long and ten-foot diameter, steel bodies. And each tank contained thirty tonnes of liquefied ammonia.

Liquefied ammonia! A murderous substance which, once released from its imprisoning cylinder, would vaporize to become a blinding, toxic cloud of killer gas. Given a major leak, such an enormous cloud of gas would float over the complex and the surrounding countryside that the evacuation of any village in its path would be imperative, and the emergency services at Forsters were always prepared for such a catastrophe. Even now, with no leak, a faint tang of ammonia hung in the air causing their noses to sting and their eyes to water. This was a property of the gas that the scientist in Wallace recognised and welcomed; he knew that the presence of ammonia in the air could be readily detected and that people would run from it in fear.

'God! It's worse than Myers' old socks,' Williams joked and he blinked repeatedly. 'Which tank is our stuff in?'

Pengelly pointed to the locked door of a smaller bund built on to the side of the main storage area. 'We are keeping it in one of the two reserve tanks,' he said. He grinned at the little man's discomfiture. 'I'll open the door, but you'll need a mask if you want to go inside.' The wearing of an emergency respirator was mandatory for everyone who entered the bund.

A dozen Draeger breathing sets hung on the outside of the wall of the compound, and each man took one down and checked that it was charged to two-thousand five-hundred pounds per square inch. It was not necessary to don the face mask, but one was obliged to sling the single bottle of compresssed air at the ready in case of a sudden gas leak. That would give each man thirty minutes of life-support.

They followed Pengelly through the door and into the reserve bund. He stopped before the tank in question, bent down and began to speak, then bent again to check his reading. 'Just over twenty tonnes,' he reported.

'That's what you said we needed.' Williams gripped Wallace's arm. 'That must be enough to do the job, eh?'

The three veterans looked at Wallace expectantly.

'It is! It's more than enough. According to my calculations it will leave a good margin of liquefied gas to spare just in case we need it.'

'Then we can go?' Oddly, it was Myers who pressed Wallace for a reply.

'We can go any time we choose.'

An air of eagerness gripped the four men. They had spent many seemingly endless months in planning, calculating, spying, but now their main weapon of attack was prepared and the project, which had appeared to be little short of fantasy when Wallace first mooted it, took a giant step nearer realization. They had enough gas!

'Now we can take another look at the prize.'

The rain had resumed a mean drizzle as they retraced their footsteps along the path from the storage bund and took to a branch of the concrete walkway which led them to the Section offices.

It was not unusual for the four men to be seen together on the plant since they were in contact with one another several times in the course of a normal working day while pursuing their legitimate affairs. Their combined presence would not cause comment, except of a derisory nature from the workmen. Wallace's yellow and black Hillman Avenger was parked in a cul-de-sac alongside the Section offices. Pengelly joined him in front, the other two in the back.

As Wallace inserted and turned the ignition key he suddenly felt Williams grasp the back of his seat and the seat jerk as the little Welshman pulled himself forward.

'I can tell you what else I want to know,' Williams breathed at the back of Wallace's neck. 'Just how many more dry runs do we have to make? We've made so many sketches of that wages office that I could get a job there as chief cashier.'

'It'll be soon, now, Steve,' Wallace said, 'I promise you. We have sufficient gas, and the other gear we need. I only have to find out exactly when the big holiday payroll is being delivered, and that must be within the next five or six weeks. As soon as I know that, then we can make the final arrangements.' The back of his seat heaved as Williams released his hold on it and dropped back into his own seat alongside Myers, and Wallace powered the car away from his office block, from Section Eight, and out into the hub of the complex.

The administration building for which they were headed lay one mile from Number Eight Section and close to the main entrance to Forsters. It was a building typical of many factory office blocks constructed in the thirties, being originally a red brick, single-storeyed structure, though later years had seen a cluster of more modern steel and glass extensions stuck on to its austere extremities, like so many out-of-place green-houses. As they approached it they could see a dark-blue van belonging to the security firm of Shuritor drawn up outside the front of the block.

'There she is,' Pengelly said in satisfied tones, 'and right on time.'

Wallace swung his car into the staff car park in front of the main offices.

'Right on soddin' time,' Steve Williams echoed as he consulted his wristwatch before peering over the driver's shoulder at the van. 'Only three boy scouts looking after it, as usual.'

'They don't look much like boy scouts to me,' Wallace muttered. 'They look like they can take care of themselves.'

'Ex-Redcaps,' Williams spat. 'I've done a few of them in my time, I can tell you! Nothin' but bloody boy scouts.'

David Wallace shrugged, but said nothing. The trio of guards wore black crash helmets strapped beneath their chins and each man carried an ugly looking baton which he looked capable of using. Wallace felt glad that his plan avoided face-to-face combat with those guards, despite his compatriot's expressed disdain.

'Three Shuritor guards—always three—never varies.'

'Three, plus the driver, remember, who never leaves the locked van. He's the one in

24

radio contact with their headquarters.'

'And those three bastards never allow anybody to get within fifteen feet of them when they are carrying the boxes of money,' Myers chimed in, with a grimace. They had learned this during the early days of planning when a tentative, probing attempt by the big man to venture close to the payroll, as it was being conveyed from van to cash office, had been halted by a warning wave of a yard-long baton.

Wallace had decided, very early on, that confrontation was not to be the way. He had no wish to indulge in, or to instigate, physical violence to the person of anyone and the entire concept of his plan was based on the avoidance of any brutality. For him, this operation was to be a success for scientific knowledge, both in design and execution. They were to walk in, scoop the pool, and dispose of their prize in a matter of minutes, then return to their normal work-places before anyone noticed their absence. Nevertheless, he had seen to it that his team was aware of every move in the routine the Shuritor guards followed when delivering the payroll; every move, from the time they pulled up in the pre-emptied courtyard in front of the administration building, until they wheeled an empty trolley out again and drove away. Wallace and his companions had learned that, although the Shuritor van varied its delivery route to the plant, it always had to get the cash to Forsters sufficiently early in the morning to allow the cashier's office staff enough time to do their accounting before paying the money out, and that meant that the time of delivery was virtually the same on every occasion.

Wallace's one big success had been with Barnfield, the chief cashier at Forsters. The big Welshman had painstakingly developed a friendship with the pompous little man for month after weary month, until they had a fairly close relationship which allowed him to call on Barnfield at any time to discuss trivia, which he usually managed to do on pay-days. He found that it was ridiculously easy to confirm the amount of each payroll through judicious questioning of the chief cashier, combined with flattery. Like most pompous men, Barnfield was always ready to impress friends by divulging important facts which he had acquired.

The Shuritor guards wheeled a rubber-tyred trolley into place at the rear of their vehicle, and the four Forsters' men watched from their vantage point in the Avenger as a hatch in the rear of the van swung open and three black, metal boxes were passed out by unseen hands, to be lifted down on to the trolley by two guards while a third stood by, baton at the ready. The hatch quickly closed, and the three guards began to wheel the loaded trolley towards the deserted main door of the administration building.

'Clever buggers, eh?' Pengelly observed. 'The driver never leaves the locked van; that's him inside, passing the boxes out.'

'No change in routine,' Myers whispered. One or other of the four had watched half a dozen similiar off-loading operations during previous deliveries.

Wallace and the three foremen left the car and followed the retreating trolley into the building, and as they did so, each man watched keenly for any change in routine, for any alteration in procedure or in the guards' usual habits that might affect Wallace's scheme, but there were none. Then, as they moved, sharp-eyed, towards the entrance in pursuit of the payroll, they suddenly found their path blocked by an elderly man, dressed in a crumpled, black serge, messenger's uniform, who barred their progress with outstretched arms.

'Sorry, gentlemen. No passin' until the containers are h'inside the strongroom.'

The elderly man was Jack Froggart, a retired process worker who now worked as a messenger in the administration block to supplement his pension. The white-haired pensioner stiffened importantly and bristled as he again said:

'No passin' until—'

'Okay, Jack, I know who my friends are,' Steve Williams chided.

'You can't come inside yet! It's regulations!' They were forced to wait outside while the payroll was transported through the foyer of the building and into the corridor leading to the cash office. The flustered old man then allowed them to enter and the quartet sauntered after the retreating Shuritor guards and their precious load while Jack Froggart fussed and fretted around them like an anxious sheepdog. The cash office lay along a corridor to the right of the foyer, and they had no option but to wait patiently as the black containers were trolleyed in through a door which bore the inscription: 'NO ENTRY. WAGES STAFF ONLY.' A rotund, bespectacled man stood just outside the open door of the cash office; this was John Barnfield, Forsters' chief cashier, who postured self-importantly and issued a barrage of instructions to his staff as he supervised the delivery of the payroll.

'Hello, John. I've come to take a look at those photographs,' Wallace called along the corridor. 'Perhaps it's a bad time to call,' he added vaguely.

'You come on in,' the cashier said, and he beckoned insistently in Wallace's direction before disappearing into the office.

Wallace acted on the invitation, and was about to enter the cash office in pursuit of Barnfield when one of the baton-carrying guards stepped forward to block his path.

'Sorry, sir! I'm afraid—'

'That's all right, Brown.' The chief cashier reappeared and gave Wallace a greasy smile of apology. 'Mr. Wallace has my permission,' he said to the guard, who stood aside for the big Welshman to gain admission.

The room Wallace now entered was divided into two sections by a waist-high counter, topped by a wire-mesh grille which rose to the ceiling, much in the manner of a bank-teller's counter. The smaller section of the room lay on the opposite side of the counter partition, and was entered through another door further along the corridor. Those employees and staff who were paid in cash came here, to receive their wages or salaries over the protected counter. The section of the cashier's office in which Wallace stood was quite large in comparison, being some forty feet square, and on one wall the massive, steel-plated door of the strongroom lay open. Inside, Wallace could see two girl assistant cashiers busily checking the contents of the newly arrived containers.

'Shan't be a minute, Dave.'

Barnfield spoke briefly to the girls and he seemed satisfied with their reply, for he quickly signed an acceptance note which he handed to one of the helmeted Shuritor guards. The security men filed out, and Barnfield carefully locked the 'NO ENTRY' door after them, then he turned to Wallace and fished in his coat pocket for a handful of photographs which he eagerly held out for inspection. 'Got some good ones of the boat,' he said. 'Not bad, are they?'

His victim groaned inwardly as he took the proffered snapshots. 'No, not bad at all,' he smiled. He had a clear view straight into the strongroom, and he could see that the lids of the three money containers were thrown back to expose their contents. He drew his breath in sharply as he saw that each box was crammed full with treasury notes of all denominations.

'That one is Betty and the kids.'

He had seen the payroll containers many times during the preceding months, but never like this. This was his first glimpse of the amassed wealth which those black boxes contained, and surges of excitement rippled through him as his eyes flickered from the photographs to the bundles of banknotes in that Aladdin's cave. The girl assistants were still fussing over the boxes as Pengelly, Williams and Myers entered the public side of the wages office via its second door.

'That one is the boat again. We had smashing weather, too—'

The three foremen handed their salary slips through the grille to one of the girls, and Wallace caught the gleam of three pairs of eyes through the apertures in the mesh which separated them. His own eyes widened in a silent signal and he swivelled his gaze in the direction of the hoard which lay open to view on the strongroom floor.

'That's us with the wife's parents—'

Wallace caught a glimpse of Steve Williams, and he almost smiled as he saw the little man staring open-mouthed as though transfixed. Wallace moved slightly to one side, as if to see the photographs in a better light, but in so doing afforded the three ex-sergeants a clearer view of the containers, and he felt that luck was truly on their side to have descended on the wages office when, by chance, the supreme prize was on display. Even he had never seen the boxes open, as they now were; this was just the fuel his stormtroopers needed to fire their enthusiasm. On the other side of the counter, they were absorbing details of the open strongroom with professional expertise.

'Very nice, too, John. You have some first-class snapshots there, I must say. You must have a good camera?'

'An Olympus OM-1N, Dave. I'm in a camera club in Bristol, you know.' The cashier responded happily to the other's flattery. 'And by the way, we call them "photographs", not "snapshots". You must come out with me in the boat some time,' he suggested. 'You and I could have a great day out.'

At that point, Wallace could have cheerfully hit the man, but he managed to nod in an enthusiastic fashion before taking his leave. The chief cashier unlocked the door to the corridor, and as Wallace stepped outside he heard the lock click behind him. Barnfield might have no social graces, but he was an efficient guardian of the firm's money and he took no chances.

The three veterans were whispering together in low monotones when David Wallace rejoined them in the deserted corridor.

As Wallace had guessed, the chance sighting of the payroll boxes lying open on the strongroom floor had aroused the three ex-sergeants to new enthusiasm.

'What a prize, Dave! What one hell of a prize!'

'That'll compensate for a lot.'

They drove back to Section Eight in a state of elation.

'Jesus, boy,' Steve Williams chortled, 'this little mission is going to go like clockwork, I can feel it in my bones. Make it soon, that's all I ask. Make it soon!'

TWO

David Wallace had had enough of Forsters for one day as he headed for the main gate of the industrial complex. It was already six o'clock which meant that he was an hour late, but there was nothing unusual in that. He had spent one hell of a time in organizing repairs to the Iron Lady and also in dealing with other frustrating production problems.

The Welshman felt absolutely shattered as he weaved his car through the milling horde who were headed for the same exit, as eager as he to come to the end of their working day, but his ill mood quickly evaporated as he motored steadily westwards, past Lulsgate airport and on through rolling countryside. The winding highway careered across the Mendips before suddenly descending on to the broad plain of the Somerset wetlands, over which it meandered to pass close to the small, coastal town of Burnham-on-Sea in which he lived.

David Wallace had been married. Married, separated and finally divorced. He thought about his ex-wife, Claire, as he drove along. He did not miss her in the meaning of any great, emotional loss, though of course there were times when, in the loneliness of his bachelor apartment, he missed her feminine company. Theirs had not been a marriage of great passion, they had known each other for a few years and just seemed to drift into an official union without it having any emotional import, rather because it seemed the thing to do. He had graduated from Cardiff University with an Honours degree in chemistry, the years until his move to Somerset being occupied in several industries. He also married Claire. After they moved to Somerset they simply drifted apart; there was no enmity, no third person came between them, it was quite simply one of those marriages that was not meant to be, and Claire had remarried and was now living the uncomplicated life she needed.

Since the divorce and the sale of the house in which they lived out their brief sojourn together, he had rented the top floor apartment of a two-storey house on the South Esplanade of the town, overlooking a lawn-lined, sea-front road.

By the time he reached Burnham the rain showers had fled to Wales and the evening sun was still quite high as he rolled off the Esplanade into the driveway of his house. As he garaged his car he gave a cheery wave to Mrs. Warren, the elderly widow who lived in the ground floor apartment.

From the rear of the garage a door opened out on to a small courtyard and garden at the back of the house. From here he climbed the external iron stairway which led up to his apartment, and unlocked the door at the top. His rooms were pleasant and large; a comfortably furnished lounge-cum-living-room, one bedroom, a bathroom and a kitchen. A three-inch Zeiss telescope which stood, permanently mounted on its tripod, in the bay window at the front of the living-room was a prized possession which gave him much pleasure in the detailed views it afforded.

He showered away the grime of Forsters and of Section Eight, then, refreshed, he dressed in more casual clothes before eating. He found that meal times were among the few occasions when living alone bothered him, when he felt any sense of loneliness. After tea he sat at a writing-desk and, unlocking one of its drawers, brought out a sheaf of papers. For a good ten minutes he studied the pages, making odd notes on a single piece of notepaper until he had copied out a list of items. When he was satisfied he folded the piece of notepaper and slipped it into his shirt pocket, then he gathered up the sheaf of papers and carefully locked them away again in the desk drawer.

It had turned into a beautiful evening. He slipped on a light windcheater and left the house; he crossed the sea-front road and walked some four hundred yards along the promenade until he reached the jetty, then he walked along the jetty and down on to the beach.

The tide was out and, as the man walked, the evening sun glistened on wet sand and sparkled on the acres of mud left uncovered by the receding waters of the Bristol Channel. Two miles to the north, along the gentle curve of the beach, stood the Low Lighthouse, and David Wallace strode out purposefully as he followed the ribbon of clean sand, past the row of buildings which lined the Esplanade and on past Saint Andrew's church until he reached the curious structure. The Low Light was a forty-foot high, box-like, white-painted, wooden structure which squatted in a fine balancing act on nine timber baulk legs, slap-bang in the middle of the open beach and below high tide level, looking like some stranded Martian. Its sister, the High Light, was a much more conventional lighthouse, and she rose as a magnificent, hundred-foot high landmark half a mile inland, alongside the main Berrow Road, amongst the houses, and oddly out of place. The dual lighthouse arrangement was such that mariners could line up both lights to be guided up the treacherous inlet of the River Parrett. He was now at the far end of town from his apartment and, soon after turning to retrace his steps, he drew level with the five-storey apartment block overlooking the North Esplanade, where Steve Williams lived with his married sister.

They had arranged to meet that evening, David Wallace, Steve Williams, Dan Pengelly and Ian Myers, in the Old Pier Tavern, a popular bar-cum-restaurant in Pier Street close to Wallace's house, where the four men often met to drink and to talk in one of its secluded, alcove seats where they could not be overheard. As Wallace entered the Pier Tavern a background noise of subdued chatter greeted him; he peered through the smoke-filled atmosphere and spotted the three veterans seated at the far end of the long room. He walked up to the bar and ordered a drink, and as he did so he looked at his wristwatch.

'It's eight o'clock!'

Wallace glanced up to see the landlord nodding a welcome.

'Your friends have been here for some time. They'll be well ahead of you in the drink stakes.'

'I thought they might be,' Wallace said, but he winced at the readiness with which the landlord associated them in his mind. 'Not many people about yet,' he added as he gazed about him.

'They'll be in later. Folk just don't have the money these days to start drinking early.'

The three men greeted Wallace with alcoholic benevolence and Myers slapped him playfully with one of his huge hands. 'You're late, Dave,' he scolded amicably. It was like being cuffed by an affable bear.

'I've been for a walk on the beach,' Wallace said. 'I was just bloody glad to get away from the plant.' He sat at their table and took a long sip from his beer before setting the glass down, then he fished in his shirt pocket with thumb and forefinger and drew out the folded sheet of notepaper. He slid it across the table towards Dan Pengelly.

'Bloody hell! Not more paperwork?' Steve

37

Williams leaned back and raised his eyes to the ceiling.

'Knock it off, Steve,' Pengelly said quietly. He picked up the paper and unfolded it.

'That's a check list of the items we need.' Wallace ignored Williams and looked at Dan Pengelly. 'I just want each of you to read it through to see if you agree with it.' He took another sip from his glass.

'But we've been through all of this before,' Williams groaned.

'You read it,' Pengelly ordered, and he dug the Welshman in the ribs as he passed the list to him.

'Yeah, yeah,' Williams grunted. He gave the sheet of paper a cursory glance before passing it to Myers. 'I tell you, I've had my fill of planning, boy. When are we going to knock over those boxes, that's what I want to know?'

'For God's sake, keep your voice down,' Wallace urged. He looked around to see if anyone was listening.

'Aw, what the hell—' Steve Williams raised his glass. 'Here's to war!' He drained his glass with great gulps.

'There's not much point in talking to you tonight.'

'You can please yourself about that, too.' Williams was in an offhandish mood, intent only on enjoying the night.

Wallace turned to Myers. 'The chain is your department,' he said. 'What should we use?'

'A three or four-legged lifting sling with a safe working load of three tonnes will be strong enough with plenty to spare. I can get hold of one easily.'

'When can we have it?'

'This week, sometime. I'll collect one from the tackle stores and have my crew use it on a plant job, then I can hold on to it and return it to the stores when we have done.' The big ex-diver saw the query in Wallace's eyes and sought to reassure him. 'There'll be no questions asked, just leave it to me and I'll have it in the back of the Land Rover by the end of the week, I promise you.'

Steve Williams pushed his seat back and rose to his feet. He swayed perceptibly as he fixed Wallace with eyes which were more than slightly glazed, then he pointed his fingers at the seated man in imitation of a revolver, squinted along an imaginary gunsight, cocked his thumb, then let it fall. 'Got you, Dave, boy—right in the head.' He gave a quick grin. 'Want a drink?' he invited. Without waiting for affirmation he gathered up four empty glasses from the table and steered an imprecise course for the bar.

The youths had entered ten minutes earlier. There were two of them; mean looking fellows who had taken their beers to a centre table where they slouched sullenly with legs sprawled across the gangways in an openly aggressive attitude, ready to take real or

39

imaginary offence. They looked exactly what they were, nasty and dangerous, and most of the other customers took studied care not to look their way twice, while from behind the bar the landlord watched carefully.

The trouble started as Williams was making his way back to the alcove with four full glasses gripped gingerly in beer-wetted fingers. As he passed the table at which the pair were seated, he brushed against one of them, a bearded youth with greasy, blond hair, dressed in a stud-decorated uniform of worn leathers. As the Welshman wobbled precariously he spilled some liquid on to the younger man's jacket.

'Sorry, lad—'

' 'Ere! Watch your step,' the youth snarled over his shoulder at a bemused Steve Williams, 'or I'll 'ave you!'

Williams stopped in his tracks, swayed unsteadily and beamed amicably down on his fair-haired aggressor. 'Now don't you go apologisin', lovely,' he said magnanimously. 'I won't hear of it.'

Dan Pengelly gave a long-drawn-out sigh and eased the alcove table away from him. 'Hell's bells,' he muttered, resignedly, 'just when I fancied a quiet night, too.'

Steve Williams approached their alcove with a weaving gait, and he winked broadly at his companions as he set the glasses down on the table with a rattle. 'Sorry they ain't full,' he informed the three men loudly. 'I spilled some over Goldilocks, there. First wash he's had this year, I 'spect.'

The words were loud enough to carry and Wallace felt his stomach knot as the unkempt couple stiffened in their seats. 'For God's sake, Steve, leave them alone,' he whispered placatingly.

Williams sat on his stool and eyed the peacemaker. 'Okay,' he said, 'they are no problem.' He paused for a moment, then said: 'I'll tell you what is a problem, though, since you are keen on making money-talk. I'm telling you straight, it's the Feeder idea of yours that bothers me.'

'What is wrong with it?'

'What the hell is right with it? No sooner do we lay our hands on the cash-boxes, than we dump them again! I don't like the thought of that one little bit. Not one little bit.'

'Can you come up with a better way?'

'Share it out and let everyone take their own chances.' The little man glared around the circle of faces. 'Each man ought to look out for himself once we've done the job,' he continued pugnaciously. 'I never have been one for playing nursemaid to people who can't take care of themselves.'

'What does that mean?' Wallace demanded. He knew full well what the little man meant and so did the others; it was another snide remark directed at him. 'My God!' he snapped. 'As soon as they realise that the payroll is missing, there'll be the tightest security clampdown on Forsters and the surrounding area you've ever seen. The guards at the plant and the civil police will be crawling all over us. Your idea of an immediate shareout is a daft notion.'

'Daft, is it? Not as daft as your Feeder idea, lovely,' Williams snarled.

'Take it easy. Do you want the whole town to hear you?' Myers cautioned.

David Wallace lowered his voice. 'Well, Steve,' he said, with well deserved exasperation, 'my way will enable us to drop the money out of sight within five minutes of our taking it, and no one the wiser until we want to send Ian down for it.'

Williams muttered something inaudible under his breath and glanced at the other two veterans for support, but they stared back impassively, prepared to allow the temperamental Welshman to grumble on until he ran out of steam. Wallace knew the two were with him on this.

'Now, if you have a better method of disposing of four sizeable cash-boxes in a very short space of time, without being seen and without leaving the plant, then let's hear it.'

Steve Williams scowled but said nothing, then, as if dismissing the disagreement from his mind, he raised his glass to his lips and emptied half of its contents down his throat with a seemingly continuous but barely visible swallow. 'Ah!' he gasped with a smack of his lips, then, turning once more to David Wallace, he added: 'Right you are, College Boy, have it your own way, but let's all hope that young Myers, here, hasn't lost his nerve when the time comes, or we'll have to tie a couple of bricks to those big feet of his and throw him in the Feeder after them.' He reached over and slapped Myers resoundingly on the knee. 'That's what we'll have to do with you, old son.'

Myers gave no sign of having heard what was said. He had drunk several pints of ale and he was now slumped back in his seat, blinking through glazed eyes at the duo of leather-clad ruffians with whom Steve Williams had just brushed, and through an alcoholic haze his eyes came to rest on their swastika badges. 'A land fit for 'eroes, that's what old Churchill said we were fightin' for. A land fit for 'eroes, and just look at that bleedin' lot over there.'

'Eh?' Steve Williams swivelled on his seat to follow the line of Myers' belligerent stare. 'Oh, them!' he expostulated, 'you don't want to worry about them, lovely. They are just a couple of kids who want their arses smacked. Anyway, it was Monty, not Churchill, . . . or was it Lloyd George?'

Once again the words were loud enough to carry and a hush fell over the adjoining tables as the two looked up sharply. The little man from the valleys waggled his fingers cheerfully at the lowering pair, and that, it seemed, was enough. The bearded one hissed something to his companion and together they rose and began to edge their way between the intervening tables towards Steve Williams' nonchalant back.

Myers studied their approach. As they neared, he dropped his eyes to meet the little man's hooded gaze. 'Company coming, Taff,' he advised softly.

'Now I'm worried.' Steve Williams chuckled, then he raised his eyebrows as he caught an expression of apprehension on Wallace's face. 'You don't want to get too worked up about these Girl Guides, Dave,' he said, and he grinned mischievously. 'They can only kill you once, you know.'

Without saying a word, Dan Pengelly stretched out one long leg and with his foot slid a vacant stool into the gangway behind Williams' back.

'You look after me like a mother,' Steve Williams said, but he made no effort to turn to meet the approaching menace. 'How close are they?' He studied the tall Somerset man's face as he spoke, ready to take his cue from the first hint of a reaction.

'Damn close!'

By this time the youths had sidled up behind the Welshman's seat, but because of the proximity of the adjoining tables and the position of the stool that Pengelly had pushed into the gangway, only one youth could stand close to the dark-haired Celt. The newcomer glared down at Steve Williams' unmoved back. 'Your mate here is askin' for trouble,' he snarled at the remainder of the quartet in general over the top of his potential victim's inoffensive head.

'Who? Him? Never!' Dan Pengelly stuck an accusing finger in Williams' lugubrious face. 'Steve! I hope you haven't been upsettin' these two lads,' he admonished.

The aggressive snarl on the youth's face faded slightly. He wasn't used to such indifferent behaviour from potential victims. It wasn't suppose to be like this. He paused, unsure of himself.

'If I were you, I'd leave now, friend, and that's good advice.' Myers spoke so quietly that his words barely reached the youth, but there was no mistaking the message they conveyed. The smiles vanished from the faces of the three ex-sergeants; they glanced at each other, and each man gave the minutest nod of agreement in answer to an unspoken question. Suddenly, almost imperceptibly, they assumed a menacing aspect. No longer were they merely three friends enjoying a drink together, suddenly they were hard and capable men. 'Shove off!' Again Myers spoke quietly, but the tone of his voice held a new and ugly edge.

The foremost intruder hesitated, taken aback by the changed situation. These older men had seemed to be easy marks at first but now he was not so sure. In fact, each one of those bleak, grim faces staring up at him sent warning signals rippling through his nervous system.

David Wallace sat still and glanced at the three veterans with increasing apprehension. Dear God! he thought, they frighten me, and they are on my side.

It was the second youth, blustering from behind his friend, who caused the grief by leaning around his partner and bawling: 'You bastards are goin' to catch a cold, and that's the truth!'

Steve Williams twisted, cat-like, on his stool and his dark, Celtic eyes were hooded with the passion of his race as he spat a string of searing curses up into the face of his blond aggressor. The final words were so viciously insulting that the youth flushed to the roots of his matted hair in rage and fear.

'Now—get lost, lad!' The last was the shouted command of a British army trained sergeant and it demanded instant obedience.

'Taffy, don't try—'

That was as far as the youth got. In a purely reflex gesture of defence he had flung up his hand and jabbed an extended forefinger in Steve Williams' face in the process. The Welshman half rose from his stool and spun on the balls of his feet. His right hand, fingers bunched stiffly, punched lightning-fast to strike with wicked precision at a vital nerve complex in his victim's belly. The action was so swift and so professionally executed that few people in the room actually witnessed the violence which caused the young trouble-maker to jack-knife with a strangled groan, hands clasped to his stomach as he fought for breath. Almost casually, the man from the valleys caught at the young lout's side and pinched a roll of dirty T-shirt and underlying flesh in a grip of steel.

'When I say get lost, you get lost! Understand?'

Steve Williams continued to support his squirming adversary in that agonising grip as he mouthed the words slowly and patiently, as if instructing a recalcitrant child.

'Understand?'

He twisted cruelly at the roll of flesh to force a gasp of obeisance from the blond youth, who writhed in vain to free himself from that paralysing hold.

'Understand?'

The owner of the bar was anxious to quell trouble as soon as possible and he reacted quickly; the entire confrontation had taken barely a minute but he managed to thrust his way through the crowd just in time to stop the place erupting. 'You leave this to me, now,' he said to Williams, and he hustled the youths back from the fracas with a skill born of experience. Both men blustered and cursed, although it was obvious that they were more than willing to break off the encounter since they allowed themselves to be propelled the length of the room towards the door, albeit to the accompaniment of a barrage of vengeful yells from them.

'You wait, you Welsh bastard. We'll have you!' The final threat echoed along the bar before the landlord finally pushed them outside.

A hubbub of excited conversation broke out among the tables as the publican returned to the alcove table. 'Sorry about the disturbance,' he apologised, 'they were some out-of-town trash. Haven't seen them in here before and they certainly won't come in again. Any damage done?'

'Not to us,' Dan Pengelly grinned. 'I thought Steve was very gentle with the blond lad, though,' he added, with a sly wink at Myers. 'There was a time when he wouldn't have walked out of here on his own two legs.'

The little Welshman grunted. 'Aye, I'm getting mellow in my old age, that's the trouble,' he acknowledged.

The remainder of the evening was an anticlimax. The other customers soon settled down again and the three veterans continued to drink steadily. David Wallace had pocketed his list; it was obvious that there would be no further sensible discussion that night, and after about another hour he took his leave of the trio and threaded his way through the now crowded room to the door.

Wallace stepped out into Pier Street. It was dark now, about ten p.m. and the short street which led directly down to the Esplanade and to the jetty itself was deserted. A chill night mist had draped itself along the sea-front and, though the vaporous moisture was by no means dense, it restricted visibility to a hundred yards. He turned right and headed along the pavement towards the sea-front road which would lead him home. It was as he neared the Queens Hotel, which sat directly opposite the beach, that he heard a sound, a slight sound, like the scuffling of rats, which caused him to turn his head sharply in its direction. His eye caught a movement in a darkened shop doorway just behind him, and his pulses raced as he realised who it must be.

The ruffians from the pub! There were more of them, at least five, who lay waiting in ambush for their targets to leave the bar.

Alert and agile, he slid silently into the murky gloom of a nearby shelter. He knew that he could not call the police; the last thing he wanted was attention from that quarter at this particular time, but what of his three companions, about to walk into ambush when they left the bar? The thought of telephoning a warning to the trio in the bar had hardly crossed his mind when he found himself hesitating. He had chosen the three foremen to be his allies in crime on the basis of their toughness and combat experience, but, although they had already demonstrated these qualities, in part, during their fracas with the two young hooligans, eighteen years had gone by since they had served as warriors in time of war. Here was a further opportunity for him to see how they would conduct themselves now; after all, they were all close to forty years of age and maybe time had tempered their aggression.

It was typical of the scientist in the man that, having reasoned the situation out, he should act accordingly. It was cold-blooded, detached thinking, but once the decision had been made then there was simply no logical alternative. He nodded to himself in the darkness. Yes! that was what he would do.

He stalked a swift and silent path to the edge of the large municipal car park which lay across Pier Street from the Old Pier Tavern, and kept well into the shadows as he threaded his way cautiously between the parked cars until he reached a vantage point from which he could see the length of Pier Street. Yes! Like the writhings of rats in a sewer, there were movements in the shadowy recesses of a shop doorway where the band of thugs now lay in wait for Steve Williams, Dan Pengelly and

Ian Myers.

Over the entrance to the bar a pale bulb splashed its half circle of light on to the night-shaded pavement. It was ten-thirty, closing time for the public house, but throwing out time was eleven p.m. and he guessed that the three foremen would be among the last to leave. He waited, shivering in the chill of the night's mist as he watched the other customers leave in the various states of gaiety or depression until, at last the glass front door opened and the tall figure of Dan Pengelly emerged, followed by the short, dark form of Williams and the stocky Myers. As Pengelly stepped out on to damp paving stones he ruffled his coat-collar against the dank, Bristol Channel air.

'Hello—?'

Denim-shrouded forms moved in the backdrop of darkness, then slowly emerged into the curtain of light which hung around the doorway.

'It's 'im, Steve!'

David Wallace was close enough to hear Pengelly's exclamation of surprise.

'Who?'

'The fairy from the bar. You know, the fair-haired laddie.'

Dan Pengelly had recognised the foremost figure of the group as the youth with whom Steve Williams had clashed earlier in the evening.

Ian Myers was perceptibly unsteady on his feet as, hands in pockets, he leaned forward and peered at the Unclean. 'God dammit, but you are right,' he belched. He took a second look around the unwelcome visitors. 'I thought there were only two of them inside, though. I can see—three—four—'

'You are drunk, Myers, you old fool. Seeing double again.'

The youths grew more tense with each bantering exchange between the three ex-sergeants. Had they been wiser they would have noticed that their would-be victims had sobered rapidly, that they had surreptitiously moved to adopt a back-to-back defensive posture which had been perfected in bar brawls around the world.

'If it isn't our two little playmates come back for more, and they've brought their friends along, too.'

'I told you, you were a bit too gentle with the pretty one, Steve.'

'Aye, but I shan't make that mistake again, Dan boy.'

The blond leader of the gang gave vent to an enraged snarl as he delved into the pocket of his fringed, leather jacket and swept a curved object into view. A loud, metallic 'click' echoed through the night as a seven-inch steel knife blade snickered open with oiled precision.

'Not so big, now, are we, Taffy?'

In the instant that the weapon was revealed, Steve Williams went into a low, feral crouch. Wolf-like, he watched his attacker's face; searched for the eyes, then held them with his own in an hypnotic stare which probed for that momentary, fractional warning they must sub-consciously give of impending movement. The youth's gaze flickered nervously under the hooded menace in the Welshman's dark eyes, and with that hint of weakness, that minute sign of submission, Steve Williams knew that he could take this man.

'I'm goin' to slice you proper, you Welsh bastard!' The blond bully swathed the blade through unresisting air and his loose mouth worked convulsively.

'Well now, lovely, you really shouldn't have brought out the penknife—' Williams breathed the words slowly while all the time inching and sidling into position, '—because now I'll have to crack that arm for you, lovely,—' and smiling, but frighteningly profane, the little Celt hissed his final, verbal ploy, '—and then I'm going to kick your balls off!'

The young aggressor licked his lips and glanced around at his companions for reassurance. He obviously began to wish that he was elsewhere.

'Go on, Clive! Let 'im 'ave it!'

Unwisely, one of the pack urged the young knifeman to the attack. The advice was bad.

'Clive! Jesus Christ, his name is Clive! That's the boy, Clive, let me have it!'

Goaded beyond reason by Williams' derisive call, the youth lunged forward and slashed desperately at thin air. For the ex-sergeant, trained as he was in unarmed combat, it was ridiculously easy. Almost contemptuously he parried the first knife thrust, then, allowing his opponent's momentum to carry him off balance, Williams stepped past the gleaming blade. The next moment the weapon spun from the youth's grasp as the Celt took a grip on his knife arm, then deliberately bent the limb back on its elbow joint. There was an audible 'crack' as its radius bone splintered and broke.

'Ahhh! Me arm—'

A retching scream bubbled from the luckless youth's lips and he came to his knees.

'Yes, yes, good boy,' Steve Williams agreed.

Though the shorter by at least two inches, he dragged his victim upright by his jacket front, then, with savage cruelty he brought his knee up sharply into the youth's genitals. Three times he kicked upwards and each time Wallace saw the body in his grasp jerk with the force of the impact. When Williams finally released his hold, saliva frothed from the corners of the young thug's mouth and he collapsed in a sobbing, moaning heap at Williams' feet.

The destruction was over so quickly that the other members of the gang had no time to interfere. Now, seeing their leader fallen, they moved forward threateningly.

Ian Myers had already drawn two beer bottles from his pockets.

'Dan!'

Big Dan Pengelly caught the bottle which Myers threw to him in a fist like a sledge-hammer. As one, they each swung a bottle and dashed it against the stone pavement at their feet. Frothing liquid cascaded from the bottles amid a shower of broken glass and the two men raised their jagged, improvised weapons menacingly. These two were veterans of countless brawls in long forgotten dives and brothels in North Africa and in France. They were well used to back-street fighting.

'Who's first?' Dan Pengelly beckoned to the youths. 'Come on, lads! Who wants it first?'

It was enough. The remainder of the group made no move to pursue the confrontation; instead they clustered around their fallen leader, with much muttering to restore their damaged pride.

'We'll catch up with you three another time.'

'You'll know where to find us, lovely.'

David Wallace left then. He had forgotten the chill of the night air as, fascinated, he watched the drama unfold before him. Now, unaccountably he began to shiver as he turned thankfully for home, both glad and frightened at what he had seen.

THREE

The fracas with the gang of youths seemed to mark the beginning of a new and more positive phase in the attitude of the three ex-sergeants, Wallace was soon to realise. He sensed a mood of increased belligerence among the trio of veterans, as if in some way they too had been reassured of their capabilities by their mastery of their young attackers that night outside the Old Pier Tavern. As they entered July, the month which was to furnish the heaviest payroll of the year, they became charged with the tension of warriors close to battle, and Wallace knew that it was now or, maybe, never.

From discreet vantage points, the arrivals and movements of staff who worked in the administration building, especially the personnel who worked in the wages office under the watchful eye of the unprepossessing chief cashier, were timed and noted with stopwatch precision. As services foreman, Steve Williams could move freely over the entire factory area, and he had already made the electrical alterations to the wiring of the industrial complex's fire-alarm system that

Wallace's plan required. Even though the two men had little in common except their Welsh ancestry, David Wallace had no doubt about his compatriot's technical ability and was the first to acknowledge the competence of the other's handiwork. The alterations involved the insertion into the fire-alarm circuits of a number of wires and clips which enabled the circuits to be activated remotely by means of a single switch. This switch would enable false alarms to be initiated as required at a number of separate sites about the complex, and the beauty of those temporary insertions was that they could readily be removed after their task had been completed, by Williams, who would undoubtedly be called upon to repair the 'faulty' alarm circuits. What made this feasible was that false alarms were not all that unusual and their cause was usually blamed on water seeping into underground cable channels from the marshy ground on which Forsters was constructed.

There had always been the problem of Steve Williams' impatience. A few weeks earlier they had made the vital pipework connection from ammonia reserve stock tank 'A' on Section Eight into the domestic water supply to the administration block, and once this had been done the scheme became viable. To the little Celt's mind there was no point in waiting and the only thing that held him in check was the fact that the pay bill for either

July or August would be boosted by holiday pay and bonuses.

They were using an empty storeroom on Section Eight as a base for operations. The room was housed in the basement of a disused process building from which the chemical plant had long been removed, and since it was below ground level there were no windows to the spacious room, so unwanted visitors could not see inside, but there were double doors which could be securely locked and which opened on to a ramp leading up to ground level. Wallace, or Dan Pengelly as senior foreman, could also control the movement of process personnel to keep them well away.

June had been a wet month but, to Wallace's slight dismay, July came in with little rain and high temperatures. He was praying that the weather on the day of the raid would prove to be wet, with little wind, since, although it was not absolutely necessary, a damp atmosphere would keep a gas cloud low and concentrated and an absence of wind would keep gas dispersal to a minimum. For these reasons he noted the evening weather forecasts with increasing anticipation as the month wore on.

It was on such a pleasant July day that he called at various offices in the administration block on business of one kind or another, and finally called on Barnfield, the chief cashier, ostensibly to talk about sailing boats. It was one of the visits the Welshman regularly made to glean what information he could about the routine of the cash office, and what he learned during the course of this visit sent him scurrying excitedly back to Section Eight and the basement storeroom.

He walked down the sloping ramp, unlocked the door, and entered the room quietly. The basement was large, some eighty feet square, intersected by concrete pillars which supported the floor above. Wallace locked the door behind him and stood watching the three foremen who were grouped around one of the Land Rovers which belonged to the Section. It had been decided that a passable imitation of a Land Rover belonging to the factory Fire-Brigade could be achieved with the aid of red-coloured, adhesive flashes and they had just completed a trial camouflage as Wallace entered. They had not yet seen him and Steve Williams was surveying the vehicle moodily.

'Turn the bloody tap now, I say!'

'I reckon that's good enough to fool anyone,' Dan Pengelly said as he smoothed down the Land Rover's false covering. Both he and Ian Myers ignored the grumbles of the little Welshman.

'Everything's ready. We could have gone for last month's lot and I could be in the bloody Canaries by now.' Williams kicked angrily at one of the Rover's tyres. 'What the hell are we waiting for? Tell me that? We could damn well go without him, and that's the truth!'

'Dave is planning this job, Steve. He's got it sorted. Best to wait until he gives the word.'

'Christ Almighty! I can't have a crap without his wantin' to enter it on his friggin' charts. I never was on a job like this before, boy. When in hell do we go?'

'In two weeks' time,' Wallace said.

They turned, startled by his silent approach, and as he stood gazing at them he felt his stomach tighten with tension and excitement at the finality of his decision. He gave no hint of having overhead any of his fellow countryman's insults.

'I've just left Barnfield. The July payroll arrives on Friday the twenty-sixth, and it's the big one!'

'Thank God for that!'

They crowded around the newcomer and an elated Steve Williams threw one arm around Wallace's shoulders in an unusual display of camaraderie. Eventually, when they had quietened, Myers said: 'You've come in time to see me test one of the incendiary devices, Dave. I've set it up in a vice, but with only one-quarter of the full igniting charge.'

At the far side of the storeroom stood a workbench on to which was bolted an engineer's vice, and in the vice Wallace could see one of the ignition devices which Myers and Williams had constructed, with advice from Wallace as to the chemical content of the incendiary charge. It was planned to place two such devices in the hydrogen and petroleum-cracking plants on Section Ten, a Section at the opposite end of the complex from the administration building, so that diversionary fires could be started when required.

'Okay, lads?' Myers queried. In his hands he held a shoe box-sized generator from which a pair of thin command wires led to a fuse in the device.

'Get on with it, old son,' Steve Williams instructed in typical fashion. 'It's this July we are aiming for.'

Without another word Myers spun the generator's handle, then thumbed its firing button. Instantaneously there was a puff of acrid smoke from the device, accompanied by a sheet of white flame which shot towards the concrete ceiling of the storeroom.

'Your mixture works, Dave, but it's a bit smoky.'

'That's due to the magnesium I added, to give a hotter flame; the smoke doesn't matter. What I want now is one of those little beauties in the main duct of the hydrogen plant and one in an inspection port on the lighter distillate section of the petroleum-cracking plant.'

'No problem. Myers and I can slip them in when we do a maintenance inspection on Ten.'

61

Later in the week David Wallace was alone in his office when there was a knock on the door and Myers entered.

'I've got the suit for a week-end job in Plymouth, Dave. Come to my place tonight and I'll show you.'

'What time?'

'Make it about nine o'clock, eh?'

That evening David Wallace walked through the back streets of Burnham until he reached the house in which Myers lived on the Highbridge council estate. He came to the door in answer to Wallace's knock.

'It's in the car. Mother is watching television, so I shan't ask you in, but come and see what I've got.'

They walked to a lean-to garage alongside the house and Myers swung the garage door open, then unlocked and opened the boot of his car to disclose a large, tin box. He lifted its lid and Wallace bent over and peered inside.

'Where the hell did you get it?'

'Brixham. I've just finished a job there. It's a Siebe Gorman heavy-duty suit.'

'Jesus Christ! Is it all there?'

'All except the pump and hose.'

'Will anyone be suspicious if you bring the gear home when we want it for the Feeder?'

'I do it all the time, Dave, to take with me

on various jobs. I can get hold of it whenever we need it.'

'Jesus Christ!'

*   *   *

It had been easy for Steve Williams to secrete his Draeger breathing set and his outfit of fireman's clothing in the boiler-room of the administration building. The oil-fired heating system for the block was turned off during the first week of May each year as an economy measure and the boiler-room was kept locked unless maintenance by the little Welshman's engineering crew was required.

Section Ten lay at the far end of the complex from the administration building, and this was the Section which operated a hydrogen manufacturing unit and a petroleum-cracking plant, both of which carried a high fire risk due to the explosive nature of the volatile products arising from each process. As the great day came nearer, one of Williams' and Myers' last actions was to place a small incendiary device in each of the ducts which drew flammable gases from these processes.

*   *   *

One day to go! Wallace had arranged a final meeting with the three ex-sergeants in his office for one last rehearsal, and was studying the blue-pencilled plan on his desk when a rattle of knuckles sounded on the door.

He quickly slid a covering sheet of paper over the drawing before him. 'Yes?' he called.

The door opened to disclose the inquiring features of Dan Pengelly, and bunched in the narrow corridor behind him, Williams and Myers.

'Come on in.'

The three men filed into the dingy room.

'Mornin', Dave.' Of the four, only the little Welsh foreman appeared to be completely at ease and his eyes twinkled at Wallace's obvious state of tension. 'Here we are, then, your three willing monkeys: Hear No Evil, See No Evil and Speak No Evil,' and he chuckled at his own joke.

David Wallace stepped along to his secretary's room and opened her door. 'I don't want to be disturbed, Susan. Any callers can wait,' he instructed, and he shut the door firmly before returning to his own office. He sat at his desk and eyed the trio expectantly. 'Well, any questions before I go over the plan?'

'It's just—' Dan Pengelly hesitated. Clouding, white steam had condensed on the dirty window of the office, further obscuring its view with a coating of tiny water droplets. The rangy West Country man fastened his gaze on the opaque glass, then he shrugged.

'No, I suppose not,' he said quietly.

'Good.' Wallace pulled his chair up to the desk and with a flourish uncovered the plan. 'Now gather round.'

The plan was a layout of the main administration building in relation to Number Eight Section; other production sections were lightly sketched in with pencil but obviously the most important parts of the diagram were those which had been scored in with heavy, blue lines.

'This is the plan of the area,' Wallace indicated, using his forefinger as a pointer. 'Admin.—Section Eight—Number One Feeder Pond. Okay?' The gathered men nodded. 'Here,' he continued, pointing to his own Section, 'are the liquefied ammonia storage tanks which supply our Pressure Oxidation Plant, and here is the reserve tank, storage tank 'A', which now holds the twenty tonnes we will be using. This road, here, passes through Section Eight, and running in a trench at the side of the road are service pipes—water, steam, and telephone and electricity cables. The service pipes then pass on,' and he followed the line of the road with his finger, 'to feed the Admin. block. Through the pipe connection we have made between our liquefied ammonia storage system and the domestic water supply pipe in that trench, we can now pump ammonia along the water pipe at will. We can flood the entire administration building with highly concentrated ammonia gas. When we open that valve tomorrow, liquefied ammonia will spew out from water taps and bubble out from every attic tank and water cistern in the place.' The scientist in Wallace had taken command of the man, and his eyes took on the gleam of a fanatic as he recounted each step of his plan. It was almost as if he derived so much pleasure from the mere telling of it, that to have given birth to the idea was enough. 'Liquefied ammonia will pour from a dozen inlets simultaneously, then vaporize to fill every room with ammonia gas within minutes. Imagine it! With the amount of liquefied gas we hold in that reserve tank we are capable of producing clouds of gaseous ammonia; thousands of cubic feet of the stuff. Nobody will be able to remain in or near the building; there will be a complete evacuation.'

'For us to walk in and pick up two-hundred and fifty-thousand quid!' Steve Williams' eyes shone again, but this time with visions of looted wealth.

David Wallace glanced up at his process foreman. He sensed a return of the earlier hesitancy which Dan Pengelly had shown, and he said: 'Anything wrong, Dan? You seemed to be unsure of something just now.'

Pengelly shrugged. 'It's a bit late in the day for me to have any doubts, I know, but I've made the point all along that somebody could get gassed, and I don't like that. Nobody could stay alive in the gas concentration you are planning to use.'

'But we've covered that point,' Wallace reasoned. 'The timing of my plan will allow people to get to the exits from the building before the gas arrives, and once it has arrived they'll soon run for fresh air.'

'Yes, old Dave is right,' Steve Williams interrupted, eager to quash any opposition. 'They'll all run like rabbits when they get a whiff of ammonia. You know, we don't hang about when we get a leak on the plant.' It was obvious that he did not care too much either way.

'Yes, but we are trained to handle ammonia. The admin. people—typists, clerks—are not. Maybe they won't run in time.'

'And maybe they will!' The little Welshman's tone was metallic. 'It's bloody well up to them. Anyway, like you said, it's a bit late for all this chat, ain't it, lovely? Not having last minute thoughts, are we?'

The warning flash on the face of the tall West Country man would have slowed the anger of lesser men, but not so in the case of the little Celt. The difference between the characters of these two was purely racial in origin; Steve Williams, mercurial, with standards of his own choosing, but nevertheless warrior-like in temperament and in courage; Dan Pengelly, steady as an English oak, slow to rage but insatiable in temper.

And it was Williams who would not let go. His dark brows knitted as he slid derisive eyes to meet the frown on the taller man's face.

'Don't you like the sound of maybe sixty thousand quid all to yourself, boyo?'

'I'll tell you something, boyo!' Pengelly spat the celticism with emphasis. 'When I risk ten years on the Moor for a wages job then I want to be sure of everything—but everything!— down to the time you dip your bloody wick, boyo!'

'Look here, Dan,' Wallace interposed hurriedly, 'I don't want anyone hurt, to avoid that has been one of the main aims of my planning. That's something I definitely do not want.' He also did not want the little Welshman's aggression to spark the raging temper he knew Dan Pengelly capable of. 'I've thought and thought about this,' he continued placatingly, 'and I'm sure that it is safe as long as Steve gives that warning before the gas hits, to get them started.'

'If that's my job, it will be done, without you wet nursing me.' Williams turned to Pengelly. 'If you are so worried about people getting hurt then what about the lads on Section Ten, Dan, boy? You worry about those pricks in admin. getting a whiff of gas, but you are happy to fire the cracking-plant and the hydrogen plant. What's the difference?'

'The difference is that the process men on Ten are trained to deal with an emergency and they are unlikely to panic.'

The ex-sergeant snorted angrily, but he was as much annoyed with himself as with anyone, for allowing himself to be rattled by the little Welshman.

Myers had been quiet until now. 'Tell me, Dave,' he queried, 'you are sure the cash-boxes will sink when we throw them in?'

The little man from the valleys instantly forgot his quarrel with Pengelly. 'What if the bastards float?' he asked anxiously.

Wallace leaned back in his chair, glad that the developing quarrel had been effectively interrupted. 'Disposal is okay,' he answered. 'I calculated the weight and volume of a metal wages container full of paper money, and I'm sure they will sink in that Feeder. Don't worry on that score.'

*   *   *

David Wallace did not sleep well that night, although he desperately wanted to, since he knew he would need all his physical and mental powers for the day that was to follow. When he awoke from a restless night to the startling jangle of the alarm clock, he found that his bedclothes were strewn about the floor at the foot of his bed.

He could eat little breakfast, he was on an adrenalin high as he drove to the plant and his nerves were on a knife edge of anticipation. If he wanted a good omen, it lay in the fact that the weather was exactly what he had prayed for; overcast with a ground mist over the low-lying wetlands, and he only hoped that the mist would last for most of the day. He forced himself to deal with office matters for half an hour, though with scarcely concealed impatience, then made his way to the underground basement. When he entered he found the three ex-sergeants busily engaged in workmanlike attention to their equipment; Pengelly was checking the Land Rover, Williams was testing the three breathing sets and Myers was examining the portable generator that was to activate the explosive devices.

Wallace hesitated. 'This is it, then,' he said. He felt awkward, out of place even, in the company of these combat-experienced veterans as they made their final preparations for attack.

No one answered him. Dan Pengelly looked up briefly and nodded, but immediately returned to his equipment check.

'It's nine-thirty,' Wallace ventured.

Steve Williams was momentarily distracted from his inspection. 'We know that,' he answered shortly. Normally the rebuff would have been followed by further sarcasm but he voiced none. He had no time for inconsequential matters.

* * *

'Take off!'

Steve Williams hissed the instruction as he slid into the passenger seat of the Avenger. David Wallace slotted the automatic gear lever into 'Drive'. He suddenly realized that his hands were perspiring as he felt his moist palm slip on the smooth, plastic coating of the lever, and as he depressed the accelerator pedal he felt his right leg tremble uncontrollably so that the car jerked away from the Section Office as if driven by a novice.

'Easy!'

His companion gave a warning growl and Wallace glanced at the man alongside him. Steve Williams looked coolly confident in his own ability and Wallace drew a deep breath; the air of self assurance exuded by the veteran at his side was the steadying influence he needed.

'I'm all right, Steve.' David Wallace was looking to the front as he spoke, but he felt the other man's eyes study the profile of his face.

'You'd better be!'

Wallace drove slowly along the concrete ribbon which led from Section Eight to the administration building. He was dry of mouth and his heart pounded as they neared their destination. When they were yet some distance from the building they saw the dark-coloured Shuritor security van parked outside its main front entrance.

'The van is in, Steve. We've timed it just right.'

'Aye. So far, so good. Now, pull over to the side and park where we can keep an eye on that van. There's no sign of the guards, so they must be inside offloading the cash-boxes on to your mate, Barnfield. We'll wait here until they clear off.'

There had been a sudden and dramatic change in the relationship between the two Welshmen, and Wallace was intelligent enough to recognise the fact and to accept the change. During the planning phases of the operation when meticulous attention to detail was required, the ex-sergeant had been less than positive, even childishly argumentative and obstructive at times. But now the planning was over, now there was only need for fast, physical action, and Steve Williams' stature grew. As if in an instant, his earlier petulance disappeared and in its place emerged a dominant character who revelled in the promise of aggression and its rich reward. He was now on the field of battle and it was quite natural that he should take command.

They were to wait a further ten minutes, ten minutes of steadily accruing tension for Wallace, before they saw the Shuritor guards emerge from the main entrance to climb into their van and drive away.

'They'll miss all the fun,' Williams muttered, then: 'You drive on.'

They cruised past the main door and swung around the end of the red brick building until they neared the lesser used south, side entrance.

'Get as close to the door as you can,' Williams rapped tersely.

When the car reached the side entrance Wallace slowed almost to a halt and both men looked around warily. The area was deserted and, at a nod from his companion, the driver drew the car up alongside the panelled door.

'Listen, boy. I'm going in now,' Steve Williams consulted his wristwatch, 'at ten-thirty hours exactly. Plus thirty minutes—that means you start the gas at eleven hundred hours. Check?'

'Eleven hundred hours. Check!'

Williams slid from his seat and peered back in through the open car door at the driver. 'Are you okay?'

'Yes, yes. Of course I am!' The pallor on the younger man's face belied his words.

'Christ! You look as if you want to puke.' Williams' lip curled in disgust. 'Don't you go soft on us, College Boy. You hear me?'

'Curse you!' David Wallace ground the gear lever into reverse and at the same time he felt nausea rise from the pit of his stomach. 'I'm fine, I tell you. Get on with your part of it, and

I'll do mine.'

'The gas—eleven hundred hours. Have you got that?'

'Yes! Yes!'

Steve Williams gave Wallace a calculating look which lasted brief seconds, then he turned on his heel and sprang up a few steps to the green-painted door. He sent one last, quick glance back towards the car, and he was gone.

'Hell! Hell! Hell!'

David Wallace hissed the word over and over through clenched teeth, as he reversed out into the roadway then headed back towards Section Eight. As he tried to still the shaking in his limbs, he told himself that he should not allow Steve Williams to rile him, but in the back of his mind he knew that he was being less than honest and that Steve was right on this occasion. The veteran had seen sufficient armed combat to make him wary of entrusting his personal safety to incompetent allies. Wallace clenched the driving wheel tightly and prayed that the ague in his limbs would cease.

By the time he reached his Section he had managed to compose himself. He drove directly into the maze of plant and nosed the Avenger towards the basement storeroom where Pengelly and Myers eagerly awaited his return. The two men came running to meet him as he rolled down the ramp and pulled up

74

alongside the red-veneered Land Rover which stood ready for action.

'Is he in?'

'Yes. He wants the gas onstream at eleven hundred hours.' Wallace clipped his words to disguise his shortness of breath.

'Any problems in getting him inside?' Pengelly asked, but he was looking at his wristwatch as he spoke and he half ignored the muttered reply. 'That gives us twenty-five minutes before we feed ammonia into the water pipeline; time for a last check on the Saunders valves. You get your suit and your PVC on first though, Dave.'

The two ex-sergeants were already clad in thick, black serge, firemen's suits over which they had drawn the yellow plastic leggings and tunics which the fire-brigade personnel wore as waterproofs, since ammonia gas in high concentration would penetrate ordinary clothing to sear and blister underlying skin. He hurriedly divested himself of his own outer garments before climbing into the fireman's clothing, and as he pulled on the protective plastic tunic, he suddenly caught a glimpse of himself in one of the wing mirrors of the Land Rover. The white, strained face that stared back at him was that of a stranger; an unreal face whose mouth split in a mirthless grin of greeting.

When he was dressed, Myers picked up the hand-cranked generator and the three men left the storeroom to make their way to the bund wall which surrounded the massive cylinders containing liquid ammonia. The critical pipework connection between the ammonia line and the domestic water line had been made in a service pit which lay outside the bund wall. The trio grouped around the pit and gazed down at the cluster of pipes, among which was the interconnecting tee-piece, with its isolating, three-inch Saunders valve, which Myers and Williams had surreptitiously installed. That single valve now gave viability to the whole nefarious scheme.

'Twenty minutes to go.'

David Wallace stared into the pit. There was yet time to call it off; to cancel the entire, crazy operation.

'Better check your watches.'

'Ten forty-three hours?'

Wallace nodded his agreement. Could only thirteen minutes have elapsed since Steve Williams slipped through the side entrance into the administration block?

'Fifteen minutes to go, by God!' Above his high, Romany cheek bones, Dan Pengelly's eyes shone with the light of battle as he cried: 'Time to let all hell loose on Section Ten.'

'I'll do my monkey act, then,' Myers grinned. The ex-navy diver handed the generator to Pengelly, grasped the bottom of a metal ladder which was bolted to the side of the bund wall and hauled himself up the first few rungs. Dan Pengelly hefted the generator up for Myers to grasp in one huge hand and then shin up the ladder to the top of the wall with a facility born of years of naval training. The command wires to the ignition devices secreted on Section Ten had been laid amongst a maze of legitimate wires and cables which ran in an underground service channel. On Section Eight this channel passed near the bund wall. There the command wires surfaced, but ran along the top of the wall where they lay out of sight and ready for use. In the same hiding place, Williams had also connected the switch which was to activate the fire-alarms.

The man on the ladder clambered on to the top of the brick wall and sat astride it. He placed the generator on the wall in front of him, then connected the ends of the hidden command wires to its terminals. He looked down expectantly at the upturned faces below him.

'Now?'

Wallace looked at his wristwatch, then at the Somerset man by his side. 'Twelve minutes. Yes?' At Pengelly's nod of agreement he jerked his thumb upwards in signal to the man on the wall.

A discernible whirring sound echoed from the set as Ian Myers cranked its handle. He pressed a red button marked 'Fire', to despatch an electric impulse to the deadly incendiary devices which he and Steve Williams had so cunningly inserted in the hydrogen and petroleum-cracking plants on Section Ten. At that precise moment, on receipt of the electric current the fulminate in the fuses would be detonating to ignite the attached incendiary chemical composition. This primary ignition would, in turn, cause a secondary ignition turning several thousand cubic feet of explosive hydrogen gas into a sea of fire and making a raging inferno of the petroleum plant. Each of the three men could imagine what chaos and consternation that simple press of a button had unleashed; two hundred men at work on those hazardous, toxic processes would be scurrying to take emergency measures before evacuating the Section.

Quickly, Myers released his hold on the generator and grabbed for the switch to trigger the fire-alarm circuitry about the complex. In the radio room of the fire-brigade's headquarters, alarms would be sounding from a dozen sites across Forsters' spreading acres. For maybe two minutes the ex-diver crouched in a listening attitude atop the bund wall, then: 'There go the fire-brigade!' he called. He disconnected the command wires and dropped the generator into the safe hands of Dan Pengelly before sliding down the ladder, navy style, so that he seemed almost to fall from the wall. The

78

distant sound of urgently ringing bells reached the ears of the other two, and they knew that the first part of Wallace's plan was succeeding and that all of the fire station's vehicles and manpower would be despatched to the major emergency on Section Ten, or to investigate a series of false alarms. Forsters' fire brigade would be unable to respond to any further calls.

'Nine minutes!'

As one, they turned and ran for the basement storeroom.

'Get the life-support sets on!'

The Draeger emergency respirator sets each had a single, black and white, back mounted cylinder which held a thirty minute supply of life giving air at two-thousand eight-hundred and forty pounds per square inch pressure. Now, each man shouldered his way into his set and tightened the buckle of its leather waist strap. Skintight rubber gloves completed each man's ensemble. They were ready for the attack!

'Check your cylinder pressures,' Myers ordered, and the three scrutinised the pressure indicator gauges which were clipped to their chest straps.

'Mine is low. The dial only reads two-thousand five-hundred p.s.i.' Wallace said in dismay.

The two veterans crowded around him. 'It can't be low, Steve checked them all,' Myers snapped impatiently.

'She must be sticking. The set is okay, it's just the gauge.'

'Even at that, there's more than enough air. If we aren't out of the cash office by the time that much air is used up, then we'll be in trouble anyway.' David Wallace tried to speak firmly, but he had gone dry-mouthed.

'You open the doors, Ian. It's time to go.'

Pengelly clambered into the driving seat and Wallace joined him in the cab of the vehicle. The air cylinders on their backs restricted their movements, but they had practised this stage of the operation many times and had adjusted the cab seats to allow driver and passengers to sit while wearing the breathing sets. The masks of the positive pressure respirators hung loosely in front of them, ready for instant use and held in place by a supporting loop of tape. The driver headed out of the basement and up the ramp. He waited for Myers to lock the storeroom door and then climb into the back of the Land Rover. As they drove towards the ammonia-storage bund, Wallace caught sight of a pall of smoke rising skywards in the distance and he knew that the hydrogen plant was burning. He hoped, desperately, that no one had been injured and that the only damage would be to the plant itself; he had planned it that way but although he had constantly assured the three foremen that no one should get hurt by a controlled ignition in the parts of the hydrogen and cracking plants he had chosen, he knew in his heart of hearts that injury and even death was possible when such hazardous processes were sabotaged, no matter how carefully.

Pengelly drew to a halt alongside the storage area. 'Just five minutes to go! Time to get inside the bund and open the feed valve from reserve tank "A",' he said as they clambered from the vehicle.

Wallace and Pengelly pushed their way through the door in the bund wall and made their way to the delivery valve at the base of the reserve storage tank. The Somerset man craned his neck to look at the pressure indicator mounted on the tank. 'One hundred and twenty-five pounds per square inch.' He glanced at his companion. 'That's plenty of pressure, Dave. I'll let her go; you get outside and see if Ian needs any help.'

David Wallace had just reached the door leading from the bund when he heard the ammonia pipes bounce and hiss as liquefied ammonia under pressure hurtled through them. Now all that stood between the administration building and twenty tonnes of liquid ammonia was the three-inch Saunders valve in the service pit outside that door.

At a signal from the big Welshman, Ian Myers dropped into the pit and stood poised above the crucial tee pipe connection which, in an instant, would turn an innocent water-pipe into a pipe which supplied life-quenching ammonia gas.

'Two minutes!'

A grunt of satisfaction rose in Myers' throat as he stooped over the water inlet valve. His gloved fingers closed on the wheel and with deft movements he drove the spindle down into its housing to cut off the through flow of water. Dan Pengelly stood over him, arm raised like the starter of a race. The man in the pit glanced at his wristwatch.

'Time check. Eleven hundred hours!'

'Let the bastard go!'

Even as Pengelly swept his upraised arm downwards, Myers spun open the ammonia isolating valve with a quick twist. Immediately, the banshee wail of whistling gas echoed inside the steel tube as gallons of pent-up liquefied ammonia jetted on-stream and pulsed along the isolated water-pipe towards the office building and its unsuspecting occupants.

*   *   *

Steve Williams' eyes gradually grew accustomed to the gloomy half-light which pervaded the boiler room in which he crouched. There had been no trouble, and, as far as he could tell, no one had seen him enter the building. The long corridor into which the south side-door opened had been providentially empty, and it had taken only a few seconds to walk to the boiler room and slip into this prearranged hiding place, locking the door behind him. Obviously, the room was little used; the boiler was shut down for the summer, but it and its associated paraphernalia were clean and well maintained, as was the air-conditioning plant which was installed alongside the boiler.

Dust lay thick on several empty shelves which ringed the bare walls of the room and a network of ancient cobwebs draped a pile of antiquated files stacked on the floor in one corner. He lifted the Draeger respirator and the bundle of clothing down from the shelf on which he had previously secreted them, and after doing so could feel the dust clinging to his fingers.

The little Welshman grinned to himself as he remembered the sickly pallor on Wallace's face when they parted. 'Stupid jerk!' Williams muttered to himself at the memory. 'Christ, Wallace, you've got a lot to learn that you won't find in books. Maybe you won't be quite so bloody wet after this little outing is over.' The intruder checked his wristwatch. The luminous coating on its hands gleamed sulphurously at ten-forty.

'Not long now, Stevie.'

Faintly, through the walls of his hide, he could hear the tap-tap-tapping sounds of typewriter keys being pummelled. Further along the corridor a door squeaked as it opened; muted tones of conversation reached the hidden man; the voices were suddenly cut off with the closing of the door. Clacking high heels rattled noisily on the tiled floor of the corridor as an office girl passed the small boiler room, oblivious to the danger that lurked behind its blank door.

'I'll soon have you twats out of it!'

The prospect of the chaos he was to unleash throughout the building added to his relish. He unrolled the bundle of clothing and picked a smoke canister from amongst its folds. He placed the canister down carefully, then quickly dressed himself in the fireman's tunic and trousers over which he donned the PVC suit. He finally adjusted his gloves with particular deliberation, so that no part of his skin was exposed to possible contact with concentrated ammonia gas. It was as he was completing the adjustments to his clothing that the distant sounds of fire-engine bells made him pause and look up. A babble of excited voices broke out in the surrounding offices as clerks and typists speculated on the reason for the alarm. Williams now knew that the incendiary devices which he and Myers had inserted into the process plants on Section Ten had done their work. He also guessed that fire-alarms would be calling for attention from all over the industrial complex's extensive installations. It only remained for him to buckle on the compressed air life-support set, but he could do that after—ten fifty-five hours! Now!

The air-conditioning system was fed by a positive pressure fan unit which sent clean, fresh air from outside the building through a filter mesh and then along a series of ducts into each office. The main duct first passed through the boiler room, and a perforated, wire grille in this duct allowed air to be drawn off into the boiler room itself. On a previous visit the Welshman had taped a square of cloth over the apertures of this grille to make an air-tight seal. Being careful not to tear the cloth, he lifted the grille from the duct and placed it at his feet, then he grasped the smoke canister and thrust it deep inside the air duct. Holding the canister in a left-handed grip, he sprang its release pin with his right hand. Instantly thick, acrid smoke spewed from the device, catching the little Welshman off guard.

'Christ!'

He flung the belching container into the duct and quickly slammed the covered grille back into place. His eyes streamed as the chemical smoke bit into them and he fought to suppress a racking cough as choking vapour reached his lungs, but fortunately for him, the cloth cover over the grille did its job and no more smoke seeped past the covered mesh, so that he was able to recover his breath without making a lot of noise. The little man realised, with much silent blasphemy, that he should have donned his breathing apparatus before releasing the pin of the smoke canister.

'Eleven hundred hours!'

The moments before the actual launch of an attack during his years in the front line of combat had always brought Steve Williams to an exhilarating high, to a crest of excitement, and so it was now. He mouthed the words as if to unseen comrades whose ghosts awaited his call to arms.

A hubbub of complaining voices broke out at several points deep within the building and the sounds filtered through the walls of his shadowy lair.

'Smoke shell on target!'

The Welshman licked his lips and his teeth gleamed in the half-light. The smoke must have hit them, he thought exultantly, and by now would be pouring from air-conditioning grilles into offices throughout the block. He unlocked the door of the boiler room and pulled it ajar. His head swung to and fro with stealthy, ferret-like movements as he peered out to scan the corridor; he saw two girls running in panic at the far end of the building, but they were scurrying in the opposite direction and so had their backs turned towards him. Luck was on his side! The glass-covered fire-alarm button jutted from the wall of the corridor some three feet away from the boiler room door. Williams stepped out and swung a sledge-hammer blow at the button with such violence that the glass plate shattered into smithereens and the button was depressed simultaneously. With shrill, ear piercing shrieks the activated klaxon system blared forth its warning and even as the first strident notes echoed throughout the offices, Steve Williams leapt for his refuge. Hell! He hadn't expected such a bloody racket. Clamouring voices called and yelled. Somewhere, a woman screamed, and her thin hysterical wails keened through the general uproar of anxious shouts like a slicing wire.

Now he worked swiftly in the shadows. He hefted the Draeger life-support pack, propped its twenty-inch long, steel alloy, compressed air cylinder on a waist-high shelf, then twisted his body and backed up to the set so that it leaned against his shoulders. With deft, agile movements, he slipped his arms through the shoulder straps and buckled the leather harness around his waist. When he had fastened the cross strap with its critical pressure gauge over his chest, he began to follow a detailed drill with a curious, dogged, military precision.

'Open cylinder valve. Pressure reading two-thousand eight-hundred pounds per square inch. Sir! Shut valve. Mask on. No leaks. Sir!'

Steve Williams was hardly aware that he uttered the staccato 'Sir!' as he repeated, *sotto voce,* the sequence of instructions that he had learned off by heart from the Draeger instruction manual. The mode of speech was instinctive, an automatic reflex for a British army trained sergeant in a combat situation. From the corridor outside the boiler room came the sound of rushing feet as people fled from the building.

'Open cylinder valve. Check bypass valve closed. Sir!'

He mouthed the drill tersely into the rubber mask which covered his face. In some bizarre fashion his mind spun back to his war.

'Sergeant.'

'Sir!'

'Check your weapons.'

'Sir!'

The oiled barrel of the sleek, black Luger reflected a satin sheen as he eased the automatic pistol from under his tunic. He slid the spring-loaded magazine from the handgrip of the gun and checked the row of wicked looking, snub-nosed bullets it held before he clipped the magazine back into the weapon. Cautiously, the Welshman eased the boiler room door open and stepped out into the long corridor. Skeins of smoke wreathed from gaping office doors which had been left wide open in the panic of evacuation, adding to the pall of thick, grey vapour which hung from the ceiling of the corridor. But the corridor was empty! They were all out, fleeing like frightened sheep at the threat of danger. Behind his gas mask Williams' face broke into a contemptuous grin as he shrugged the weight of the breathing apparatus further up his back and then checked his watch. Eleven zero three hours. The gas was on stream!

His body stooped slightly beneath the weight of his life-supporting burden as he shuffled along the corridor to the men's washroom and pushed his way through its swing doors. To his left, a row of water-closet cubicles ranged the length of the room, while from the opposite wall two dozen china hand-basins projected on iron-work pedestals. At once he made for the chipped and battered hand-basins. He tucked the German pistol into the waist-band of his trousers in order to free both hands, then quickly worked his way along the row, opening fully the taps of each basin as he went. Next, he stepped into each of the water-closet cubicles in turn and yanked at each cistern chain as he did so. Above him, in the attic of the single-storeyed building, the ball-valves in the cold-water head tanks began to vibrate as the diverted ammonia supply backed up behind the rapidly draining water seal which remained in the water-pipe supplying those head tanks.

As he watched the flow of water gushing from the taps, the Welshman knew that the water supply must soon run out, drawn from the path of onrushing, deadly, liquefied ammonia, and that at any moment a searing blast of liquid gas would jet from the ball valves in the attic. Once released from that restricting pipe the liquid gas would vaporize in the warmth of the roof space and then spread in billowing clouds along the length of the building until it penetrated downwards to fill the rooms below. Also, once the water-tanks themselves were drained of water, a choking, stinging stream of ammonia would surge from the open taps in the washroom and—

' 'Ere. Where be the fire?'

'Christ!'

Williams spun on his heel. The inquisitive, frowning face of the messenger, Jack Froggart, peered perplexedly into the Celt's face-mask.

' 'Ere, fireman, what's on? Where's this fire?' The old messenger waved his arms. 'I've been all along the offices,' he said, 'an' there's a deal of smoke, but I can't see no fire. I reckon they've runn'd away for a false alarum,' and the old fellow cackled delightedly at the prospect.

Steve Williams felt his heart hammer with the shock of this unexpected intrusion. He gritted his teeth; obviously the old fool had mistaken him for a fireman because of the camouflaging effect of his ensemble.

'You shouldn't be here. Get out!'

Williams' frantic shout was muffled behind his visor.

'What say?'

'Get out, you stupid bastard. Get out!'

'Well now, son,' the old man said obstinately. He was slow in his ways and he spoke with an air of heavy wisdom which infuriated the impatient Welshman. 'There ain't no fire, as far as I can see, and I ain't about to make a fool o'meself by a'runnin' after that lot.' Froggart chuckled to himself; then, before Williams could take avoiding action, the messenger stepped forward and grasped his arm. 'I tell you 'tis a false—' Froggart paused in mid sentence and craned his scrawny neck to stare into the other's visor. The pensioner screwed up his rheumy eyes. ''Ere. I know you! You ain't no fire-brigade man. You'm that foreman from the plant.'

'Let go of my arm, you doddering old idiot,' the Welshman snarled savagely, and he jerked his arm from the claw-like grip of the messenger.

'What's goin' on? What's the game, eh?'

'You just wouldn't listen, would you?'

The old man's gaze widened in astonishment as he found himself looking into the vicious, black eye of the Luger automatic pistol. Involuntarily, he took a pace backwards, and in doing so collided with one of the overflowing wash basins. His hand slipped on the edge of the bowl as he fumbled for support, plunging his coat sleeve up to its elbow in the foaming water.

'Now—you wait, son—'

'You just would not listen.'

In mortal fear the old man was suddenly older, weaker. Yellowy eyes blinked back tears of surprise and his aged body sagged visibly as he struggled to comprehend this alien confrontation with violence.

'Please, son—'

Steve Williams regarded the pleading pensioner dispassionately. He had gunned younger men in France. Some of those had pleaded, wept for wives, babies, a chance to live. He could never remember their faces, only the fright in their eyes, as they faced the unwinking, metal tube of extinction which he alone controlled. He had never been able to understand the fuss his own infantrymen had made over executing prisoners, so he had always done it himself, surreptitiously, easily, a few fields back from the front lines. After all, the bastards were trying to nail him, they just ran out of time. There had been murmurings among the soldiers of his own platoon, veiled threats about reporting him to an officer. Then they had seen him chopped down at Rouen; that had shut their snivelling mouths and reminded them what war was all about, though it had taken a Schmeisser bullet in their sergeant's belly to do so.

'Turn around!'

'What are you goin' to do?' Stark terror showed in Froggart's eyes and saliva dribbled an erratic course down the stubble on his chin.

'Turn around!' Williams ordered, and emphasised his repeated command with a jab of the Luger in the old man's stomach.

'For God's sake, don't shoot. Please, don't shoot me.' The messenger trembled uncontrollably as he begged for his life. A sob rose in his throat. 'Please, son. I shan't say anything about this. I shan't let on that I saw you.'

'Okay, okay,' the masked man rasped impatiently, and nodded his head. 'Now, turn!' His mind worked furiously. The old fool had recognised him and would undoubtedly identify him, despite the fearful assurances given while faced with the gun.

With much hesitation and with many fearful glances over his shoulder, Jack Froggart turned to face the white-tiled wall of the washroom. Through the eyepiece of his mask, Williams could see the skin at the back of his victim's thin neck crease into folds as the old man flickered nervous glances from side to side in futile attempts to determine the gunman's intention. The fear of death, held the messenger in its black embrace.

Williams took one quick step forwards and brought the butt of the Luger arcing down on the exposed nape of the man's neck. The messenger's knees buckled, he flapped down like a stranded flatfish and in doing so struck his face a sickening, bone-crushing blow on the concrete floor. The Welshman tucked the gun into his waistband and regarded the insensible figure of the old messenger who lay curled in the foetal position at his feet. He toed the prostrate body on to its back; gobs of bright red blood pulsed from the old man's nose and, diluting, spread in crimson waves on the layer of water which now swilled across the washroom floor.

A blast of ammonia coughed first from one tap, then another. Hissing liquid choked on a last water-lock before spitting into the room with pressurised force; gas delivery multiplied along the row of open taps and, as liquid ammonia jetted into cold water, each wash basin became a boiling cauldron from which gas vaporized and expanded voluminously into pungent, invisible clouds. In the roof cavity of the building, the same process continued to spew volumes of deadly ammonia from the gurgling ball valves.

Steve Williams checked his wristwatch. 'Eleven zero eight, Stevie, boy,' he cautioned himself. 'Got to get moving!' Already more than five minutes of precious air had been used from the thirty minute supply on his back because of this unforeseen interruption. The man from the valleys frowned down on the frail, limp body of the messenger.

'Pity you saw me, lovely,' he whispered to the blueing face. 'Aye, it's a pity, that.'

The man on the floor made small, gargling

sounds in his throat as his lungs filled with the stifling gas. Though senseless, he retched violently around a swollen and protruding tongue, as his body tried to reject the all-pervading ammonia. He gasped for air, but there was none. Only more gas, to bind his chest and still his mind.

FOUR

'There's the smoke, by God! I can see the smoke!'

Ian Myers screamed the words from behind his mask. He gripped Wallace's arm in his huge, gloved fist so tightly that the Welshman could feel the pressure of the big man's iron fingers through the double thickness of his tunic and plastic oversuit. Then Wallace and Pengelly could see it too, swathes of greyish-black smoke, pouring from the side doors of the administration building and from a number of partly-opened windows at the rear of the block.

The three men sat alongside each other in the cab of the disguised Land Rover as, with Dan Pengelly at the wheel, it cruised slowly along a road which passed close by the rear of the building. With the despatch of Forsters' fire-fighting appliances to the inferno on Section Ten and to attend to the false alarms, the trio had slipped away from Section Eight and headed towards their target. They knew that further fire-engines would be sent to Forsters from Bristol fire stations, to give assistance to the over-stretched firemen at the plant, but Forsters was nearly fifteen miles from the city, and so it would be at least half-an-hour before extra appliances arrived.

'And he's got them out! That bloody, beautiful Welshman has got them on the run.'

As they closed on the building they could see small groups of office workers milling about the lawns near the side entrances to the block, and a few hysterical typists who clutched at each other for comfort.

'Hold tight! It's time to join Steve,' Pengelly bawled, and he wrenched the Rover into low gear.

They came in fast on the curving road that skirted the rear of the administration block and was separated from it by a three-hundred yard wide strip of grass and shrubbery. When they reached a point nearest to the barred windows of the cash office, Dan Pengelly swung the driving wheel over so violently that the tyres of the Land Rover squealed in protest at the sudden stress and the smooth passage of the vehicle became a juddering, bouncing nightmare as it careered across the rain-softened verge. The driver mouthed wild curses as he tried to thread a route between the straggly shrubs which grew in haphazard clumps about the lawn, but most of the bushes which lay in their path were flattened beneath their threshing wheels.

Inside the jolting cab the three gloved and suited men braced themselves as best they could. They looked like a trio of demented, goggle-eyed, alien beings beneath the paraphernalia of their Draeger breathing sets as they grappled for hand-holds with which to anchor their flailing bodies. Their air cylinder supply valves were still in the closed position; there was insufficient in those single cylinders to use any of it needlessly, but they wore the identity-concealing masks loosely over their faces so that, although their features were hidden, they were able to suck air in past the loose rubber hoods.

'The smoke is thinning,' Myers warned.

He was right; the initial density of the chemical fog belching from the building lessened visibly even as they watched.

'They'll be going back inside,' Pengelly shouted despairingly, and he stood on the brake pedal and brought the Rover to a sliding halt so rapidly that the vehicle slewed broadside on. 'Where the hell is the gas? It was on-stream before we left the Section.' He hunched awkwardly behind the steering column as the bulk of the alloy cylinder strapped to his back forced him forwards. A muffled roar of rage came from inside his mask. 'Where's the bloody gas?' he screamed.

'Look! The bastards will be back inside the building soon.'

He gesticulated with gloved fingers towards the group of evacuees of whom one or two of the more adventurous male clerks were reconnoitring the side entrance through which they had recently fled in panic, no doubt emboldened by the arrival of the Land Rover and what they mistakenly took to be a fire-fighting crew. Then, abruptly, the clerks jerked back from the doorway like so many puppets plucked by unseen strings. They clutched at their throats and knuckled their eyes as they turned and ran from some terrible but invisible power. Shrieks rose from amongst the crowd as the retreating, blinded men careered into them until the milling onlookers turned and fled in a state of utter confusion, coughing and spluttering as they went.

Wallace thought he detected faint wisps of whitish vapour mixed with the thinning smoke, but that was the only visible indication of ammonia and the fronds of white soon disappeared from sight as the gas expanded and vaporized further. He had seen process workers on the plant run from the invisible hand of leaking ammonia gas on a number of occasions, but only now, as he watched the spectacle of the frantic mob being driven from the administration building did he feel vindicated in his choice of an ideal weapon.

'The gas, Dan,' he cried with relief. 'I just knew it would work. The whole building must be flooded with the stuff!'

'Look at them run,' Myers breathed in awe at the sight of the scampering office workers.

The sharp tang of ammonia caught their nostrils and stung their eyes as a warning that the noxious cloud had reached them, though they were yet fully a hundred yards from the building. There was no wind and the still, misty weather served to keep the gaseous cloud low and compact.

'It's getting pretty thick. Tighten your masks and open your air valves.'

Wallace yanked the nylon web fastenings of his mask tight at the back of his head and sucked a great lungful of rubbery-tasting air from inside his mask in order to test the seal around his face. The soft rubber of his mask buckled against his cheeks in response to the vacuum, then, satisfied that his mask was air tight, he spun open his main supply valve to give his lungs access to one-thousand two-hundred litres of pure, clean air. The two men at his side did the same.

'Thirty minutes' working time.'

The masked apparitions nodded in unison. They could rely on their life-support systems for this length of time, allowing for a normal breathing rate of forty litres of air per minute, but heavy work would increase their oxygen requirements and shorten the thirty-minute period by an unknown factor.

'This is it!'

Pengelly's muffled voice reached an urgent crescendo as once again he slashed the engine into low gear. The motor whined momentarily without apparent effect, then the vehicle's spinning wheels took grip on solid ground beneath the soft surface of the grass lawn and they shot forwards so violently that Wallace's head whiplashed back and he thought for one agonized moment they must accelerate straight into the brick wall of the building. He should have known better; Dan Pengelly spun the driving wheel with all the skill of a Formula One racing driver and brought the Land Rover in a four-wheel skid to halt exactly level with the barred windows of the cash office.

Myers was out of the cab before they slithered to a stop, with Wallace close behind him. Pengelly yelled encouragement as they clawed the coiled, three-legged chain from its housing on the flat bonnet of the Rover. There was the crash of breaking glass as the pane of one of the barred windows disintegrated and fell away; wraiths of smoke and gas funnelled out from the break in the window, then, through the vertical, iron security bars they saw the plastic suited figure of Steve Williams inside the room. In his hands he held the burnt out smoke canister and the cloth he had used to cover the air conditioning grille. There was now no sign of his having used the boiler room for any nefarious purpose, and Wallace reached through the bars, took the items from him and threw them into the back of the Rover. It was well-nigh impossible to converse, encased as they were in the Draeger masks, except by muffled shouts which were unintelligible at a distance of more than three or four feet, but they were well rehearsed and the two men quickly passed the three hooked ends of the triple lifting chain through the window to the little Welshman. It took only moments for him to fasten the hooks to individual bars, then Myers reeled in the free end of the chain and hooked its case-hardened steel links to the chassis of the Land Rover.

'Go!'

Wallace had been crowding Myers, anxious to prove his worth in action. He heard the veteran shout and saw him signal to the driver, but was not quick enough to avoid a collision of bodies as Myers jumped back from the tightening chain and the metal air cylinder strapped to Myers' back caught Wallace a painful blow on his cheek bone, filling his eyes with tears and causing him to stagger. He stood stock still, dazed and unable to wipe his brimming eyes.

'Get bloody moving!'

As Wallace's eyes cleared he saw Myers waving a clenched fist as he shouted the angry

101

instruction. There was no place for weakness; no time for it.

Pengelly wrestled with the plunging vehicle as he powered it into reverse. The chain tightened and hummed with tension. Tiny chips of brickwork flew off the window surround; the steel bars buckled, but held. The ex-sergeant eased the Rover forward, then there was a crash of gears and it rocketed backwards with the full power of its two-and-a-quarter litre engine. As the chain slammed tight, a rending, cracking noise split the air and the brickwork which entrenched the ends of the bars split asunder. Suddenly, the entire, barred framework was plucked out bodily and fell to the ground to leave a gaping hole in the wall.

They were shrouded in billowing vapour as they scrambled through the demolished aperture to join Steve Williams inside the gas-filled cash office. The little Celt had begun work on the wire mesh above the paying-out counter, and one corner of the grille was already loose. Then Dan Pengelly fell on the barrier that stood between him and the payroll. Wallace did not know this man; a tearing, ripping machine who literally smashed the mesh from its mountings with an immense and terrible strength. Wallace found himself carried along with the tide of ferocity, yet he felt overwhelmed by the naked power emanating from the three ex-sergeants; Dan

Pengelly raged before him like a colossus no man-made barrier could withstand; Steve Williams, cool, calculating and deadly; Ian Myers, competent and reliable. Curiously, Wallace remembered the feeling he had experienced in his youth when caught at some nefarious prank with a gang of older boys. He remembered how they had scattered and eluded pursuit, but how he, younger and less sure, had been caught and punished. He felt vulnerable, weak to his bowels now, as then.

The grille buckled, held momentarily, then fell before the onslaught. Pengelly and Williams swung their encumbered bodies on to the counter which divided the room and slid, belly down, across it. The strongroom door stood ajar; obviously the wages office staff had had no time to lock it before the smoke had driven them out. Wallace scrambled across the counter to join the two veterans who were already swinging the heavy strongroom door wide open.

'There they are, by God!' Williams' throaty roar echoed in his air hose. 'Four of them!'

The three intruders crouched in the open doorway. Four cash-boxes lay before them in a neat row, ranged against one wall, with the cover of each container thrown open to expose the contained wealth to their excited gaze. The sight of serried layers of banknotes, neatly bundled in brown paper bands, held them spellbound and they hovered like three enormous, carapaced insects, blinking at the trove through disked and shining eyes.

'What is it? Get a move on, before the gas thins.'

They heard Myers call from the far side of the counter, and Wallace turned and held four fingers aloft.

'We've got four, and each one full to the brim,' he mouthed, though the other could never have picked up his every word.

Their pause was fractional, a fleeting moment of appreciation, then they were moving swiftly again as, one by one, they manhandled the money containers from the strongroom. Williams closed the lid of each box and snapped its clips shut before sliding it from the strongroom to Pengelly, who heaved each metal container from floor to counter with one, muscle-raking lift. There was little talk, the rubber masks made speech distorted and difficult anyway, so the few exchanges were made in guttural grunts.

David Wallace had clambered back over the counter to help Myers carry the boxes out to the waiting Land Rover. He glanced at his wristwatch and bawled: 'Five minutes gone!'

Ian Myers' spaceman-like figure came stumbling in through the hole in the wall where the window had been as Pengelly and Williams followed the last of the containers over the counter. Five minutes! It seemed impossible to David Wallace that the driving, reckless automatons who surged around him had taken so short a time to achieve so much. He felt hot. Dear God! he felt so hot, but that was only to be expected when working hard while dressed in the enveloping uniform and PVC overclothes. He could feel perspiration running in a stream down the small of his back; waves of dizziness engulfed him and a band of steel tightened round his chest. He realised that the gasping sound he could hear was the sound of his own lungs sucking plaintively for air.

'Ian—something wrong—wrong—wrong—'

Wallace heard his own frantic call for help as a recurring echo inside his Draeger mask, moments before his senses hazed and clouded. He felt strong arms grasp him and hold him upright in a darkening world. Pinpricks of light danced crazily through his night as his knees buckled and he felt hands grappling at the intolerable burden on his back.

'The bypass, Dave! Use the bypass, man!'

The nightmarish features pressed close to his face appeared to be those of some alien being until, with recovering consciousness, he realised they were a replica of his own. Myers' eyes stared into his through the misted windows of their visors.

'Wait then—I'll reach it. Just help me to my feet—'

'No, no, man. I've opened it for you,' Myers shouted, and he knocked Wallace's hand away from the forgotten valve. 'We have to get out of here!'

Dismay struck Wallace like a physical blow as comprehension returned to his oxygen-starved brain and he realised the enormity of his error. Despite all his lecturing and preaching during their training and planning sessions, he had been the only culprit to omit that one vital function. They had been moving hard and fast; their work rate had been high enough to raise their bodily oxygen requirement by a considerable factor, but he had forgotten to bypass extra air from his back cylinder to meet the increased need of his heaving lungs.

As his faculties returned, Wallace felt himself being half-dragged, half-carried over the pile of demolished masonry where the window had been, then he was lifted bodily and virtually thrown into the cab of the vehicle. He felt the Land Rover leap beneath him.

'The money? Have we got the money?'

Wallace ripped his mask from his face, oblivious to any danger. Instantly, the residue of ammonia inside the cab seized his throat and he retched noisily, then vomited into his lap.

A cursing Dan Pengelly fought to keep control of the bucking vehicle as it ploughed a return path across the grass strip, then veered on to the road. As he accelerated along the firmer surface he opened his side window to disperse any remaining gas before tugging his own visor free. 'Shut your mouth!' he yelled. 'Just shut your mouth and hang on.'

'But—wait—' Wallace protested as he fought down rising waves of nausea.

Steve Williams and Ian Myers sat crouched in the rear of the Rover. The little Welshman reached through into the cab and slid open the window on Wallace's side, and as more fresh air swept through the length of the vehicle, Williams slipped his own mask from his head.

'Shut up, Dave! It's okay, I tell you,' Pengelly snapped savagely without taking his eyes from the narrow road. 'The cash-boxes are in the back.'

'Aye, it is okay, but not because of any bloody help from you.' Williams leaned over so that Wallace could feel the little man's hot breath on the side of his face. 'You very nearly poxed up the whole operation,' he sneered. He sat back, then leaned forward again to increase Wallace's sense of humiliation by adding: 'You stink of spew, Wallace, boy.'

The speeding Land Rover swayed round a bend in the road and headed for the distant Number One Feeder.

'Leave that, Steve, and unbuckle me,' Pengelly snarled, and he coughed over residual wisps of gas which clung to his clothing. The alloy cylinder strapped to his back meant that he had to lean forwards at an awkward angle. 'Get this flamin' lot off me, will you?' As he spoke he swung the machine through a series of curves that centrifuged his passengers to the side walls.

Williams reached for the driver. 'Easy, boy. This way a bit—there—' He swore profusely as he fought taut buckles. 'Now steady yourself as I pull—'

'Wait!' Pengelly crashed through the gears without toeing the clutch.

'Okay now?'

'Aye. Get on with it!'

Aided by Myers, Williams peeled the restricting apparatus from the driver's shoulders and flung it to the floor. The Draeger sets of the other men quickly followed suit.

'Almost there, lads,' Pengelly warned. 'Keep your eyes skinned for unwelcome guests.'

As they closed on the Feeder Pond, the white, concrete strip which surrounded the margin of the reservoir came into view, then suddenly they could see over the edge and down on to the broad expanse of deep water. Pengelly drove close to the rim of the Feeder, then turned in a half circle and came to a halt, so that the Land Rover faced away from the water. Gears whirred as he engaged reverse and rolled backwards to place the rear wheels on the concrete surround within a yard of the waiting depths.

'Can anyone see any movement?'

Four pairs of anxious eyes scanned the deserted, scrub-littered acres of rough ground that lay around Number One Feeder. Contours of uneven ground shielded them from the factory buildings, though from the direction of Section Ten they could see a billowing column of black, hydrocarbon smoke which rose higher and higher until it merged with the overcast sky. As expected, the Feeder and its vicinity were deserted, but Wallace found himself wondering how these three violent men would have dealt with an intruder.

'All clear.'

Myers lowered the tailboard of the vehicle and leapt out to join Wallace and Pengelly as they continued to scan the area.

'Aw, come on, for Christ's sake.' Williams was already sliding one container out to them. 'Quick about it, boys.'

'Heave!'

It took only seconds for them to hurl the four cash-boxes, one after the other, in a swinging arc into the calm water of the Feeder. As each metal container hit the surface it immediately sank, carrying its valuable contents down to obscurity in the gloomy depths.

'You were right, Dave, they were heavy enough to sink.'

'At least you've done something right, Mastermind,' Steve Williams grunted. There was another splash as he dropped the empty smoke canister, into which he had stuffed the piece of cloth, after the boxes. 'Now let's get the hell out of it.'

As they scrambled aboard the Land Rover once more, Pengelly said exultantly: 'I think we've done it.' He thrust his foot hard down on the accelerator pedal but they found themselves flung forwards in their seats as the vehicle lurched once, twice, then settled back with its wheels churning uselessly in a cloud of dust and loose scree. Pengelly's face blanched as he stabbed at the foot controls. 'The bastard's stuck. Get out and push.'

The three passengers sprang from their seats and heaved and strained at the heavy waggon with a strength born of desperation.

'Keep at it. She's goin'—she's goin—'

Pengelly gave a sudden stamp on the accelerator and the embedded Rover catapulted free from its self-made trap.

'A-g-ggh! My arm—'

A shrill bellow of pain rent the air.

'Ian. What the hell?'

They ran to the prone figure of Myers who lay in a cursing heap clutching his right arm.

'I slipped and the rear wheel caught me. Pull me up.' The man's upturned face contorted in agony and he yelped in pain as he was helped back to his seat. 'What a bloody carve-up,' he grimaced.

'Forget it,' Steve Williams muttered, tight-lipped. 'Let's just get out of here.'

Their journey to Section Eight was mercifully free from further incident. Pengelly drove quickly but steadily and they were soon rolling down the ramp and into the basement storeroom. Once inside, they ripped the disguising, red flashes from the side panels and bonnet of the Land Rover and divested themselves of the PVC oversuits and firemen's uniform. Steve Williams had kept his own clothing on underneath, and the other three hastily pulled on their own clothes which they had left in the storeroom, though Myers needed some assistance to dress. To all outward appearances they were once again a Section Manager and three foremen.

'First we turn off the ammonia and isolate the storage tank,' Wallace reminded his companions. 'We reconnect the pipelines in their normal sequence and resume the water supply to admin. as quickly as possible to avoid the line being traced to this Section.' He spoke with more authority than he felt, and he carefully avoided Steve Williams' mocking gaze. 'Ammonia is extremely soluble in water, so as soon as we get water running through the pipe again, it will dissolve all traces of the gas and flush it away. Analysis won't find any sign of gas in the water supply after that.'

They had driven out of the storeroom in Wallace's car, locking the door to the basement behind them, and reached the Section office before meeting anyone. As they dismounted, a Land Rover belonging to the fire-brigade came rushing up and stopped alongside them.

'Steve! We've been looking for you.' A harassed looking assistant fire-chief leaned out of his side window and addressed the little Welshman.

'What do you want?'

'You know about the trouble on Ten?'

'I can see it, boy.' Williams pointed to the cloud of smoke which still rose to the heavens. 'What the hell happened to cause all that?'

'They've had a fire in the hydrogen plant and a small explosion on the cracking unit.'

'Anyone hurt?' Wallace interjected hurriedly.

'No. Not as far as we know.' The man looked at Williams. 'There's also been an incident in admin., some fool said it was an ammonia leak, but that's not possible. We haven't enough men to cover everything, but I'm on my way there now. The thing is, Steve, alarms are going off all over the place, and we've wasted a hell of a lot of time in chasing false calls. Can you find out what's wrong with the system before we go crazy?'

'What do you think I'm doing on Section Eight?' Williams said. It was a piece of quick thinking on his part. 'I'm going around with Mr. Wallace, here, trying to sort out the alarms on his plant. The rest of my crew are checking the other Sections, so we'll know where the fault is soon enough.'

'Thank God for that!'

As the fire vehicle drove away, Pengelly grabbed Wallace's arm. 'You take Ian to the surgery; tell them he fell off a catwalk, or something. I'll make for the ammonia tanks and get the water flowing to admin. again. Steve must first reset the alarm circuits and recover the command wires. Then I'll give him a hand to reconnect the ammonia and water pipework as they should be.'

'What about the ignition devices we used to fire Section Ten?' Myers asked. The three veterans automatically looked at David Wallace for an answer.

'There'll be nothing left of them,' Wallace said. 'Steve will be removing the command wires, and he can nose around Ten later, just in case, but all trace of the incendiary devices should have been destroyed in the fire and explosion.' He shrugged. 'Besides, even if they do find some bits, well, so what?'

'I must telephone my instrument fitters, or they'll be wondering where I am,' Williams said, and he grinned. 'They'll be running around like headless chickens without having me tell them what to do.'

'Best hurry, now, before the bloody balloon goes up!'

When Pengelly and Williams had gone, Wallace said: 'You sit in the car, Ian, I won't be a minute.' He opened the outer door to the

Section offices and shouted: 'Any calls, Susan?' along the corridor.

'No, Mr. Wallace.' The girl peered round the door post. 'Everything's been quiet here, but there's something going on. The fire-engine bells have been ringing something awful.'

Wallace heaved a sigh of relief. No one had noticed his absence from Section Eight. 'Mr. Myers has injured his arm and I'm taking him to the surgery.' He hesitated. 'If Dan Pengelly or Steve Williams turn up, ask them to wait for me in my office.'

He walked to the car and the waiting Myers. 'How is it?'

'I'll live; my own stupid fault,' the big man grunted but he was obviously in a great deal of pain.

'You couldn't help it.' Wallace turned the key in the ignition. 'Steve isn't too tolerant of mistakes, is he?'

'There's no room for mistakes in an operation like this. I know some of the men who served under Steve during the war; he saved more than one member of his platoon by being the way he is. I'd rather have him with me than against me, but don't cross him, Dave, he's a dangerous man to cross.

'Aye, that much I know,' Wallace said, then added: 'Dan will have refilled the pipeline to admin. with water by now.' When they arrived at the surgery he parked to one side of the space marked 'Ambulances Only'. 'I'll come in with you and try to find out if anyone's been hurt,' he said. 'Come on, old son, let's get you inside.'

The white-coated doctor examined Myers' arm. 'Nothing broken,' he reported, 'but I'll ask Sister to strap it up for you, then you'll have to excuse me. We have some casualties coming in from Section Ten. By the way, how did it happen?'

'He fell.' Wallace had his story ready. 'He fell off the catwalk over the fuel oil tanks in the hydrochloric acid plant.'

'Fell, eh?' The doctor frowned. 'With the severe bruising, it looks more like a crushing injury than a fall.'

'That'll be the sample box, Doctor,' Myers said quickly. 'I was carrying this heavy sample box, you see, and it fell on my arm as I hit the ground.'

'Mmm. Well, it's not too bad. You'll live. Now I really must leave you to the tender mercies of Sister.'

'I hope the casualties aren't serious?' Wallace asked, before the other could leave.

'I don't know any details yet; three or four process men from the hydrogen plant with third degree burns, apparently. There's been an incident in the administration building, too. Some story about a gas leak,' and with that the doctor hurried away.

They were leaving the medical unit, and

had pushed open its glass swing doors to step from the antiseptic-smelling hallway, when the flashing, blue lights of an ambulance appeared. The white-painted vehicle came rushing towards them and drew to a halt in the reserved space immediately in front of them.

'What the hell is this, Ian?' Wallace whispered apprehensively.

'Excuse me, but you'll have to move from here!'

They turned to see the senior nursing Sister standing behind them, then quickly moved aside as two ambulance men jumped from their seats and ran to open the vehicle's rear doors. The body lay on a wheeled stretcher, shrouded by an all-enveloping blanket and between them, the ambulance attendants sledged the corpse from its resting place and carried it towards the foyer of the surgery.

As they passed within arm's length of him Wallace was unable to tear his gaze from the awful, immobile mound which lay beneath the blood red blanket. 'Dear God! What's happened?' he hissed through clenched teeth to his stunned companion.

Myers face was set, as if carved in stone, and no trace of emotion showed to betray his shocked senses. 'Who is it?' he whispered to the man who bore the rear of the stretcher.

'Old Jack Froggart.' The ambulance man nodded briefly at the cadaver as he spoke. 'There's been one hell of a massive gas leak inside the admin. block, and poor Jack bought it.'

David Wallace felt his cheekbones numb with sudden fear and his scalp prickled as he indicated the covered form with a feeble wave of one hand. 'Is—is he dead?'

'He's gone, sure enough,' the attendant nodded grimly. 'Gassed to death, I'd say, from the colour of his face and the way his tongue has swollen out of his mouth.'

Wallace felt the vomit rise in his throat, then running footsteps rang on the foyer floor as the doctor and nurses rushed to meet the stretcher bearers. The Welshman watched through the glass-panelled door as the ambulance men whispered urgently to the doctor; saw the doctor raise one corner of the blanket and peer underneath, then drop the cover into place with a shrug.

'No! No! It can't be!'

'You come on, now,' Myers urged, and he took the younger man by the hand, and led him like a child from the place that smelled of death.

*   *   *

When Wallace and Myers entered the office on Section Eight, Williams and Pengelly were waiting for them.

Steve Williams' face wore a wide, satisfied smile as he rose to greet them. 'Well, my

beauties, that must be the easiest fortune—'
The little man broke off in mid sentence as he
caught sight of the expression on Wallace's
face and he flickered wary eyes in Myers'
direction. 'Anything wrong?'

'Wrong? Wrong?' Wallace was beside
himself with rage. 'We killed a man, that's all!'

Dan Pengelly leapt to his feet. 'What are
you saying?' he demanded. 'Who is supposed
to be dead?'

'There is no "supposed" about it,' Myers
said flatly. 'It's Jack Froggart, the messenger
in admin. They brought his body into the
medical centre as we were leaving.' He raised
his eyebrows at Pengelly in some unspoken
question before turning to face Steve
Williams. 'The old man has had it, believe me.
He was gassed.' Myers studied the little
Welshman's face in silent appraisal.

'Well—' Steve Williams' eyes were hooded
like a cobra's as his gaze swung to each of his
companion's faces in turn. He pursed his lips
and made a hunching gesture with his
shoulders. 'Well, that's war.'

'How did it happen, Steve?'

'How should I know? The old fool must
have collapsed somewhere out of sight. Now
leave it, Ian, boy.' The little Welshman's voice
was ominously quiet.

No one spoke. Wallace raised his head from
his hands and stared at his fellow-countryman
unbelievingly, then he rose to his feet and

118

rounded his desk to stand face to face with him. 'Don't you understand?' he cried in bewilderment. 'Don't you understand? We've just killed an old man, you stupid fool.' Unwisely, he grasped the collar of the little man's coat as he accused: 'You said they were all out.'

He did not see Williams move until he felt the Welshman's fist drive deep into his solar plexus and the sudden pain made him jack-knife to his knees, then through watering eyes he saw Williams step back, cat-like, from the encounter.

'Keep your voice down and your bloody hands to yourself,' Williams rasped venomously, 'and take care what you call me.'

Pengelly stepped between them. 'That's enough, Steve,' he warned quietly as he helped Wallace to his feet.

'Okay, okay, but I'm not having College Boy, here, gettin' heavy-handed with me, see?' Once again he made that curious, hunching gesture, and appealed with outspread palms to the other two. 'For God's sake, we didn't murder anyone. It was just bloody bad luck, that's all.'

'But he's dead, you fool. Jack Froggart is dead!' Wallace had recovered his breath though his stomach muscles were still knotted with paralysis from the blow.

'There's only one fool here, Wallace,' Williams exploded, 'and that's you.' He stabbed a finger in Wallace's direction. 'Now I'm only going to say this once, so you had better damn well listen, and listen well. I've seen a lot of men die, but I never did have over sixty thousand quid before, so you forget the old feller and stop squealing like a stuck pig just because we met a problem.' The ugly tone of his voice whiplashed the room. He glanced sharply at Pengelly and Myers before returning to the attack. 'You crack, and you'll drop all four of us in the mire, an' I'm not doing twenty years on the Moor because of your snivelling. Do you understand me, College Boy?'

Wallace slumped into his chair, a beaten man. He had reacted hysterically, and he knew it. 'All right, Steve, have it your way.'

'Do you understand?'

'Yes. Yes. I said so, didn't I?'

'Then by God, boy, I hope you do!' The little Welshman turned to address Dan Pengelly. 'You'd better put him straight, old son,' he said. 'He's likely to blow the whistle on all of us, just because one bloke got the chop.'

*   *   *

For several minutes after Williams and Myers left the office, David Wallace sat motionless, staring at the top of his desk yet seeing nothing. Dan Pengelly stood, looking out

120

through the rain-spattered window. The overhang of mist, which had so admirably aided the raid on the administration building by holding down the gas cloud, had given way to light rain. Neither man had spoken since the departure of their two partners in crime until, finally, it was Wallace who broke the silence.

'I can hardly believe it. Nothing like this should have been possible.'

'The best-laid plans, Dave.'

Wallace looked up. Pengelly seemed outwardly cool and collected as he continued to gaze out through the droplet-specked panes of glass.

'When I think of all the calculation and preparation I put into the planning in order to avoid injury to anyone—it simply should not have happened. Everyone should have been out of the building long before the ammonia was released. My God! there was fire and explosion on Section Ten, and that only resulted in slight injuries. Compared with Ten, the routine for admin. was almost foolproof.'

Pengelly shifted his stance without averting his eyes from the dismal view outside. 'There's not much point in moaning about it now,' he said quietly. 'We all knew what we were into, and besides,' he added, turning to regard Wallace through clear, grey eyes, 'you can't say I didn't give you fair warning of what to expect if we used Steve.'

Wallace dropped his eyes as he remembered the numerous cautions his companion had given him about the difficulty of controlling the little Welshman, once having set him on a path of violence. 'But Steve claimed it was an accident, which could have happened to any one of us in the same situation.'

Dan Pengelly remained silent and expressionless. Another man might have taken note of that silence and given it some interpretation, but Wallace's senses were too numbed to respond.

'I never wanted anything like this to happen, Dan.'

'No, neither did I, but there it is.'

'You are like the others,' Wallace said bitterly. 'You don't seem to understand that we killed a man today, and all it means to Steve is that "a bloke got the chop".'

'That's enough,' Pengelly growled, and the tone of his voice stilled Wallace's rising hysteria. 'I'm as sorry as you are, Dave, but what's done is done, and that's an end to it. Steve is right. We must keep cool if we are to get away with it.'

'Steve! He didn't really care about Jack Froggart's death, you know that.' Wallace was calmer now, but he could not stop his hands shaking. 'You sound as callous as Steve.'

Pengelly's mouth tightened. 'I knew Steve during the war, he was a cold-blooded killer; a shooting never bothered him like it did me, he could gun a man down without giving it a second thought. When we were home on leave, talk was, amongst the Bristol lads who served in Steve's mob, that he had the job of escorting prisoners from the front line to internment compounds, until they found that many of his prisoners never made it.' Pengelly's neck reddened as he realised that Wallace had not understood. 'He only took them a couple of fields back—you see? Does that shock you? Then you should have learned more about the people you were recruiting, before you started all this.'

'I wasn't prepared for anyone being killed,' Wallace said miserably, but his protestation faltered weakly.

Pengelly slammed his balled fist on the desk. 'But it happened! Now we all have to be hard-headed, or we've had it; like Steve, I'm not getting landed with a life sentence just because you had a late attack of conscience.'

The sudden jangle of the telephone bell made both men jump like coiled springs.

'God!' Wallace stared at the instrument as if it were unreal.

'Answer it, then. Dave! Pick the damned thing up, man.'

The big Welshman made no move, as if his mind had congealed and in congealing had ceased to function.

'Move over, then,' Pengelly snapped, and he

thrust Wallace aside as he grabbed the receiver. 'Hello? Pengelly speaking. Ah—Mr. Carter—yes, yes, I'll call him. He's just along the corridor.' The tall man held one hand clamped over the mouthpiece as he offered the instrument to Wallace. 'Pull yourself together. It's Carter,' he hissed, 'now take it!' and with that he forced the telephone into the other's unwilling hands.

'Wallace? Are you there, man?' The bullying tone of the Production Director pierced the Welshman's consciousness.

'Yes, sorry to keep you waiting.'

'Well, come along! This is an emergency!'

'Emergency? The smoke from Ten, you mean?'

Dan Pengelly sat on one corner of the desk and leaned close so that he was able to overhear the agitated voice of the caller.

'Hasn't your Area Manager been in touch with you yet?'

'No. I've been out of my office for a while.'

'Worst of all, we have lost a man. The doctor has just informed me that Froggart, the messenger, has died.'

'I know, Wallace whispered. 'I happened to be at the surgery when they brought him in.'

'Do you know any details of what happened?'

'No. No details.' Wallace's voice broke slightly. 'Only that he was a dead man.'

'Well, he was killed by a voluminous release

of ammonia gas inside the administration building, from which everyone else managed to escape, by the grace of God!'

'Ammonia?' Wallace drew in a deep breath and tried to make his reply that of an innocent man. 'Are you sure, Mr. Carter? There is no ammonia plant anywhere near admin.—'

'Don't you think I know what ammonia smells like, Wallace?'

'No—yes—'

'Of course it's ammonia, and you carry ammonia on your Section. Yes?'

'So do Sections Three and Five,' Wallace said quickly, 'and they are nearer admin. than we are.'

All he got for his pains was a mollified grunt, then Carter proceeded to tell him about the raid on the Cash Office.

'My God! No, what robbery? I hadn't heard. What? What's that?' Wallace's grip tightened on the receiver. 'Over four-hundred thousand? Did you say four-hundred thousand?' He stared wide eyed and unbelieving at Dan Pengelly, as the voice on the other end of the line droned 'Four-hundred thousand, Dave,' Pengelly hissed excitedly. 'That gives us one-hundred thousand each!'

A sharp word from the earpiece jerked Wallace to his senses. 'Sorry, but I was listening. It was just the shock of hearing that dreadful news. Yes, yes, I'm sure that our

125

stocks of liquefied ammonia are intact and accounted for, but I'll have them checked at once. Pengelly or myself would have been informed had there been an ammonia leak from Section Eight.' The seated man listened intently for a minute or two longer before replacing the receiver, then, momentarily lost for words, he gawped up at Pengelly.

Dan Pengelly seized him by the shoulders. 'We grossed a hundred thousand apiece! That covers a lot of mistakes, Dave, lad.'

'For ten minutes work!'

David Wallace heard himself laugh. It was a thin, high-pitched laugh with a crazy edge to it.

*   *   *

Within five minutes Rossiter, Wallace's Area Manager, was on the telephone.

'You've heard what happened, Dave?'

'My God, yes, it's incredible. Carter's been ranting on the telephone.'

'He's upset about Jack Froggart.'

'Almost as upset as he is about losing the cash.'

'You knew? About the messenger dying?'

'The ambulance brought him in to the medical centre as I was leaving. I could have touched him, had I reached out,' Wallace said sombrely.

'Sweet Jesus!' Rossiter was silent for a few

126

seconds. 'All hell has broken loose, Dave, and the civil police have been called in. There is some senior detective named Cox from Bristol in charge. Anyway, I've rung to tell you that an emergency meeting has been called for two o'clock this afternoon, in the conference room at admin.'

David Wallace glanced at his watch and saw that it was only twelve-thirty; he could hardly believe that the events of the morning had been compressed into so short a time span. 'Do you want me along?'

'Yes. This fellow, Cox, wants all senior staff, including Section Managers and their Senior Foremen, to attend. By the way, the press have got hold of the story and are waiting at the main gate; television cameras—the lot! Carter doesn't want any member of Forsters' staff giving interviews until he releases a statement later today. See you at two.'

Duly at two that afternoon, Wallace and Pengelly threaded their way between several police cars parked outside the front entrance to the administration building. A uniformed police constable stood on duty outside the door and a faint tang of ammonia bit their nostrils as they entered the foyer. Staff from other Sections wrinkled their noses and chattered animatedly as they headed for the conference room; a hum of query and speculation arose as new arrivals noted that doors and windows were open wide to vent the now reoccupied offices of remnants of the gas. Two of Forsters' own security men guarded the corridor which led to the Wages Office, though police activity was obvious in that area.

Wallace walked along the opposite corridor and slipped into the washroom. The floor was still swilling with water, but the taps were turned off. He turned one on and cupped some water in the palm of one hand and sniffed at it, then he rejoined Pengelly in the foyer. 'We are in the clear,' he said, in answer to the other's questioning look. 'There's no trace of ammonia in the pipes; any residual gas will have completely dissolved in the water and will have been flushed away down the drains. There is no evidence to tell how the gas was delivered into this building.'

They were heading for the conference room when Wallace felt a nudge in the small of his back and a voice whispered: 'Have you heard? There's a rumour goin' round that it's well over four-hundred thousand quid.'

'Shut up, Steve,' Wallace muttered, 'or someone may hear you.'

'Aye, but don't that cheer you up a little bit, lovely?'

The long, oak-panelled conference room was almost full as Wallace and the two veterans filtered into the room. Myers was already there, standing amongst the crowd of about a hundred other assembled members of Forsters' staff.

Williams winked up at Dan Pengelly. 'This is a touch of luxury, boy. Just like the old officers' mess, eh?'

Carter and several of his fellow directors were conversing with a number of strangers and when the room had filled, Carter raised his eyebrows at one of the strangers and, on receiving a nod of confirmation, turned to address the gathering.

'Gentlemen—' The buzz of conversation ceased. 'Gentlemen, I have called this meeting of all Area Managers, Section Managers and their senior supervisory staff, at the request of the police as a preliminary to any further enquiries they may wish to make. As most of you will by now be aware, a terrible crime was perpetrated inside this building earlier today. Someone, somehow, after driving all the occupants from the offices by means of ammonia gas, has stolen the entire pre-holiday payroll from the Wages Office. Not only was company money taken, but also that belonging to a number of contractors who use our strongroom facilities. This considerable sum of money was contained in four metal boxes.' He waited for an outbreak of chatter to subside before he continued. 'In order to effect the robbery, the thieves managed to evacuate the premises by generating smoke, followed by the release of a massive volume of ammonia which flooded the entire place with concentrated gas.' The fleshy-faced Scot paused, and added gravely: 'It is my sad duty to inform you that Mr. Jack Froggart who, as you will know, was one of our oldest messengers and a loyal, long-serving employee, has died after being trapped in the gas. His body, I am told, was only discovered after the building had been cleared of fume. We do not know how the gas was brought into the building and released. There is no plant processing ammonia near the block and first reports from those Sections which use ammonia in their chemical reactions indicate that no factory stocks are missing. Now the police have put forward the theory that the miscreants, by some unknown means, secreted the gas on or near the premises beforehand. I must say that those of us who know the problems involved in handling large volumes of ammonia are baffled as to how it was accomplished.' He half turned to a dark-suited stranger at his side. 'A road tanker is a possibility, I suppose.' Carter returned his gaze to the assembled staff. 'I am sure that any theories from plant personnel will be welcomed by the police. Now I would like to introduce Detective Inspector Cox of the Bristol Criminal Investigation Department, who wishes to speak to you.' The paunchy Scot nodded to the man who had been waiting at his side with every sign of growing impatience at the protracted introduction.

The detective hardly waited for Carter to

conclude his last sentence before thrusting himself forward to adopt a straddle-legged stance, like some sailing master on the bridge of an old time clipper ship. He was about six feet tall and heavily built, almost to the point of being overweight. His short, straw-coloured hair was plastered plate-flat with a wide, centre parting. His eyes were of a light, indeterminate colour, set in a coarse, broad-featured face which bore several deep pock marks. His pin-striped, city suit had obviously seen better days. His manner was brusque and offhand from the outset; he wasted no time on the niceties of introductions, but spoke in a harsh, bludgeoning tone which matched his appearance. His curiously searching eyes swept the room, selecting faces at which to stare, and it was noticeable that several of those present shuffled uncomfortably under his openly hostile gaze.

'Gentlemen.' It was as if he were questioning the fact. 'It can only be a matter of time before we bring this case to a conclusion and I warn anyone who knows the culprits to come forward before it is too late. I can now add a piece of further information of which Carter—Mr. Carter, is unaware. The messenger, Froggart, who was found dead on the floor of the men's washroom, had been struck a severe blow at the base of his skull before the ammonia reached him. He was deliberately left in an unconscious state, and therefore unable to save himself from the gas.' Cox paused momentarily, allowing his words to sink in. 'That makes it murder,' he said slowly. 'Premeditated murder.'

As the Inspector's words echoed in his ears, Wallace could only stare at the profile of Steve Williams' moody face. Intuitively, the little Welshman turned to meet his countryman's gaze. The dark eyes held a gleam of pure malice, daring Wallace to speak and so accuse himself of complicity in murder. A pulse fibrillated uncontrollably in the taller man's temple, and he heard the voice of the detective as if through an echo chamber.

'That means we are now looking for killers, not thieves, and this has become a murder hunt. During the course of the next few days, my men will be visiting the Sections and talking to you individually, but I want to put some general points to you so that you can think about them before we take written statements. As you know, there was a sudden release of ammonia gas in this building to shield the robbery. If anyone present has any idea as to how the gas could possibly have been brought in, they should say so now.'

At the murmur of dissent which arose in the room the policeman spread his hands wide, displaying frayed shirt cuffs to his audience.

'That is one of the most puzzling aspects of this crime. How, in a busy office block with people working in almost every room, and in broad daylight, could the gas have been brought in and released? I am told that it would require a fairly large container or tanker to transport that much ammonia, even in liquefied form, yet no one saw anything unusual until the smoke and gas drove everyone from the building. Then again, the money was in four, fairly heavy, metal containers. How did the criminals get them past the security men on the gates? The complex has been scoured and so far there is no sign of them, so where is the loot now?'

Cox swung his gaze around the room and as he did so his eyes met Wallace's with that disconcerting stare before the big Welshman could take avoiding action. As Wallace stared back he wondered, frantically, how an innocent man would react, but the Inspector was the first to break off the exchange, and he concluded: 'Should anyone remember anything, no matter how trivial, he should let me or one of my men know. That is all for the present. You can go!'

After this curt dismissal a buzz of excited conversation broke out, and the assembly began to file out of the conference room.

Detective Inspector Cox took a stub of pencil from his pocket and made a brief note on a dishevelled pad which he withdrew from the inner recesses of his coat. He sucked the pencil reflectively. 'We can be sure of one thing,' he said to Carter.

'What's that, Inspector?' Carter asked, regarding the pencil with some distaste.

'Whoever did this job had inside knowledge.'

'An employee, you mean?'

'Past or present, yes. The villains had to handle ammonia gas and to use breathing sets, the type of work your plant men are trained for.' Cox sucked vigorously at the soggy pencil. 'Also the thieves knew the geography of the administration building. Well now, is it in order for my men to wander around the complex?'

'Of course, only warn them not to go near any chemical plant without first asking whether it is safe to do so. We handle some pretty dangerous things, you know, Inspector.'

Deliberately the policeman withdrew the pencil from between pursed lips, and as he did so it made an audible 'plopping' sound. He eyed the Production Director steadily. 'So do we sir,' he drawled. 'So do we!'

*   *   *

Outside, in the pale sunlight, the three ex-sergeants waited on the pavement in front of the administration building for Wallace to emerge. Without ceremony he strode up to them and pushed his way past the two Somerset men in order to reach Steve Williams. He gripped the little man's arm

134

accusingly.

'You left Jack Froggart to die. You clubbed that old man, and left him senseless on the floor of the washroom to suffocate in the gas!'

'Get away from me,' Steve Williams snarled, and he ripped his arm free. 'You stupid, stupid swine, Wallace. He saw me, didn't he? He recognised me through the Draeger mask; do you think I could let him get away after that?'

'For Christ's sake, cool down,' Pengelly warned, and he and Myers looked anxiously about.

Wallace refused to be calmed. 'You said it was an accident,' he raged, 'but it wasn't! You murdered him! Because he saw your face, you murdered him!'

'I didn't murder anybody, you crazy fool. I had to clobber him when he recognised me, and he took his own chances after that.'

'He didn't have any kind of chance, lying unconscious in concentrated ammonia gas, did he?' Wallace demanded passionately. 'You bloody, bloody killer.'

'Calm down and start walking,' Pengelly urged. He and Myers grabbed the outraged Wallace and began to propel him along the pavement towards his waiting car.

'For God's sake, fellers, not here! We're in the open for anyone to see,' Myers hissed.

As they forced Wallace along, Steve Willliams fell into step behind them and began to curse profanely at Wallace's back.

'You'd better tell this boy scout a few facts of life, Dan, boy. He's goin' to get us all put away for life if he doesn't shut his mouth, so if he opens it just once more, I'll shut it for him. Permanently!'

FIVE

Wallace remained in his Section office until seven o'clock that evening, waiting for his turn to be interviewed by Detective Inspector Cox or one of his minions. For the remainder of the day he had been in a kind of stupor and made little contribution to the work of removing all traces of his team's complicity in the robbery. The three ex-sergeants had lost none of their capability; between them they removed the command wires, reset the fire-alarm circuits, burned the red, plastic flashes used to disguise the Land Rover and changed the vehicle's tyres so that it could not be traced from imprints left in the grass at the rear of the administration building. They also destroyed the firemen's tunics and PVC suits and returned the breathing sets to the plant where they would become mixed with dozens of other Draeger sets. Finally, they hosed out the basement storeroom to wash away any telltale signs.

136

At five minutes to seven the telephone on Wallace's desk rang, and he picked it up.

'Mason here, sir.'

'Who?'

'Detective Constable Mason, sir.'

'Do you want to see me now?'

'I'm afraid not; not until tomorrow. We are taking statements from staff on Sections closer to the incidents than Section Eight, and that is taking some time. Can we contact you in the morning, Mr. Wallace?'

'Eh? Oh, yes. Yes, of course.' Wallace felt enormously relieved. 'It's Saturday tomorrow, remember. We only work half a day, until twelve.'

'I'll be here all day, sir, and all day Sunday, I expect,' the detective sighed. 'Sorry to keep you hanging about, sir.'

'That's all right.'

As Wallace drove through the gates of the complex, he passed television cameras and their crews gathered in search of interviews, and could see several self-conscious looking workers being filmed and questioned.

That evening, television news reports carried the story of the robbery at Forsters and of the murder of Jack Froggart. Wallace could only stare at the screen in horror when a picture of the messenger suddenly appeared, for, from God knows where, the reporters had managed to obtain a photograph which showed a youthful, smiling Froggart in army uniform. At last he could stand the tension no longer and he picked up the telephone and dialled Dan Pengelly's number.

'What do you want, Dave? You shouldn't be calling.'

'I know. I only phoned to ask if you got away from the plant—without any complications, I mean?'

Pengelly understood his meaning. 'No. No complications to worry about,' he said quickly.

'Dan?'

'Yes?'

'Why don't you call round some time tonight?'

'That's not a very good idea. I'm hanging up, I'll see you at work tomorrow.'

The following morning the telephone was already ringing as Wallace entered his office, and he lifted the receiver to hear the voice of his Area Manager.

'Look, Dave,' Rossiter said. 'Two of Cox's detectives are on their way to see you, and Carter has given instructions that you have to give them your full co-operation and priority over your other work.'

'Naturally.' Wallace hesitated. 'Presumably the police are visiting other Sections, besides mine?'

'Cox has a dozen men out, visiting all production plants, but beginning with those which use ammonia in their processes. That means two others, of course, as well as Eight.

138

The 'tecs were here until late last night, crawling all over admin. and Section Ten.'

'Have the police any ideas about how it was done?'

'The robbery? I don't think so, not according to the conversation that went on in Carter's office this morning. It's got me baffled too; I'd give my eye-teeth to know how the thieves got that much ammonia into admin. That was some trick, eh?'

'Some trick!' Wallace echoed.

'Did you see the plant on television last night?'

'Yes.'

'And did you see the photograph of poor old Jack?'

'Yes, I did,' Wallace said, shortly.

He had hardly replaced the receiver when there was a knock on his office door and, at his shouted invitation, two men entered.

'Good morning, sir. Detective Constables Mason and Hardwick. I'm Mason, and you are—?'

'Wallace. It's on the door as you come in. You spoke to me last night.'

'Right, sir. Perhaps you could tell us a little about your Section and its processes, but don't make it too technical, sir. We wouldn't understand anything too technical.'

Wallace gave the two men a description of Section Eight and its processes, though it was noticeable that their interest concentrated mainly on any part of the plant associated with the processing of ammonia. After about an hour's discussion, during which both detectives took extensive notes, Mason said: 'I think that's all I can take in, for now. Perhaps you could show us something of your Section, sir, to give us some practical idea of what you've been talking about, so to speak.'

They were making their way towards the ammonia bund when they turned to the sound of a call, and Mason hissed to his companion: 'It's the Old Man!'

The doughty figure of Detective Inspector Cox walked towards them with slow, unhurried steps, so that they were forced to stand and wait until he reached them.

'Now then! You'll be —?'

There was no hint of courtesy of politeness in the manner of Cox's address.

'Wallace,' the Welshman said, nettled. 'Manager of Section Eight.'

'Ah, another manager,' Cox sighed. 'There's one hell of a lot of managers about the place.' He rambled on without once deigning to glance in Wallace's direction. 'Section Managers! Area Managers! Managers of Managers! I suppose someone actually does the work, eh?'

Wallace's cheeks flushed at the rudeness of the man. He felt uncertain how to react, and ultimately he simply shrugged and said: 'I suppose so.'

Cox fumbled in his pocket and withdrew a typewritten list which he made great play of perusing. 'Yes, here you are. Wallace—a qualified chemist, I see. Lives at Burnham—your senior foreman is Pengelly.' It was as if Wallace was not present, and Cox raised his eyebrows in the direction of his two assistants. 'Well? Well?' he demanded. 'Where are you taking me?'

'Ammonia storage area, sir,' Mason said quickly. 'Section Eight is one of the three on the list which uses ammonia in its processes.'

'So it is!' Cox seemed to be amused by some hidden joke which no one else present was privy to. 'Section Eight makes nitric acid, using ammonia, for fertiliser manufacture. Also makes and concentrates sulphuric and hydrochloric acids. Also has a chlorine plant.' He suddenly raised his straw-coloured brows once more, this time to fix Wallace with an hypnotic stare. 'Or so my piece of paper tells me.'

'Well, that's right, Inspector.'

'Then suppose you show us exactly where you keep all this ammonia, and then you can explain just why you think you haven't lost any.'

'I was taking your men to see the storage bund when you arrived.'

'Lead on, and by the way, Pengelly is your senior foreman?'

'Yes, he is.'

'Then let's have him here!'

Cox stayed on Section Eight for over two hours, by which time he had questioned Wallace and Pengelly about every item of plant that had to do with ammonia storage or processing. He left them, then, without a words of thanks, but before leaving he folded a batch of plant drawings, records and chemical stock sheets that he had collected during his excursion and tucked them under his arm.

'I'll take these with me. Mason will return them later.'

'We can manage without them for a while,' Wallace said, without warmth.

Cox paused, and looked at Dan Pengelly. 'How would you get four boxes out of Forsters without being found out, Mr. Pengelly?' he asked, without preamble.

The veteran was sharp-witted enough to counter the faceted question. He shrugged and replied in his Somerset drawl: 'It all depends on what size boxes you are talking about, I suppose.'

'Are you trying to tell me that you don't know what the stolen cash-boxes look like?'

Pengelly had been controlling his precariously balanced temper, but two hours spent subject to Cox's abrasive manner had brought him to the limit of his patience. 'Damned right, I don't,' he exploded. 'I work here, on this plant, not in bloody admin. Of

142

course, I've a vague idea because, like most people, I happen to have seen the Shuritor wages van arrive at one time or another, but I don't know in detail. No!'

It was exactly the right thing to have said, exactly the right tone of indignation to have adopted. The Detective Inspector gave no outward sign of being perturbed by the ex-sergeant's outburst, instead he behaved as if he had heard not a word of Pengelly's heated reply by simply turning on his heel and marching away.

'Good for you.'

Wallace hardly picked up Detective Constable Mason's quietly whispered congratulation to Dan Pengelly.

'Cheeky bastard,' came the veteran's succinct summary of his departing inquisitor.

Days went by, during which police activity heightened and the attentions of Cox and his men to some of the staff at Forsters increased almost to the point of blatant harassment, but they found nothing, and when Forsters closed for its annual holiday period the employees found some respite from the persistent enquiries. The enquiries continued in an abated form throughout the two week vacation, only to be resumed with gusto when the employees returned, finally reaching a fever pitch as Cox and his men realised they were no nearer the truth. The period since the robbery gradually lengthened from days into weeks, and as August came and went, the intensity of investigation began to diminish. David Wallace was still distressed by the death of Jack Froggart, but there was nothing he could do about it, and slowly he adjusted to the fact although he felt revulsion every time he found himself in the company of Steve Williams.

By the time September arrived, each man was ready and eager to recover the cash-boxes from their hiding place in the depths of Feeder Pond Number One. They rehearsed with the diving equipment in the safety of Myers' locked garage, until the diver was satisfied they could keep him alive when he made the dive into the Feeder.

'Why the hell don't you use one of those skin-diving outfits, Myers, old son. Like James Bond does, you know? I reckon you could be in and out of that reservoir like a randy frog,' Steve Williams said during one of these training sessions.

Myers quashed the suggestion unhesitatingly. 'I'm not trained in that type of equipment, but the water is too deep anyway. If this were only a shallow dive, then I might chance it, but I have to go deep to reach the bottom of that Feeder, and I have to stay deep for maybe a couple of hours. It's cold, hard work down there; I need all the protection I can get.'

They waited until the darker evenings of

September, and settled on the second Saturday in the month as the day on which they would pluck their reward from the depths.

*   *   *

It was late evening. The dark, moonless sky was filled with scudding cloud through which an occasional star could be briefly seen. Splashes of artificial light fell from the front windows of the sedate Burnham and Berrow Golf Club clubhouse, to illuminate verdant areas of smooth putting green and then to fade into inky darkness over the buckthorn lined eighteenth fairway. There were less than a dozen vehicles in the car park alongside the Victorian building; Saturday was normally a quiet night in the club, and the only noise to disturb the peace was muted chatter emanating from the bar and the chink of glass on glass.

The dark-green, elderly Jaguar was parked well away from the clubhouse. It stood, without lights, at the furthest boundary of the parking area and in the deepest shadow; a red pinpoint of light glowed momentarily inside the vehicle as one of its occupants drew deeply on a cigarette. The fifteen-year-old Jaguar was Pengelly's pride and joy. He had bought it secondhand, two years ago, and although the coachwork had seen better days, the machine

145

was mechanically sound and tuned to perfection.

David Wallace had been preparing himself throughout the day for the coming foray. When it was time, he left his apartment and drove through the sleepy town and along Berrow Road towards the golf club. He turned into Saint Christopher's Way and wheeled along the twisting road until he entered the golf club's car park. He cursed his stupidity in driving his own brightly hued motorcar; its waspish colours seemed to shout aloud his presence to the world. Once inside the car park, he braked to a halt, then peered out into the dark night. Across the park twin headlamps gleamed for an instant, at which the big Welshman pulled his automatic gear lever into 'Drive' and eased the tyres of his car over loose, crunching stones until he rolled to a halt alongside the waiting vehicle. He stepped from his car and closed the door behind him as quietly as possible.

'Dan?' Wallace whispered hoarsely. 'Is that you?'

The electrically-operated window of the Jaguar slid silently down, and a laconic: 'Okay, Dave. Have you got the key?' came from the shadowy interior.

Wallace could just discern the figures of Steve Williams and Ian Myers in the back seats. 'Who the hell does he think it is?' Wallace heard his little fellow countryman grunt. 'Father bloody Christmas?' He climbed into the front passenger seat. Coils of hose, rope and cable lay on the floor at his feet.

'Yes, I have the key. Are the suit and air pump in the boot?'

'No. We left them behind for Ian's old mum to play with,' Williams snorted. 'For God's sake, Wallace, where do you think they are?'

'Are you happy with the suit, Ian?' Wallace said insistently. He craned his neck and tried to distinguish the features of the two men as he spoke.

'Yes, yes, he's happy. We are all happy. Now let's shove off, for Christ's sake!' Williams rasped.

'Have you made a last minute check?' Wallace persisted. 'Does everything work as it should?'

'Do you think Myers, here, is an amateur? At least he won't forget to open the right valve, lovely.'

As Wallace concealed a surge of irritation at the snide reference to his error during the raid on the wages office, he noticed that Myers had placed a placating hand on Williams' knee.

'The rest of the gear is in the boot, Dave, and everything is in good, working order, I've checked it thoroughly. All you three have to do is to keep the hand pump working,' the diver said quickly.

They left the secluded car park and drove

rapidly along back roads towards the curious, hump-back silhouette of Brent Knoll, then past the knoll and out on to the A38. The shades of night deepened as they headed north-east, in the direction of Bristol and Forsters, and conversation became minimal. Steve Williams made a few flippant remarks concerning Myers' inability to swim, but they were all much too tense, too near to the pot of gold once again to do more than grunt in reply and soon Williams also lapsed into silence.

One mile before the side-turning which led off the A38 to Forsters, Pengelly slowed the Jaguar and turned off the main road on to a roughly laid track used by local farmers and occasionally by contractors working on, or just inside, the perimeter fence of the industrial complex. The endless potholes and bumps along the track were testimony to the passage of herds of cows and heavy vehicles.

They were halfway along the track when Wallace said: 'I think this is far enough. Stop the engine and switch off the lights, then we can find out whether the security patrols are awake.' He delved into a pocket of his jacket and brought out a two-way radio which was a duplicate of the radios used by the security guards in Forsters and which he had purchased quite openly from a radio shop in Park Street in Bristol. He partly opened his window and slid the telescopic aerial of the hand R/T set through the aperture; his gloved fingers played restlessly with the tuning control.

'—Patrol Able Three—come in Able Three—over.'

The voice of the afternoon-shift radio controller crackled in the confined space of the darkened Jaguar.

'This is Able Three—this is Able Three—over.'

'What is your position, please?—over.'

'We are on Number One Section—' Section One was at the other end of the vast complex. 'Now moving to patrol the east boundary fence—over and out.' The patrol leader sounded tired, he was coming to the end of his afternoon shift and his thoughts lay with home and supper and a late football match on television.

'We'll have no trouble from that quarter,' Steve Williams said as he leaned forward in his seat. 'They'll be having a crafty smoke somewhere nice and quiet until it's time to go home.'

Wallace suspended the radio by its carrying strap from the rear view mirror, with the control switched to 'Receive'. The next patrol to tour the west perimeter fence, towards which the Jaguar was headed, was not due until the middle of the night shift, and that was not for five or six hours.

'It looks quiet enough,' Pengelly said cautiously. He started the engine and began to move forwards at a snail's pace, then grunted an oath as the front wheels hit a particularly deep pothole. He had switched on dipped headlights to illuminate the twisting track ahead, and as the vehicle rode the humps and dips of the undulating surface, the twin beams of light alternately rose skywards to pierce the night sky like searchlights or plunged downwards.

Wallace cast an anxious gaze through the windscreen. The plant was clearly visible against the sky as dark silhouettes of criss-crossed girder work which stood out against the paler shade of night; on working plant the lattices were festooned with blazing fairy lights.

'Can you make it without headlights? Someone may spot us.'

Dan Pengelly flicked at the light switch, and they found themselves plunged into sudden, blinding darkness. Pengelly began to curse, and he cursed continuously as he edged the heavy vehicle along the rutted causeway, guided only by the dim glow of sidelights. Forsters was set in open country, bounded on three sides by wet, low-lying fields and marshy moorland, while along its southern boundary the notorious A38 road snaked a tortuous route between Bristol and Bridgwater. The dirt track they were following dithered across several sparsely hedged fields until it brought them to the steel mesh, perimeter fence of the complex and there the track turned to skirt the security fence. They turned with it, and travelled parallel to the eight-foot high fence for several, spine-jolting minutes until at last they came face to face with a double gate set in the fence. Even by the limited illumination of the Jaguar's sidelights it was obvious that the gate was little used, in fact it was only opened when engineers from Bristol Waterworks wanted to inspect Forsters' reservoirs or when contractors were engaged in maintenance work in the area of the Feeder Ponds; probably twice a month in all. However, as Wallace had ascertained, the heavy padlock which secured the gate was well greased and would present no problems.

'Let me have the key,' Myers hissed. He reached over Wallace's shoulder and held out one huge, upturned palm. 'You two stay put. Steve and I will open the gate.'

David Wallace had the duplicate key to the padlock ready, and as he dropped it into the diver's hand he said: 'Leave the gates wide open after we drive through, just in case we want to leave in a hurry.'

The rear doors of the Jaguar opened noiselessly as Myers and Williams slipped from their seats and the only sound to be heard was the soft crunch of feet on the earthen drive as the two men ran lightly to the gate. Williams adopted a crouching, crab-like gait as he moved forward in the darkness, and watching him, Wallace could imagine the veteran moving just as stealthily years earlier when on patrol in the sombre forests of war-torn Europe, a killer ready to strike.

'I hope to Christ Steve doesn't meet anyone tonight. One dead man is enough.'

'Forget it! You've got other things to think about,' Pengelly snapped. He sounded angry, and his voice rose a pitch as he stuck his head out through the open window and snarled at the shadowy figures ahead: 'Come on! Get a bloody move on, you two!'

The faintly visible outlines of Myers and Williams were crouched, motionless, over the padlock. Then they began to move, to the accompaniment of a slight rattle, as one half of the fence-high gate swung wide.

'That's it—we're in!' Pengelly feathered the throttle of the Jaguar impatiently as he prepared to drive through the gateway. 'Come on, Steve. Jesus Christ! Come on!'

Steve Williams remained bent double over the other half of the gate, fumbling amongst the grass and weeds which grew around its base.

'What on earth are they waiting for?' Wallace agonized.

Myers dropped to his knees alongside the little Welshman and they began an animated discussion which was interspersed with frequent examinations of something close to the ground. Then Williams got to his feet and trotted back to the Jaguar, and as he approached, Wallace could tell from his set, white face that something was dreadfully wrong.

'What is it, Steve?'

'Just one small problem, Mastermind.' Williams glared at his fellow countryman. 'The soddin' gate won't open!'

'What?' Wallace jerked his door open and literally jumped from his seat. 'But it must open! The waterworks' engineers use it for access to the plant reservoirs. I know they do! They go through in a van.'

'In a van, maybe. Not in a flaming, great Jaguar, they don't.'

Wallace was aghast as he realised that he had not actually checked that both halves of the service-gate opened. He had assumed that since the engineers from Bristol Waterworks entered and left via the gate, in order to inspect Forsters' water supplies, all one needed to gain admittance was a key to the padlock. Wallace pushed his way past Steve Williams and rushed to the recalcitrant section of the gate. He took hold of it and tried to force it back on its hinges.

'It's useless,' Myers said soberly as he pointed to the ground. 'It's welded to an iron plate.'

'Oh, God! I don't believe it, Ian.'

'See for yourself.'

David Wallace fell to his knees and tore

feverishly at the foliage that intertwined the gate's lower bars. It was difficult to discern detail in the dark, but he could see that the length of angle iron, which formed the base of the frame of this half of the gate, had been fractured at some time. It had been repaired by spot welding the angle iron along its length to a large iron plate which was set firmly in a bed of concrete. Wallace bit his lip and rose slowly to his feet. This half of the gate was permanently closed; to prise it open would leave visible signs of forced entry which might lead to detection.

'What's happening? Get it open!' Dan Pengelly had joined them at the gate.

'It won't open. This is what I call detailed planning and—'

'Shut up, man!' Pengelly let forth a blast of sulphurous language that cut Williams off in mid-sentence. 'Stand back, and I'll rip the bastard open!' he gritted.

'No, Dan. Wait!' Wallace knew just how strong Pengelly was and he grabbed at his arm as he lunged for the gate. Dan Pengelly would have torn the gate from its hinges had he not been restrained, and Wallace never quite knew how he managed to hold back the raging bull of a man. 'They'll know someone has broken in, if we damage the gate; they'll check for tyre-marks and finger-prints and that detective, Cox, may get a lead. There's another way,' Wallace urged.

The three ex-sergeants crowded around him. They had been baulked, and because of it they were hard and dangerous.

'What is it?' Myers tone was uncompromising.

'We are going in for those cash-boxes tonight, boy, I can promise you that,' Williams snarled.

'Yes, yes, but do it without damaging the gate. That's one sure way to get the police on our backs.'

'Okay, College Boy!' Steve Williams was venomous by this time. 'We must have been mad to let you have your way about dumping those boxes in the Feeder. You just spit out your next brilliant brainwave, and it had better be good!'

'We leave the car here.' Wallace spread his hands in supplication. 'The Feeder is only two hundred yards inside the gate, surely we can carry the equipment that far?'

Number One Feeder Pond was not visible from where they stood. Inside the gate, a narrow track climbed a short incline before reaching a plateau some twenty feet higher, and the reservoir that was their target lay hidden from their present position by the rising ground. Across the plateau grew small, footling trees, interspersed with denser clumps of undergrowth which overhung the water's edge in parts, and it was these bushes that Wallace had counted on to provide cover for the parked car.

'We do it that way?' Steve Williams rapped the question to Pengelly and Myers and received an equally rapid confirmation. 'Okay. Wait here while I do a recce,' the little Welshman said. He was back in a short space of time. 'It's all clear; no sign of any patrol.'

Then they were moving again. Pengelly ran to the rear of the Jaguar, opened the boot and hauled out the portable pump, which was bolted to a cradle so that two men could carry it. Quickly and efficiently, Pengelly and Williams manhandled the pump through the half-open gate, up the short slope and across the intervening ground to the concrete rim of the reservoir. David Wallace grabbed the two-way radio from the rear view mirror, then helped Myers to carry the case containing the Siebe Gorman diving suit. Before they had climbed halfway up the slope, Pengelly and Williams were making the return journey to the Jaguar in order to collect the coils of hose, rope and cable.

It must have taken only ten or fifteen minutes from the moment they discovered that the gate would not open wide enough to admit the Jaguar until they were all standing alongside the Feeder preparing for the dive. Wallace found himself breathing rapidly, due in part to the physical activity and in part to the slugs of adrenalin that were pumping into his bloodstream.

'—Able Three. About to inspect Butane Tank Farm, east of Number One Section—on foot—'

Wallace had hung the lightweight radio by its carrying strap from the branch of a small fir tree that grew conveniently close to their place of operation. The pocket set continued to crackle staccato messages from the unsuspecting security patrol; with the device permanently switched on while Myers was making the dive, the intruders would be continuously informed of the movements of Forsters' security men.

Wallace had never liked deep water, whether open sea or enclosed like the Feeder, and as he stood there in near darkness and looked across the rippling surface of the reservoir towards the myriad lights of Forsters, he felt awed by the thought of Myers piercing that interface of air with water and descending through sombre depths into the unknown.

Eager hands had already divested Myers of his outer clothing, and he shivered in the night air as his comrades helped him don the thick, rubber suit. It had been decided that he should not partly dress for the dive beforehand in case they were stopped. They might have explained away their proximity to the plant, but not with Myers wearing diver's apparel.

'By God, it's cold!' Myers hissed. 'I should

have worn more underwear. I'll bloody freeze!'

'You'll be like a friggin' duck in water, boy,' Steve Williams grinned as he slipped the oval, brass corselet over the diver's head and married the holes in the metal ring to the protruding studs of the suit.

They had practised this part of the operation repeatedly and had absorbed Myers' detailed instructions concerning vital clamps and connections during the rehearsal sessions. They had rehearsed until they could prepare him for a dive with consummate ease, and now the hours of practice paid off as, in the darkness of a Somerset moor on a moonless night, Pengelly and Williams spun greased wing-nuts on threaded studs, then tightened them with strong, sure fingers to seal corselet to suit. Myers' last act of preparation was to slip over his head a soft, leather under-helmet with built-in receiver and throat microphone, before Pengelly lowered the bulbous, metal helmet into place.

'Good luck, Ian, old son,' Steve Williams whispered as he helped guide the helmet over the diver's head.

David Wallace peered over their shoulders. 'Half a turn to the right, to seal,' he instructed. 'Remember, now, half a turn to the right.'

'Do you know something, Dave?' Steve Williams rasped. He had already twisted the triple-windowed helmet into place, and he spat the words over one shoulder as he

158

worked. 'I once had an officer like you. Kept repeating orders; simply would not stop talking, that bloke.'

'Sorry, Steve, I was only trying to—'

Williams cut the apology short. 'Then, on one recce through a mined area he was gabbin' as usual.' The little man adopted a mincing tone. 'Don't step on a mine, chaps! Don't step on a mine!' He resumed his normal voice 'Then the silly bastard went and stepped on one himself.' Williams continued his pre-arranged check of the diving suit's connections with faultless efficiency. Finally, he stepped back from Myers' encapsulated figure, and only then did he deign to look in Wallace's direction as he added: 'After that we had some peace to carry on with the patrol.'

A query from Myers over the diving intercom interrupted any further quarrel.

'Testing. Testing. Can you hear me?'

The diver's communication set had been placed on the ground near the water's edge. It was a small black box about one foot square, with built in receiver and a separate, hand-held transmitting microphone connected to the set by means of a flexible cable. Wallace picked up the microphone and squatted on his haunches alongside the set to speak to Myers.

'I hear you loud and clear, Ian. Can you hear me?'

Dan Pengelly had begun to work the hand lever of the manually operated air pump, and that appeared to be working without fault. Myers squinted out from his protective shell like a hermit crab and his colleagues could see his lips move in synchronization with the voice which issued from the black box. 'Put the guide rope exactly where the containers went down,' the voice commanded as Myers lumbered ponderously to the concrete rim of the Feeder in weighted boots. 'Don't make me go runnin' about down there looking for them. Unscrew my front visor and then you can belay the pump.'

Number One Feeder Pond was one of four enormous reservoirs used to supply the huge quantities of cooling water and process water which the vast chemical engineering plants operated by Forsters demanded. Feeder One was the size of a small lake, constructed in the shape of a concrete-lined, rectangular basin, three sides of which dropped vertically to its shelving floor. The deepest water lay in the end of the reservoir at which they now stood, two hundred feet of cold, murky water which held their fortune as securely as any safe, and from this deep-end the bed of the Feeder sloped gradually upwards in the manner of a swimming pool.

For a moment the four men stood poised on the edge, and peered at the water's calm, reflective surface in a vain attempt to pierce invisible depths.

'Throw the guide rope a good ten feet from

160

the side wall,' Myers piped. 'That'll keep me clear of any projections.'

'Stand back!'

Dan Pengelly swung the weighted end of the two-inch thick guide rope in a pendulum like motion, and with each swing he allowed the rope to slip through his fingers to gain a corresponding increase in the length of arc. With one final twist, the tall veteran released his hold on the rope to send it plunging into dark waters.

'Is that good enough, Ian?'

Myers was now the centre of their attention, their only possible link with the payroll which rested on the bed of the Feeder.

'Yes. I think so.' The awkward, leaden-booted figure made a final assessment. 'Yes, that'll do. Now screw in the visor.'

Had anyone chanced upon them at that moment, they must surely have doubted their own sanity. The shock of seeing Myers, standing like some grotesque Martian in the Somerset night, would have been enough to make the strongest man run.

Steve Williams peered in at Myers. 'Look after yourself now, boy!' he cautioned.

'I'll be fine.'

As Williams wound the small, circular window tightly into the front aperture of the diving helmet, David Wallace was never to forget the brief glimpse he caught of the diver's face as Myers gave one last grin of assurance through his tiny window on life. The two Welshmen took Myers by his arms and led his faltering steps to the brink. Dan Pengelly was once again working the hand lever of the pump with a steady rhythm, and the three attendants heard excess air being expelled from Myers' helmet as a sibilant whisper. The uppermost few feet of the concrete reservoir's retaining wall sloped at an angle of forty degrees to the horizontal, and Myers used this slope to plod into the water while clutching the stout guide rope to steady himself.

'I'll be fine.'

He was gone before Wallace realised it. One moment he was there, the next he had disappeared beneath the surface with only a cluster of popping bubbles to mark his place. Wallace could not repress an involuntary shudder and thanked God that it was Myers, and not he, who had to enter that awful pond.

From Myers' suit an undulating umbilical cord led upwards to a convoluted pile which they had laid out on the ground close to the edge of the Feeder, and it was Williams' task to pay out this threshing combination of air-hose, lifeline and communications cable as smoothly as possible to match the diver's rate of descent. Wallace's job was to manage communications between the surface and the sinking man, and to this end he hunched once more over the small black box that kept them informed of Myers' condition.

'Forty feet,' the box said.

Part of the diver's equipment was a modern depth gauge which he wore attached to one wrist like a watch. He also carried a powerful battery-operated underwater lamp.

'Let the hose out a little faster. You've got me dancing like a puppet on a string.'

'Steve —?' Wallace prompted.

'Okay.' Williams had heard the diver's comment and was already acting on it.

'That's better,' Myers' voice advised.

David Wallace thought he caught sight of a flash of light in the depths of the Feeder, but he could not be sure and he did not see it again.

'One hundred feet, now.'

'Is everything all right, Ian?'

'It is, so far. I can't see the bottom yet though.' The box was silent for several minutes, and then Myers said: 'Are you sure this thing is only two hundred feet deep, Dave?'

A cold sweat broke out over Wallace's back. He had gleaned the information about the dimensions of Number One Feeder from Forsters' drawing office where the civil engineering drawings of the contractors who had constructed the reservoirs were filed. What if the drawings were wrong? God! He looked down at the coiled heap of hose and cable at Williams' feet. It seemed incredibly small. What if it did not reach the bottom?

'That's what the drawings said,' Wallace

163

stammered.

Steve Williams was about to say something when the lifeline in his hand twitched from a strong double pull from below.

'He's there!'

'Dave?' Myers' staccato voice echoed from the receiver.

'Yes, Ian. I'm here.'

'On the bottom now—there's too much slack in the hose. Ask Steve to take it in by about six feet.'

'Up by six feet, Steve.'

Wallace made a lifting motion to Williams who nodded and then hauled on the lines.

'That's enough!' A metallic parody of Ian Myers' voice clicked at them.

'What's it like down there?' Wallace asked. There was no immediate reply and the crouching man fingered the controls of the microphone. 'Ian?' There was a hint of worry in Wallace's voice.

'It's okay—not to worry. There is one hell of a lot of rubbish down here, though.' Myers' breathing began to sound heavy and laboured in his throat microphone. He was working hard.

'Tell him to take it easy,' Pengelly cautioned. 'He hasn't been paid this much for a dive in his life and he might get reckless.' Dan Pengelly, too, sounded a little breathless and his easy pumping action had become somewhat ragged. He had been pumping life-

164

giving air into the diver's suit since the helmet was sealed, and, strong as he was, it was obvious that he would soon need help to keep the double-cylinder air pump going.

Wallace stood and surveyed the plateau surrounding the Feeder Pond. He could see no sign of intruding lights on the wide expanse of waste ground and he crouched to the transmitter again. 'All quiet up here, Ian. We have plenty of time before the next security patrol is due on this side of the factory, so don't tire yourself by hurrying.'

Williams grasped the handle of the compressor and began to help Pengelly in his efforts.

'God! I must be getting old,' Pengelly panted, and he released his own hold on the lever.

The night was quiet as the grave, except for the quiet 'phut-phut' of the hand pump and an occasional grunted blasphemy from Myers. The trio on the surface watched the black receiver eagerly as they waited for it to deliver news of their fortune; the surface of the water was ruffled, now, by some random breeze, and they could picture the man two hundred feet below as he groped a path through unknown obstacles, guided only by a single, diffuse beam of light from his underwater torch.

Dan Pengelly leaned to the microphone in Wallace's hand. 'Any sign of the containers, lad?' he asked.

'No. Not yet.' Again the strained breathing. 'Some rotten bleeder's dumped a load of old iron down here. Got to tread carefully.'

'Don't risk getting trapped,' Wallace warned. 'We can always try another time.'

From his post at the pump, Williams glared with baleful eyes. 'The hell with that,' he snapped, 'that loot is coming up tonight.'

Wallace covered the microphone with the palm of one hand so that the diver could not hear what was being said. 'Even if it means risking Ian's life?' He was stung by Williams' singlemindedness.

'Aw, Christ, don't be so bloody theatrical. You needn't worry about old Myers. He can take care of himself.'

'There they are!' At that precise moment Myers' triumphant cry crackled from the receiver. 'I've got 'em! One, two—yes, all four!'

The trio at the waterside grew tense with excitement. 'Send down the salvage line,' ordered Myers.

Dan Pengelly gathered up the heavy, metal snap-link and a ten-ounce lead weight attached to the end. He clipped the link on to Myers' guide rope, then looked at Wallace and nodded.

'Are you ready?' Wallace said into the microphone.

'Aye, let it drop.'

At a signal from Wallace, Dan Pengelly

released the snap-link which immediately slipped down the guide rope and disappeared into the water, carrying its attached nylon line with it. The salvage rope spilled freely from a coil in Pengelly's arms until at last an acknowledgement from Myers indicated that it had reached him. For what seemed like an age to the men on the surface there was silence from the communications set, apart from an occasional grunt of exertion as Myers strained to his underwater task. At long last came the command they so desperately awaited.

'Haul away!'

'Lifting now, Ian,' Wallace said, then he jumped up and ran to help Pengelly. They hauled the salvage rope in, hand over hand, until the first metal container broke the surface, and it took but few seconds to swing the dripping prize to safety and to unfasten the snap-link from its handle. Pengelly clutched the cash-box in both hands, as if to reassure himself that it was real, before setting it on the ground, then he snatched up the microphone and crouched over it like a happy terrier.

'Myers, you beautiful old sod, when you come up I'm goin' to give you a great big kiss!'

'Take that back, or I'm staying put. Hurry with the salvage rope; the next box is ready.'

Again, and yet again, they repeated the same procedure until three of the money containers had been recovered and lay in a row on the hard earth at their feet. Throughout, the three men on the surface had maintained a vigilant watch over the area surrounding Number One Feeder, and only once did they receive a mild scare when the lights of a vehicle appeared to be leaving the process plants and be heading in the direction of the reservoirs, but the headlights eventually turned away from them and were soon lost again amongst the cluster of Forsters' twinkling lights.

Steve Williams had been relieved from his place at the pump by Dan Pengelly, and had immediately trotted over to examine the boxes. 'Hadn't we better open one up?' he suggested. 'We could just have a load of rotted paper if the boxes let the water in.'

It was obvious that he wanted to see the banknotes once more, to confirm their existence for himself, and even Pengelly eagerly said: 'We ought to check, Dave,' but the little Welshman had already opened one lid and he laid his open palm on the money. 'Dry as a bone,' he said informatively, then he resealed the box, apparently content.

As the salvage line slid down into the depths for the fourth time, Steve Williams returned to join Pengelly at the pump. After a while, Pengelly relinquished his hold on the operating lever and stretched his tall frame to ease cramped muscles.

'Dave and I could begin loading these cash-

168

boxes into the car,' Pengelly suggested. He flexed whitened fingers. 'It's taken a good twenty minutes for each lift; we could carry all three containers between us in one journey, and be back by the time Myers has the last box ready to come up, that is, if you can manage to keep the pump working, Steve.'

'Good idea, lovely.'

'Can you manage the pump and the intercom?'

'No problem. Place the set close to me, then get cracking.'

Wallace carried the two-way communication set over to the little Welshman and laid it alongside him so that he would be able to converse with the man below while continuing to work the pump.

'This will save time, Steve. You sure you can manage?'

'Get on with it!'

Dan Pengelly and David Wallace bent to take a one-handed grip on opposite handles of the centre box in the row of three, and lifted it clear of the ground.

'You okay, Dave?'

'Yes, I think so.'

Each man clutched the handle of a second container with his free hand and then, together, they stumbled over the rough, scrub-covered ground, towards the gate and the waiting car. When he and Pengelly reached the edge of the plateau, Wallace cast one last glance back towards the Feeder and, above the foliage, could just discern the silhouetted head and shoulders of Steve Williams, rocking to and fro as he worked the pump. Then he was lost to view as the two men bulldozed their way over the edge and down the slope, half-carrying, half-dragging the payroll containers as they did so.

*   *   *

Williams leaned towards the microphone as he pumped. 'You still down there, boy?'

'Aye, I'm here.'

'How's it goin' with you, matey?'

'I'm having to rest for a minute. Jesus!' Myers sounded exhausted. 'It's a good thing there were only four bloody boxes, I couldn't take much more of this.'

Below, on the bed of Number One Feeder Pond, Ian Myers swivelled his head as he searched for the descending salvage line. Normally, when he went on a diving job, he had all the equipment including powerful, generator-operated lights, and a fully trained crew above. Still, working in the dark did not worry him overmuch, he had worked under much worse conditions during the Normandy landings. He remembered those dives, when he and his mates had worked by touch, guided right or left by a code of tugs on their lifelines. This was a piece of cake compared to those,

170

and the pay was better! He didn't much like all the scrap metal that lay around, though.

'Watch your air hose, Myers, old son,' he muttered. 'Watch your hose!'

At this, the Feeder's deeper end, the bed of the reservoir was a veritable scrapyard in which great chunks of rusting iron lay piled in utter confusion on top of lengths of twisted pipe and steel girders. It was obvious that contractors, passing this end of the Feeder on their way to the service-gate in the fence, had succumbed to the temptation to use the water as a dumping place for scrap. It was, of course, a practice not officially allowed, but it saved having to haul the scrap away, and over the years an amazing assortment, including cracked dephlagmators, corroded fume ducts and burst boiler tubes, had been surreptitiously added to the rusting pile.

'Did you say anything?'

The words echoed in Myers' earphones.

'Dave?'

'No, Dan and College Boy have started loading the boxes. There's only me up here, a'pumpin' an' a'callin'.'

The bantering words crackled above the steady hiss of rubbery air.

'They shouldn't have left you alone, Steve,' Myers said aggrievedly.

'I'll be all right.' The little Welshman sounded surprised. 'It's not you I'm worried about!'

171

Myers bit his lip. One of the cardinal rules of diving was that a standby pumpsman should be available at all times in case the original pump operator became incapacitated. If anything should happen to Steve Williams before the others returned—

'They should have told me that they were leaving, Steve.'

'Aw, don't worry, boy. Everything is going like a dream.'

Myers' lumbering activities on the bed of the Feeder had stirred up a mixture of mud and algae that further clouded the water and reduced visibility, and it was not until that moment that he detected the salvage rope, snaking whitely above his head.

'Have you got that other box yet?'

'No, not yet. Give us a chance!' Myers complained. He freed the snap-link from his guide rope, then turned in a lumbering, slow-motion waltz. He knew exactly where the fourth container lay, but he had left it until last to recover because it was not as readily accessible as the others had been; between man and box, a concertina of girder work rose twenty feet in an arch of Gothic proportions. Cautiously, Myers inched his cocooned body under the precarious-looking structure. The opening of the archway seemed to be wide enough for him to reach the box without disturbing anything, though he was determined not to take any risk but rather to leave the damned box where it was.

'What are you doing down there?'

'Shut up!'

Myers leaned forward as far as the encumbrance of his diving suit would allow, and reached out one gloved hand. His fingertips hooked over the nearest, braided-wire handle of the cash-box and a miniature cloud of particles ballooned upwards as the box moved on its cushion of mud. Above the diver's head, his swaying air hose snagged on oxide encrusted iron; caught fast, then tugged at the whole, crazy framework.

The first stunning impact plucked Myers off his feet and thrust his helpless body, face down, on to the concrete floor. Remorseless pressure, as if from some giant hand, pinioned his arms and crushed into his spine. There was no noise, no crash of falling steel; instead, the dark blanket of water served to deaden the vibrations of the collision so that they reverberated only briefly as a distant rumble.

'Aggh—!'

An involuntary cry issued from Myers' lips. He lay still as death, waiting for the inward rush of water that must surely come to suffocate him.

'Please, God!'

Fists clenched in most earnest supplication, the prostrate man cried to a long-forgotten Father.

'Sweet Jesus! Save me!'

173

The diver's scream of anguish from the receiver brought the startled Williams to his feet. He heard no other noise, but he felt a slight tremor pass through the ground on which he stood.

'Ian? Ian? What the hell's the matter? Myers?'

Williams' frantic shouts ringing in his earphones steadied the diver's initial panic. The expected deluge had not poured in to engulf him, therefore his air hose was intact! Myers schooled his thoughts, forced himself to calm down, to follow his emergency training. He must try to think clearly and assess the emergency. His first logical response was to protect his vital air supply.

'Ian? Good God! Answer me, will you?'

'Keep pumping, Steve! Don't stop. Keep that pump working at all costs!'

'What's wrong, man? What is it?'

Steve Williams frowned at the silent receiver. This was trouble; he could smell it! He shifted uneasily and tried, impossibly, to penetrate the Feeder's gloomy depths with worried eyes. There was no clue to be seen to tell what might be wrong, no rising trail of bubbles. The Welshman swung steadily on the pump.

'Steve—'

The voice of the diver sounded calmer, yet Williams detected underlying terror.

'Yes? Yes? What is it?'

'I'm trapped.'

Steve Williams stared mutely into the murky water.

'Jesus Christ!'

'Oh, Steve—' The pain-filled call ended in a sob.

'How do you mean, trapped?'

'There's a ton of steel across my back and arms. I can't move! I can't move!'

'Try, Ian, boy,' Williams urged into the microphone. 'Can't you shift it a little?'

'It's no use, it's hopeless. God! I'm on my belly and I've lost the lamp.'

'What if we send a rope down? If you could tie it to—'

'Don't you understand? I can't move, I tell you! I'm stuck fast—can't do a thing.'

Steve Williams had been in sufficient life-or-death situations to know that the man below was fighting panic; that the struggle for sweet life now occupied his entire existence to the exclusion of all else.

'I need help, Steve, and quickly. Where's Dan?'

'He's not back, yet. Not just yet,' Steve Williams said. He looked in the direction of the service-gate. 'He won't be long.'

'Steve! You have to get help. Call the plant security guards on the radio and ask them to get some rescue equipment out here, fast!'

'What?' Williams asked incredulously. He stared at the mass of dark water.

'It's the only way. Call Dan. Please call him! He will radio the guards for help, you'll see.' Myers' pleading tone rose to a demanding scream. 'Call Dan—he'll get help for me!'

'You are right, boy, Dan would.' Williams looked thoughtful. 'Did you manage to fasten the salvage line on to the box?' he asked softly.

'No! Forget the bloody cash-box, we've had it now.' Myers sobbed with pain. 'For God's sake, shout for Dan.'

'All right! All right! I've got to keep the soddin' pump goin', haven't I?' There was an ugly, aggrieved inflection in the Welshman's voice.

'Oh, Christ—my legs—I think they are both broken.'

Williams made no reply. He pursed his lips in silent contemplation as he continued to swing on the lever of the pump.

'Steve? Steve?'

'All right, lovely, I'm here.'

'I'm getting cold, please hurry. Can you see Dan and Dave yet?' The whimpering voice of the diver ended in a yelp of pain.

'Don't you worry, I can see them now.'

'Thank God! Dan will call for help, I know.'

The man at the pump cast his gaze across the empty plateau. There was no sign of the two men returning. 'Dan is almost here,' he said into the microphone. He hesitated. 'No chance of reaching that last container, I suppose,' he asked casually.

'You stupid fool!' Myers screamed desperately. 'I'm trapped down here and all you can think of is the bloody money!'

'Take it easy, will you?' Williams' hand froze on the lever. 'Remember, it's you who loused up this operation, not me.'

Myers sensed the note of impatience, recognised the need to placate this selfish God of life, stationed high above his own dark world of anguish.

'Steve! The pump!' The diver's frightened yell rent the night air.

Quickly, Steve Williams darted out one hand and turned the volume of the intercom receiver down, while with his other hand he worked the pumping mechanism. He said: 'Is that better, lovely? Dan and College Boy are almost here.' He had slipped something from his pocket. There was a faint 'click' as he thumbed an oiled blade from the clasp knife in his hand. 'They can call the guards while I keep pumpin',' he said. 'It shouldn't take long to get the rescue gear out here.'

Myers spoke with child-like pathos. 'Tell the security men that we need a crane, and a diver—lights—'

Steve Williams clenched the open knife between his teeth and convoluted Myers' air hose into a loose bend.

'I am sorry, Steve, but this means we've had it.' There was a moment of silence before the entombed diver spoke again. 'Maybe two of

177

you can get away just before the guards arrive, but someone will have to stay behind to work the pump and tell them where I am.' A sob of distress filtered from the small, black box. 'God, Steve, I'm sorry!'

'I'm sorry too, lovely.'

The little Welshman released the handle of the pump. He took a firmer grip on the already-folded hose, then swept the honed blade through the tube in one easy motion. 'I'm sorry, too,' he repeated softly. He stood up and dropped the cut end of the air hose into the water, then watched a stream of bubbles pour from its open end as it sank beneath the surface.

'Steve! What's happened? The air, Steve!'

Myers felt the pressure drop a fraction of a second after the knife ripped across his hose. Instinctively, he struggled to turn off his belly, to look upwards, even though he could see nothing for the cloud of mud which he disturbed, but he was helpless as a babe.

'Help me—Steve! Help me!'

The first inrush of water quickly filled his helmet. He could see the level rising in his visor, feel it wash over his face.

'Quick—oh, God! Steve!'

Insane with fear, Myers pleaded with his executioner as he fought against the weight which pressed him flat, but it was hopeless. He tried to hold his head back, to raise his mouth above the incoming flood, but bubbling water poured into his ears, his nose, his throat. In that split second, his dying brain offered up some ancient diving lore, and he knew what he must do. He inhaled deeply, filling his lungs with water, and as his vision dimmed, the body of the prostrate man writhed and jerked in great spasms.

Steve Williams stood quite still as Myers' screaming, choking cries called to him from the receiver, but very soon they died away and the night was quiet once more. He watched as the last blossom of bubbles bloomed on the smooth water.

'You've got your boxful,' he muttered. 'Don't spend it all at once.'

He gave one quick glance to reassure himself that he was still alone on the plateau, then sprang into action. The pump was the first to go in, and he grunted as he heaved and rolled it to the brim of the reservoir before toppling it over the edge. He gathered up the intercom set and the ropes, and flung them after the pump. That was all! He had started his run into the shadowy undergrowth before he remembered the two-way radio hanging from its branch, and with a gasp of dismay he spun on his heel and raced for it. He snatched the set from its support and flung it in a high, wide arc out over the Feeder; a faint splash sounded from far out on the surface, and satisfied, Steve Williams turned and scampered across the plateau.

SIX

Dan Pengelly and David Wallace struggled across the uneven ground with the three payroll containers. It was extremely hard work, and they both felt as if their arms had been dragged from their sockets by the time they sledged their way down the earthen slope and reached the gate, but they finally arrived at the car and the three cash-boxes were safely stowed away. Pengelly reversed his ageing Jaguar so that its boot stood only a foot or so from the half-open gate.

'That'll make it easier to reload the pump and the rest of the gear.'

'Things are going well,' Wallace whispered. He looked at his wristwatch. 'We are well inside the time limit, all we have to do is pull that fourth box up, and Myers, then get the hell out of here.'

'So far, so good,' Pengelly admitted.

The two men hurried up the incline and were just breasting the top of the rise when the sound of someone crashing through the scrub reached their ears and a body came hurtling towards them out of the darkness. Before they could take evasive action, the fleeing figure of Steve Williams leapt from the crest of the slope and quite literally dropped on them.

'Steve? What is it?' a startled Pengelly cried as he grabbed at the Welshman's arm.

'Security patrol! Quick—turn back!'

The little man's momentum carried them back down the bank with him, and half-way down one of them lost his footing to send all three sprawling at the foot of the slope. Williams was on his feet in a flash and he clutched at his two companions, pulling them urgently towards the gate.

'It's a patrol. They've got Ian!'

Wallace tried to tug his arm free. 'But is he—?'

'For God's sake, run! You can't do anything, the security men have him.'

Williams made as if to run, but Dan Pengelly reached out and clutched at his clothing with restraining fingers. 'Is Ian out of the water?' he demanded. 'Is he safe?'

'Come on, you fools, or we'll all be caught. Ian is on dry land, but the guards have got hold of him.' Williams threw his arms up in despair and glanced fearfully to the top of the slope. 'I'm off,' he mouthed wildly, 'if you stupid bastards want to stay, then go to hell!'

They broke in confusion and fled for the service-gate. As they burst through, Williams stopped and swung the gate closed. 'The key?' he yelled after the men, 'who has the key?'

Pengelly had already gunned the engine to life, and David Wallace had the front passenger door of the Jaguar open and was half-way into his seat. On hearing Williams' shout he scrambled from the car and hurried half-way back towards the gate.

'Leave it, man, there's no point—'

Williams bared his teeth in the darkness. 'Don't argue, let me have that key!' he snarled.

'For God's sake!'

'The key!'

Wallace fumbled in his pocket for the key to the padlock and flung it at Williams before scurrying back to the car. Once inside, he twisted in his seat so that he was able to watch through the rear window. Williams snapped the padlock shut and turned the key to lock it, then he yanked at the gate until he was satisfied that it was secure, slipped the key into his pocket, and ran for the Jaguar as it gathered speed.

'Move it, Steve, let's get out of here,' Pengelly roared as he revved the engine into a high-pitched whine.

Williams hurled himself into the rear passenger seat as the car accelerated along the dirt-track. Pengelly drove like a madman, cursing and raging as he flung the machine along the rutted surface. Wallace tried several times to look back towards the reservoir for signs of pursuit, but his body was bounced and rattled about so violently that he was quite unable to focus his straining eyes. They finally reached the end of the track where they swung right, on to the A38.

'Slow down, Dan, take it easy,' Williams said hoarsely. He leaned over the driver's shoulder. 'You are doing over a hundred. We don't want to be stopped for speeding.'

'What?' Keeping his eyes on the road ahead, Pengelly partly turned his head. 'The police will be after us, anyway, won't they?'

'They won't know what to look for! They don't know who we are or what car we've got, and by the time they get the suit off old Ian and contact the civil police, we'll be safe at home.'

'Jesus!' Dan Pengelly hesitated, then braked the thundering Jaguar to sixty. 'How in the hell did they rumble us?'

'The first I knew about it was our two-way radio calling a patrol down on us.' He swore volubly. ' "Intruders near Feeder Number One", it said. I didn't wait to hear any more; I called on Ian to come up and I'd just got him back on the bank when they hit us. Five minutes more, by God, and I would have had him out of it.' He paused breathlessly. 'I had his helmet off him when Ian saw them coming at us through the bushes. "Run, Taff!" he said to me, "run while you've still a chance!" So I bloody well ran. Almost left it too late, but Ian made me go.'

'What a carve up.'

'I couldn't help it,' Williams complained plaintively. 'It wasn't my fault.'

'Couldn't you both have made a run for it?'

'Poor Ian didn't have a chance with all that gear on, but he warned me in time, I'll say that for him, he gave me the jump on them.'

'He won't talk, either,' Dan Pengelley said. 'The bastards will never get anything out of Ian, so it's up to us to clam up and look after his share until he gets out.'

'Gets out?' Wallace asked naively.

'Of Horfield, Dave,' the driver said sombrely, like an adult warning an adolescent of an unpleasant fact of life, 'or maybe the Moor,' he added.

David Wallace felt suddenly sick as the penalty for failure and capture was brought home to him. He had visited Princetown years before, with Claire, and he remembered making the tourist-run along the road above Her Majesty's Prison and shuddering at the thought of incarceration in those gaunt, stone blockhouses amid the dank mists of Dartmoor.

'Like Dan said, Ian won't talk,' Steve Williams agreed. 'We can be sure of that.'

They swept westwards along the snaking road in silence, but in the very back of Wallace's mind an indefinable doubt kept surfacing through a maelstrom of thoughts. Something was not quite right; some small piece in the jig-saw of the night's disastrous events did not fit into place. For the security guards to swoop and trap Myers was bad enough, but there was something else, something wrong with the sequence of events, and he relived each frantic moment in his mind until, at last, he realised which segment of the happenings worried him.

'Why did you bother to lock the service-gate?'

'Eh?'

'Why bother to lock the gate?' He guessed that Williams would take exception to the query, and he was right.

'What the hell are you on about?'

Williams went into his usual display of insulted rage, but beneath the tirade, Wallace thought he detected an element of bluster.

'I'm not quarrelling with you, Steve,' Wallace said wearily, 'I only thought it strange that you should hang about when the security patrol might have dropped on us at any moment.'

'You were the one who didn't want to leave any sign of our having used the damned gate,' Steve accused. 'If Dan had forced it open like he wanted to, we would have had the Jag parked alongside the Feeder, and we might all have got away including old Ian. As things were, the patrol had no idea how Ian entered the factory, he's an employee, so it could have been through the main gates with the shift workers. They certainly didn't see me run for the gate, but just in case they had, the locked gate would have delayed them.' He raised his

185

voice a pitch, as if annoyed at having to offer an explanation, to demand: 'All right? Is that all right with you?'

Wallace had to admit that there was some logic in the man's reasoning. 'Yes, forget it.'

The little man snorted and settled back in his seat. Wallace had nettled him, but his explanation seemed reasonable enough, even if it was given with such bad grace.

At the village of East Brent, they left the main A38 and took to unlit side roads until they reached Burnham. Throughout the journey they expected to hear a pursuing police siren, but none came and their immediate fears subsided when at last they swung in through the gates of the Golf Club. The plan had been to split the money four ways in an immediate shareout, but during the return journey David Wallace thought furiously about the changed circumstances and grew convinced that the shareout should be delayed. Obviously, Detective Inspector Cox and his men would be roused by the capture of Myers and one of the cash-boxes to renew their flagging efforts, and any display of new-found wealth would attract the police like bees to honey.

Wallace examined his wristwatch. 'Almost midnight,' he said. 'If we can make it to my apartment without being stopped, we should be safe.' As they entered the Golf Club's car park he raised his hand to caution the driver to slow down, then saw that the clubhouse was in darkness. 'Carry on, Dan—no, wait!' The professional's shop, windows a blaze of light, came into view.

'Someone about,' Pengelly hissed as he looked towards the light. 'Who is it?'

'Must be the pro. What the hell is he doing here at this time of night?' Wallace opened the door of the Jaguar and slipped from his seat. 'You turn around and clear off,' he whispered, 'and I'll walk to my car. See you at the house.'

He made as little noise as possible as he walked towards his car, but as luck would have it, a figure emerged from the shop doorway when he was almost level with it.

'Hello—Mr. Wallace?' The professional evinced mild surprise. 'Not playing in the dark?'

Damn! Wallace thought, of all the infernal luck, but he managed a chuckle and said: 'No, not golf, anyway.' He winked and gave a broad grin. It was a piece of quick thinking on his part; a hint, a suggestion of the one plausible reason for his being in the secluded club grounds late at night.

'Oh—well, goodnight.'

Wallace walked on, towards his car. If he had embarrassed the golf professional, then so much the better. The man was sufficiently discreet to avoid discussing the nocturnal wanderings of club members, so Wallace had covered his presence well, even if it might bring a few old-fashioned glances during his next golf lesson.

He drove through the sleeping town, and when he was part way along Berrow Road he saw in his rear view mirror that Dan Pengelly's Jaguar had fallen in behind. Once, when he glimpsed a patrolling police constable ahead, he turned along another route; he knew that policemen on the beat have an awkward habit of noting the registration numbers of vehicles moving late at night, just in case. When he reached his apartment on the South Esplanade, he slewed the Avenger through the front gates and parked it on the lawn to one side of the drive, then he hurried to the garage door and raised it to allow the Jaguar immediate entry. As Dan Pengelly turned off the Esplanade he switched off his engine and freewheeled up, the short drive; he judged it nicely, for the vehicle's impetus carried it the length of the drive and into the garage.

Wallace's mind worked furiously as he stood in the darkness outside the garage door. They had originally agreed to have an immediate shareout, being careful not to attract attention by overspending. Now, with Myers in the hands of Detective Inspector Cox, things had changed radically. The first and major factor was the capture of Ian Myers, of course; both Pengelly and Williams seemed absolutely sure he would give no information to his captors, but what if the police managed to trick the diver into providing a clue as to the identity of his accomplices? If that should happen, then possession of the stolen money would seal the case against them. The second and imponderable factor was Steve Williams. Since their altercation during the return journey he had lapsed into a sulky silence, which suited Wallace since it gave him a chance to consider the changed situation. The unstable element in Williams' makeup was likely to blow everything skyhigh, should Myers' capture produce further complications, for faced with complications Steve Williams would simply disappear, but he would never run without his share of the loot.

He looked up and down the South Esplanade until he was satisfied that no one had been watching their furtive arrival, then he stepped inside the garage, reached up, and swung the door down quietly behind him.

'Dave?'

'Yes, it's all right, it is me. I can't see anyone outside; doesn't look like we were followed.'

Pengelly and Williams were standing at the rear of the garage.

'Shall I switch the light on?' Pengelly whispered.

'Yes, it won't show outside.'

By the dim light of a single bulb the three men stared at one another. For several seconds they stood there in silence, each man undergoing some kind of psychological reaction to the bizarre events of the night. It was Williams who spoke first, to break the trance-like moment.

'We've done it! By God, we've done it!'

'That we have,' Dan Pengelly said, and his face creased into a wide grin. 'We've got the money, Steve, that makes us bloody rich.' He grabbed Williams in a bear hug and the two of them rolled about like a couple of gleeful schoolboys.

'Not so much noise,' Wallace urged, but it was difficult to restrain such spontaneous exuberance. Then: 'Listen!' he hissed as he suddenly heard the sound of a motorcycle engine on the sea-front road outside. They froze momentarily, then relaxed as the 'phut-phut' of the motor passed the garage and died away in the distance. 'Upstairs with the money, lads,' Wallace said, 'but wait until I check that Mrs. Warren's not about.' He pushed past the men, switched off the light, and stepped out through the rear door of the garage on to the tiny back yard of the house. He listened for a few moments but the night was still; he peered around the corner of the house to see if there were any lights on in the ground floor apartment, but the old lady's rooms were in darkness and he returned to the garage.

'All clear!'

'The old girl wouldn't be running around

outside at this time of night,' Williams said. He looked at his wristwatch. 'Hell, she's been tucked up in bed for hours.'

'I'll open the apartment and keep watch on the road, if you can manage the boxes?'

'Go ahead, Dave, and break out the whisky as well, eh?'

Working in the darkness, Pengelly opened the boot of the Jaguar and, between them, he and Williams unloaded the three payroll containers on to the garage floor, then they manhandled them, one at a time, up the iron staircase that led to Wallace's apartment. Finally, the three men stood in a circle, looking down on the containers laid out on the floor of Wallace's living-room.

'That's the pot of gold, boy, and we've reached the end of the rainbow,' Williams breathed.

'Open them up, then,' Pengelly said, and he knelt to one box and took hold of its lid. When the lids of all three containers hung back on their hinges, he looked up. 'Dave, lad!' he whispered, and Wallace saw the light of elation in his eyes.

They had seen the boxes open before, on the floor of the strongroom in Forsters' cash office, but now the long-awaited, magic moment had arrived and the piled banknotes lay at their feet, for them to do with as they wished.

Steve Williams was seated on his haunches

in a miner's squat, and from his crouched position he swept up a double handful of treasury notes and held them aloft. 'Touch it, Dave,' he urged, 'it's all ours.'

The two ex-sergeants pawed at the money and whispered together in furtive excitement.

'Three boxes of the stuff,' Williams cried. 'That's one box of cash-money apiece.'

Pengelly froze. 'There are four of us, remember?' he rasped, and he caught hold of the little Welshman's arm in a bruising grip.

'Eh?' The warning in Pengelly's voice took Williams aback. The two men's eyes met briefly before Williams' eyelids flickered and he wrenched his arm from the other's grasp. 'Yes—that's right. That's what I meant—'

'We keep Ian's share for him, regardless of how long a sentence he gets,' Pengelly growled.

'Oh, for God's sake!'

Pengelly's eyes narrowed and a muscle knotted in his cheek. 'He is all right, Taff?' The tall man was ominously quiet as he repeated: 'Tell me that he is all right!'

'Will you bloody lay off?' Steve Williams shouted and he glared at each man in turn. 'Perhaps you'd both be happier if the coppers had caught me as well, then you'd have had the cash all to yourselves. I told you, Ian was out of the water and on the side of the Feeder when I last saw him. I'm not responsible for what happened after that, am I? Why don't you just ring up that bloody detective and ask him, if you don't believe me.' He turned away, apparently in anger, then spun on his heel to face his adversaries again. 'You are getting as bad as him,' he said plaintively to Pengelly as he jabbed a thumb in Wallace's direction.

'Let's forget it,' Wallace interposed quickly. 'I'll get us all a drink, that's what we need. We are all on edge, that's the trouble. We must try not to wake old Mrs. Warren in the apartment below,' he added.

'To hell with Mrs. flamin' Warren,' Williams snarled as he collapsed sulkily into a chair.

Wallace poured three whiskies. 'Here,' he said, 'this is what's wanted,' and he downed his own with one gulp. He knew that what he had to do next would not be easy, to say the least, especially so with them in such a truculent mood, but he was convinced it was the only way if they were to avoid capture themselves. He made a sign behind Williams' back, indicating that he wanted Pengelly to follow him, and made his way into the kitchen. Pengelly's face wore a quizzical look as he walked into the tiny room.

'Close the door, Dan.'

'What is it?'

'The money,' Wallace said bluntly. 'We can't possibly share it out now, not with Ian and the other cash-box in the hands of the police.'

'Why not?'

'All hell is about to break loose again; it'll be as bad as it was before, with Cox's men questioning everyone and those blasted newspaper and television reporters will come swarming back.' Wallace paused for breath and Pengelly shrugged non-committally. 'I know I'm right,' Wallace insisted in an undertone. 'It would be fatal for Steve to take his money until things quieten down, because if he does, he'll do a bunk at the first sign of trouble, and that really would be the end for all of us.'

Dan Pengelly sucked in his breath. 'You could be right,' he said doubtfully.

'I know I'm right.'

'Maybe, but what is Steve going to say?'

'If I propose the idea to him, will you back me?'

'I don't know. It's a sudden change from thinking that I'm walking out of here with seventy-five thousand quid, to thinking that I'm not. What would you do with the money, anyway?'

'Only keep it out of the way long enough for the fuss to die down.'

'We could just as well have left it in the Feeder for another couple of months.'

'We didn't know Ian would get nabbed.'

'That's true.'

Wallace was about to say something further when the kitchen door opened and the frowning face of Steve Williams appeared.

'What's all the chat about?' he asked suspiciously. Now that he had joined them the tiny kitchen was crowded, and Wallace said: 'Let's go back into the living-room. I've got something to say to you, Steve.'

They filed from the kitchen and Wallace walked over to the containers which lay with their lids open. He turned and stood his ground.

'Well? What can be so important that you two have to leave the room for a quick board meeting,' Williams began belligerently.

'It's not like that.'

'No? Then what is it like, eh?'

Wallace toed one of the cash-boxes. 'It's a question of what to do with the money now that Ian has been nabbed.'

'Do with it? Do with it?' The little man glared at Wallace with a look of angry bewilderment. 'By God,' he said, 'I'll show you what to do with it,' and he made as if to reach for the contents of one box. 'We share it out right now.'

'No!'

Wallace gave one swift kick and the metal lid of the box slammed shut, almost catching Steve Williams' hand in the process. He jerked his hand away just in time, and there was no mistaking the look of pure hatred in his eyes as he slowly straightened.

'Just what the hell is going on?' He addressed the question solely to Dan Pengelly.

'Dave thinks we shouldn't share out the cash yet.'

Steve Williams rounded on Wallace. 'Why not?' he asked in a tone which conveyed total disbelief.

'Calm down, Steve. If you'll only listen to what I have to say, you'll see that I'm right,' Wallace coaxed. 'If the four of us were here then we could have a share-out as arranged, but with Ian taken by the police, and they'll be finding the fourth payroll container at the bottom of the Feeder, remember, we can expect the balloon to go up tomorrow. Cox will know that someone has recovered the other three boxes and he'll be watching like a hawk for anyone spending more than usual.'

'Do you think I'm that much of a fool?'

'It's not that—'

'You two buggers had this worked out all along,' Williams accused. He glanced at Pengelly. 'Have you been making some private arrangement behind my back, Dan, lovely?'

'Don't be stupid, Taff! Dave has only just mentioned the idea, and then only because of the cock-up over Ian. If you must know, I'm beginning to think there may be something in what he says.'

'Aye, boy, I bet he's only just mentioned the idea,' Williams said with heavy sarcasm, 'and now I'm just going to mention a few things—'

'Don't be a fool,' Wallace snapped as he ran out of patience. 'With Ian caught, we have to be extra careful.' He was about to add: 'If Cox had you, you'd squeal like a stuck pig to save your own skin,' but he bit his tongue and managed not to blurt out the words.

'So, what would you have us do with it?' Williams said angrily, and he kicked one of the boxes in temper. 'Shall we run down Burnham High Street in the morning and stick it in Lloyd's bank?'

'No,' Wallace replied. 'We bury it.' He caught sight of a surprised look on Pengelly's face.

'Bury it?' Are you mad?' Williams looked askance at Pengelly, but found him gazing open-mouthed at Wallace. 'God damn, Wallace, boy, but you come up with the nuttiest notions. How long were you thinking of burying the money for?'

'Six months should be enough.'

'Six—' Steve Williams broke off and a stream of curses ripped from his lips. 'You've had that! We've only just pulled the stuff out of that flamin' pond, and now you want to bury it. Well, I ain't waitin' one more day. I'm taking my share now, tonight.'

'Christ!'

'Stay exactly where you are, lovely.'

Wallace found himself staring into the mesmerising eye of a gun which Steve Williams held in an unwavering grasp.

'You mad, bloody Welshman,' Dan Pengelly said slowly, and his lean body tensed like a coiled spring.

'You'd never make it, Dan,' Williams said with a wolfish grin. 'You must be getting old. There was a time when I never would have caught you flat on your fanny like this.'

'Make the most of it, Taff. There won't be a second time, I promise you.'

'Now, now,' Williams chided. He centred the muzzle on Pengelly's chest. 'You don't think I'd gun down an old comrade in arms, do you?'

Dan Pengelly's eyes glittered with suppressed rage.

'It's a joke—a joke,' Williams grinned, but his gun still covered the two men.

'Then put it down.'

'In a minute, lovely, in a minute. I want to sort out our little misunderstanding first.'

Wallace could still hardly believe his eyes. 'Look! Be sensible,' he pleaded. 'We only need delay the share-out for a short time.'

'Aye. A very short time.' Williams swung the gun Wallace's way as the taller man shifted uneasily. 'You stand still, mate, I'm not waitin' six months. I'm having mine now!'

'What about Myers?'

Williams' eyes narrowed. 'What about him?'

'Cox has got him, and will soon get the other cash-box.'

Williams looked thoughtful. 'Well?'

'Cox will have his men crawling all over

Forsters, and Burnham, looking for anyone linked with Ian.'

'I suppose so.' Williams seemed to hesitate before replying.

Wallace noted the momentary hesitation and thought his reasoning was making ground. 'They'll especially question any friends of Ian's or anyone he worked with, and that lets us in on both counts. I tell you, Steve, if we do anything slightly unusual, buy whisky instead of beer, cigars instead of cigarettes, then we become suspects. Cox's men will be watching every pub and club in the area for high-spenders.' Williams seemed even less sure of himself and Wallace went on more confidently. 'For God's sake, man,' he said, 'leave the money alone for a few months at least, then maybe we can spend a little, if we are careful.'

'Dave is right,' Pengelly interposed. 'Old Myers getting himself nobbled has changed things somewhat. Hell, I want my money as badly as anyone, but it does make sense to get rid of it again until this new bother has died down. Now put the shooter away before I kick you all round the room.'

'Aw—hell—' Steve Williams hefted the automatic weapon from hand to hand. 'Okay!' he decided, and he grinned like a mischievous schoolboy as he pocketed the gun.

David Wallace had to grip the back of a chair to still his trembling hands, though

199

whether they trembled from rage or fright he could not tell. 'I didn't know that you had one of those,' he said in shocked tones.

Williams gazed at him with hooded eyes. 'There's a lot you don't know about me, boy,' he said insolently.

'Where—where did you get it?'

Williams drew the gun again and brandished it aloft. 'That, for your information, is a Luger P08 pistol, so beloved by the German officers that they wouldn't change to their new issue Walther P38. It was a present from a big, blond Panzer officer, deceased. I had to make him deceased to get my hands on the Luger.' He slid the gun back into his pocket.

Dan Pengelly pointed a warning finger at him. 'Remember what I said about there not being a second time,' he advised.

'Ah! That's something else again! Let's hope we never have to put it to the test,' Williams said, with an odd smile. 'In the meantime ask Mastermind, here, where he intends digging this hole.' He turned to address Wallace. 'In your back garden, I suppose.' His lip curled. 'Not flamin' likely! You might decide to gather in the harvest one dark night and do a bunk, eh?'

Wallace controlled himself with difficulty. 'No. Not in my back garden, nor in yours, come to that,' he said. He glanced at Dan Pengelly. He still had to sell the idea to him, even though Williams was the main obstacle. He said: 'It has to be in a place where one or even two of us can't get at it without attracting the attention of all three, yet a place where we could recover it reasonably quickly if all three agreed to do so.' He added bitterly: 'That's how it has to be, it seems, since obviously we can no longer trust one another.'

'Trust!' Steve Williams spat the word. 'Could we ever?'

'Is there such a place?' Pengelly asked doubtfully.

'Yes,' Wallace said. 'Steart Island!'

To the west of Burnham, one mile or more across the mouth of the River Parrett from the coastal town, lies the island called Steart; in reality little more than a lonely, dangerous, God-forsaken finger of mud, stabilised by a thin covering of sand and scree through which tufts of coarse marram grass thrust their roots in a precarious hold on life. One mile long and dumb-bell shaped, so that its twin mounded structure is split into two islets when high tides flood across its central bar, Steart Island thrusts itself just above the level of the sea at that point where the tidal waters of the mighty Bristol Channel surge and race in a battle for supremacy with those of the outflowing River Parrett. In fine weather, when the reach of the incoming tide has lost its pace, the waters surrounding Steart seem deceptively calm and the banked-up threshold of the Parrett appears like a mill-pond on a summer's day. The casual visitor should beware, however, for as the tide recedes the channel between island and mainland becomes an eight-knot tide-race that rips and rolls over floorless chasms full with quicksands and quaking mud, mud which rises from the depths in the form of fluted buttresses to support Steart's perimeter and seal off the island's approaches as effectively as if an army guarded them.

'Steart Island?' Steve Williams blinked. 'Have you lost your marbles, boy?'

'I say it suits our needs exactly,' Wallace said. 'You can see the island from your house on the seafront, as I can. Dan would have to walk to the beach from where he lives, but it's the one place where we can hide the containers, yet keep a check to make sure no man sneaks out there alone. For most of the time the place is inaccessible, when the water race or the mud exposed by the falling tide prevents a crossing, that is. During the few hours either side of high tide when the mud is covered and a boat could cross, we can keep a look out. If any one of us tried to get at the money during that time he would be easily seen.'

'And at night?'

'There's no man fool enough to try.'

They thought of cold, wet coffins of mud; bottomless pits of the stuff that ranged from Burnham to Steart and encircled the island.

The trio looked at one another and each man knew that Wallace was right, not one of them would seek almost certain death by attempting to traverse those tide-ripped mud-gullies during darkness.

'Well, what about it?' Wallace asked. 'Is it to be Steart Island?'

Dan Pengelly nodded. 'Sounds good,' he asked, 'but what do you say, Steve?'

'Okay, okay, if it makes you happy.' The little Welshman shrugged his shoulders nonchalantly and raised his eyebrows. 'When are we going to carry out this brilliant scheme, eh?'

Wallace looked at the wall clock. 'It is three a.m. now. High tide is at seven-twenty this morning; if we meet here at six o'clock we can do the job before it gets really light. Bring your fishing rods with you and we'll make it look like an angling party. Can you bring the boat, Dan?'

Pengelly was the only one of the trio who dabbled with boats, and he shared the use of a small dinghy with a friend of his, who also owned an old banger of a Land Rover which they used for fishing expeditions.

'It's at Mike's place.' Mike was the name of Pengelly's friend. 'He's on shift work at the moment, so he won't want to use it. I'll need his Land Rover, too, to carry the dinghy. He won't mind.'

'We'd better carry the cash-boxes down to

the garage and leave them there for the rest of the night, otherwise some early caller like the milkman or the postman might catch us at it,' Wallace said.

'Do you want to know something?' Williams said sadly. 'What with all the aggravation from you two buggers, we haven't even counted it!'

'God! We haven't, either,' Pengelly agreed despondently.

For months they had been anticipating this moment, the moment when they had the money in their grasp, to do with as they wished. They had talked of it and dreamed of it, and planned it to be like a party at which each man would count out his share of banknotes, and roll amongst them naked if he so desired.

'There's no time. We know roughly what a count would show.'

'It's not the same.'

Between them, they manhandled the three containers back down the stairway and placed them against the rear wall of the garage. 'They'll be safe enough,' Wallace said. 'I'll lock all the doors until the morning.'

'It's morning now. See you in a few hours, eh?'

Wallace opened the garage door so that they could drive the Jaguar straight out and be away with the minimum of fuss. They drove past him as he stood at the front of the garage, and Williams stuck his head out through his

204

open window. 'See you later, old boy,' he drawled. 'Don't you go gettin' any funny ideas about those payroll boxes between now and six o'clock, you hear?'

Wallace grimaced after the disappearing vehicle, then closed the garage door and glanced at the three containers. He carefully covered them with a couple of old coats, locked the rear garage door, and toiled back up the stairs to his rooms. He felt the sudden pangs of hunger and realised that he had hardly eaten all day, so he forced himself to cook an omelette which, somewhat to his surprise, he ate with great relish.

He set his alarm clock for five-thirty, though he did not expect to sleep during the intervening few hours until the return of his two companions. He lay down on his bed, having taken off his muddy shoes and undressed down to his underwear, and as he lay there in the darkness he cursed the ill-luck of Myers' capture and wondered where the police had taken the diver and whether they had managed to elicit any information from him. If so, Wallace knew that he might expect a knock on his door at any time. He drifted into the limbo of half sleep in which he dreamed wild, fleeting dreams of ogre-like divers who screamed at him in silent pain. Their faces, sliding beneath red-stained waters were always those of Myers! Myers! Myers!

He awoke with a start. His naked arms and

legs felt terribly cold. For one brief, sweet moment he remembered nothing, as his mind hovered in the semi-consciousness of waking thought, then the reality of life came rushing back. He rolled over on the bed and reached for the alarm clock. It was just five a.m. He twisted his limbs into the bed cover for warmth and, as he lay there in the semi-darkness, he could still see Myers' features diffracted through the water of a nightmare lake.

Finally, Wallace roused himself and dressed quickly. He only just caught the tail-end of the news on the radio but there was no mention of Myers' capture or of the payroll container they had left behind in the Feeder pond.

First light came just after five-thirty a.m., but it came over the eastern horizon as a grey, subdued dawn, and when he drew back the curtains of his living-room window and gazed out over the broad expanse of Bridgwater Bay, he could only just see past the sea-wall which lined the Esplanade. By the time the Land Rover arrived, a few minutes before six o'clock, he had opened the door of the garage and was waiting inside as Pengelly reversed along the drive and into the garage.

Steve Williams' head bobbed out through the side-window of the vehicle and he craned his neck to glance back at the waiting man. 'Still here, then?' he quipped.

David Wallace ignored him. Instead he

looked through the open back of the Rover from which the snub nose of a pram-dinghy protruded. 'You had no trouble getting it?' He patted the prow of the dinghy and addressed himself to Dan Pengelly who had swivelled round in the driving seat.

'Not really,' Pengelly shrugged. 'My mate didn't like being woken at five on a Sunday morning, but he'll get over it.

'Aye, stuff him!' Williams said. 'We've got other things to think about.'

Wallace continued to ignore him. 'You got the outboard?' he asked Pengelly.

'Under the boat.'

'We need to launch from the far end of the beach, up near the Low Light.'

'Why not run straight down the jetty? That's directly opposite the island.'

'But it's also in full view of the Esplanade and the houses along the sea-front. Anyone watching along there would be close enough to see us and the boxes, but if we launch from the far end we can work without being seen, and the incoming tide will carry us up river towards Steart Island.'

There was little further discussion. Between them they managed to load the three containers into the Land Rover without much difficulty. They drove along the Esplanade until they reached Maddocks Slade, from which a sloping ramp led directly on to the beach. Once on the beach they drove north until they reached the Martian-like, nine-legged Low Light, at which point Dan Pengelly made a ninety degree turn and headed for the water's edge. Incoming wavelets slapped on to the sand some sixty yards from the wooden lighthouse as they lifted down the pram-dinghy and slid it out to meet the oily waters. Wallace held on to the painter of the small craft while the two veterans lifted the first container from the back of the Land Rover and carried it out to the boat. They had to paddle knee deep in muddy water to do so, but nobody cared about minor discomforts and a second container quickly followed the first into the dinghy.

'Wait a minute,' Wallace said. He had been holding the boat steady but now he clambered aboard after the boxes. 'Push it out a bit, it's grounding.' Using one of the oars he poled at the sand that lay beneath the murky water. 'You'd better get in now, Dan.'

The pram-dinghy already sat quite deep in the water. It was a small craft, designed to carry four or, at the most, five people on short-haul trips. Pengelly carried a small Seagull outboard motor from the Rover and clipped it to the stern of the boat. 'We can't all go,' he pointed out. 'If we take the last box, one of us will have to stay behind. She isn't the Queen Mary, for Christ's sake!'

'In that case Steve can wait here while you and I go out to the island.'

'Why don't you tell him?' Pengelly said wryly and a faint light of amusement flickered in his eyes.

Steve Williams was waiting at the rear of the Land Rover to help carry the third container.

'I think we can manage to take the third box if you wait here with the Rover, Steve,' Wallace called, but as he made the suggestion he noticed that Dan Pengelly kept his back towards the little Welshman.

Immediately Steve Williams' face tightened and he came trotting to the water's edge. 'Not bloody likely,' he spat vehemently and he splashed ankle deep into the sea in his anxiety as he added, 'I'm not that stupid. I want to see where this little lot goes, matey!'

Wallace began to argue but gave up. He felt much too tired to enter into a prolonged slanging match.

Dan Pengelly jerked his head towards the beach. 'What about the waggon? Will it be safe to leave it with the box inside?'

'If you buggers are so worried about it, one of you two can stay,' Williams snapped.

'Okay, okay,' Wallace retorted with equal irritability, 'the beach looks deserted and there are no houses overlooking us.' He turned to Pengelly. 'Pull the Rover back to the Low Light and lock it. If you pull a cover over the box it should be safe enough; we'll have to make two runs, that's all. Don't forget the spade and fishing rods,' he called.

At first, the run out to the island went quite smoothly. Although heavily laden, so that its gunwale breasted the water by only a few inches, the pram-dinghy forced its blunt nose through the discoloured water. The sea was flat calm for the first half-mile as, with Dan Pengelly at the tiller, they headed straight out to sea along the line of the High and Low Lights, an imaginary line which indicated the sea lane for the occasional tramp vessel to steam up the River Parrett. They had rounded Number Five Buoy which lay anchored off the north-east corner of Steart Island, when they first ran into a gentle swell that rolled foot-high surges of water head on into the cut-off nose of the dinghy. Under normal circumstances that size swell would not have bothered them, but riding low in the water as they were, each wash that swept in from the Bristol Channel lapped over the gunwale and slopped a spray of water into the boat.

It had been their intention to land on the seaward side of the island so that they would be shielded from the mainland while they carried the boxes up the island's shore. Obviously they would be visible during the boat journey to and fro, but small craft were a common sight on the River Parrett when the tide was sufficiently high. By now the tide was quite high and had already flowed over the central bar of Steart Island to split the sliver of sand and silt into two separate parts. Their objective was the peak of the knoll which was always left protruding above sea level at the northern end of the island, and they had managed to cover about three-quarters of the distance to their goal although the three of them were thoroughly soaked by the splashing waves and their feet squelched in several inches of water swilling around in the bottom of the dinghy.

'Here! This is getting a bit rough,' Steve Williams said anxiously. 'We won't sink, will we?'

Both he and Wallace were taking the brunt of the waves since they sat with their backs towards the prow of the boat. Wallace was tempted to remind him that he could have stayed ashore, but he held his tongue; he was beginning to get more than a little worried himself.

'If we ship too much water we may have to land on this side of Steart, Dan,' Wallace said, but he was too intent on shielding the back of his neck from the next wave to look at the man at the helm. Pengelly made no reply. He was sitting tall in his seat in order to look at something over the heads of his companions.

SEVEN

'There's a yacht not far away, and unless I'm very much mistaken she's heading straight for us!'

Wallace nudged Steve Williams and without looking around said: 'Hold the rods up, quickly, to make them think we are out fishing.' They fumbled in the bottom of the dinghy for a rod, then each held one aloft in the pretence of assembling it.

Williams slewed in his seat and glared angrily at the yacht which was rapidly closing on them. 'Why don't they sod off,' he grumbled. 'All this water to play with and they have to sail into us.'

'It's not the police, is it?' Wallace hissed. He kept his eyes on Pengelly's face as he spoke. 'If it's Cox and his men then we are done for. There's no way we can hide the boxes if that detective is aboard, so get ready to dump them over the side.' The evidence lay on the floorboards under their feet, covered by a sheet and the fishing equipment.

'I don't think it's him,' Pengelly muttered quietly, his face deathly pale. 'It looks like a private boat but the bastard is getting too close for comfort. What do they want?'

David Wallace twisted on his seat and peered over the prow of the dinghy through a hail of spray. A thirty-five foot sailing cruiser had closed to within hailing distance and her name, painted in white lettering on her teak, chine-built prow, stood out in the grey, half light.

'The *"White Heron"* Wallace mouthed, and he cursed under his breath. 'Of all the damned luck!'

'What is it, Dave?'

'I know that boat. I know the people sailing her.'

Steve Williams leaned close to him and snarled in his ear. 'Then get rid of them, and make it quick. This ain't no social occasion for you to be hobnobbing with your flamin' golfing pals, Wallace, boy.'

The unwelcome cruiser was some twenty lengths from their prow when she suddenly turned in a wide circle and gybed to come up alongside. Wallace knew the boat well; her owner was a golfing and drinking friend who had built the yacht in the garden of his house. Wallace had seen the *"Heron"* at various stages of her construction over the past year or so, but she was the last thing he wanted to see at that particular moment.

'What are you doing out here?' a voice called, and Wallace looked up to see a burly figure gazing down at him with an expression of amusement mingled with mild concern. Wallace suspected that his friend had certain views on his seafaring capability.

213

'Jim!' He grinned weakly and tried to sound surprised. He clutched the sections of unassembled fishing rod in his hands and waved them about his head. 'Just off to do some fishing,' he called lamely.

Jimmy Wilson and his companion surveyed the bobbing dinghy and its cramped occupants in dispassionate appraisal, as if deciding whether they should be rescued from their own foolishness.

'You look a bit low in the water, Dave,' the man at the tiller of the yacht advised.

'For Christ's sake, get rid of them, will you!' Steve Williams leaned close to Wallace's ear and growled the instruction through immobile lips.

'We can manage, thanks. You carry on,' Wallace called, with an air of assurance that did not match his feelings. He was completely out of his element, squatting in that tiny, sea-tossed craft, with his head hunched into his shoulders in an effort to avoid the flying spume.

Jim Wilson shrugged and glanced at his partner. Wallace could only grin inanely up at the newcomers until he heard the shouted reply: 'Be careful, Dave. Perhaps you should make for the shore?' and with that the *White Heron* slipped away into the sombre morning.

They finally managed to round the northern end of Steart Island and chugged slowly along parallel with its seaward shore, though they had to bale water continuously from the bottom of the dinghy in order to keep afloat. They beached on soft shingle, out of sight of Burnham town, and the two payroll containers were quickly offloaded and dragged up through sparse clumps of marram grass until they were at a point where the crest of the islet just shielded them from view of the mainland. It took perhaps twenty minutes to dig a hole deep enough to take both precious containers, to cover them with scree, and to return to the dinghy. Once they had embarked on the return journey they found that without the weight of the heavy cash-boxes the craft rode the slap of the incoming wavelets quite comfortably. They passed inside Number Five Buoy and were steering towards the Low Light and the waiting Land Rover when all three spotted the brightly-coloured car more or less simultaneously.

'The Ford passing the church,' Williams gasped. 'It's the law!'

Even as they watched, the patrol car slowed to a halt on the Esplanade near the leaning tower of Saint Andrew's church, and made no attempt to drive on.

'Christ!' Pengelly muttered blasphemously, 'are they on to us after all?'

'If Myers has talked—'

'You don't want to worry about old Ian,' Steve Williams assured, cutting Wallace off in mid sentence. 'He will never tell the CID about us, I'm sure. I don't like the look of that patrol car, though; something else may have given them a lead. You never know what the devious buggers are up to.'

'I can't see any other police cars,' Pengelly observed.

The mainland was still three-quarters of a mile distant and although they studied both beach and town, from the yacht club at the south end of Burnham to the sand dunes that lined the golf course to the north, they could see no other sign of police activity.

'What shall we do?' Wallace asked plaintively. 'It could be coincidence that the car has stopped, so for God's sake let's not panic.'

'Always assume the worst, boy. Split up, I say, then if the coppers are waiting, one of us will get a chance to make a run for it.' Steve Williams pointed towards the old, abandoned boating lake, the breached walls of which lay in ruins at the far side of the town jetty. 'Drop me off up by there, then you two can land lower down the beach. Keep away from the Rover and the third box until we know that it's safe.'

Wallace looked at Dan Pengelly for guidance and received a quick nod. 'Steve is right. What else can we do, out in the open like this?'

They were certainly out in the open. Having committed themselves to the return journey

216

from Steart they were hideously exposed to observation from the town, and with the dinghy making only three or four knots they would remain so exposed for the next fifteen minutes at least. Pengelly swung the handle of the outboard engine hard to his left, at which the tiny boat spun to starboard and headed up river, away from the Low Light and the Land Rover with its incriminating load. The incoming tide was now to their advantage, but it still took well over ten anxious minutes to cover the intervening distance as they forged their way upriver in full view of the police car.

'They look harmless,' Wallace suggested as he examined the car for signs of surveillance by its occupants. The two uniformed policemen who occupied the front seats of the car were clearly visible to the trio in the boat until they passed the end of the jetty and the old boating lake. Pengelly made a ninety degree turn and headed for the beach.

'Aye, the crafty bastards,' Williams grimaced. 'Don't trust 'em an inch,' he advised, and before the craft reached dry land he leapt into the shallows. He landed up to his knees in water, and splashed his way out of the tide, racing away over the muddy strip of sand which lay between them and the sloping embankment of the sea-wall. His short, agile figure was hidden from the police car by the crumbling wall of the disused lake as he took the concreted slope at a run, topped the sea-wall, and disappeared.

As Dan Pengelly headed the dinghy out into mid-channel once more, he and David Wallace studied the patrol car closely.

'I think we may have been wasting our time, Dan, they haven't moved a muscle and I don't think they are interested in us. Shall we chance it?' Wallace suggested.

'You mean go back to the Low Light?'

'Yes.'

Pengelly shrugged. 'I suppose if they were after us then they would have picked us up by now,' he said. 'What the hell!' and with that he turned the nose of the boat downstream.

Their return passage along the open foreshore, and once again in full view of the parked police car, was even more traumatic than before, and stretched their already taut nerves almost to breaking point. At any moment they expected to hear the sounds of shouts and whistles or to see another launch in pursuit, but none came. After what seemed like an eternity they turned in towards the shore and beached.

'So far, so good, Dave.'

They were alone on the beach, but the tide had risen since their first launching and now it rolled its entrained jetsam to within twenty feet of the Land Rover.

'What about the third box?'

'Mustn't be caught with it.' The tall man grabbed the spade from the dinghy which they had dragged clear of the gentle wavelets. He fumbled in his pocket. 'Here are the keys. You unload the box and we'll dump it where we stand, beneath the Low Light.'

The Low Light at Burnham was a curious structure, set down in splendid isolation on the beach to the north of the town. A square, white, wooden tower, exactly forty-feet high, with a vertical, red stripe running down its centre, a working, automatic lighthouse whose light could be seen for nine miles. It was used as a leading light, with the High Light behind, to indicate a sea lane for vessels navigating the River Parrett, and the Low Light had stood there since 1832, on nine, foot-square, timber legs which in turn rested on a concrete raft.

With powerful thrusts of the spade, Dan Pengelly began to gouge a hiding place deep into the muddy sand to one side of this concrete block. The Land Rover and the massive baulks of timber that formed the legs of the lighthouse shielded their frantic activity from any possible observation by the occupants of the police car as Wallace manhandled the last container from the tailboard of the Rover, dragged it to the gaping hole and pushed it in. It hit the bottom of the watery cavity with a squelching sound and Pengelly quickly shovelled the pile of sand at his feet over the box.

'There,' he said as he stamped the wet sand flat, 'now we need a mark,' and using the spade like an axe, he scored the stilt-like leg of the lighthouse nearest to the hidden hoard.

'Thank God the weather's bad,' Wallace said. 'At least it's keeping people off the beach.' The earlier gloom of the dawn had not improved as the morning wore on, and it was still quite cold and the sky remained heavily overcast. He glanced at his wristwatch. 'My God, it's only half-past eight! We seem to have been in that damned boat for ages.'

His companion peered through the stilted legs of the structure that loomed above them. 'The police car is still there, Dave,' he said, and the tone of his voice indicated a rapidly growing impatience.

'Do you think Ian might have talked?'

'Like hell! Old Myers would never drop us in it.' Dan Pengelly spat vehemently at the encroaching tide, then glared in the direction of the immobile symbol of law and order. 'Come on,' he rasped, 'I can't stand this cat-and-mouse nonsense any longer. We'll drive straight past the bastards and then we'll know, one way or the other.'

They loaded the dinghy and other bits and pieces into the back of the Land Rover, then drove slowly towards the town, past the waking houses in Grove Road and along firm sand to the slipway at Maddocks Slade. Once off the beach, Pengelly pulled the Rover in a tight circle on to the Esplanade and then drove warily by the leaning tower of Saint

Andrew's church. As they glided past the parked police car, one of its occupants looked up, briefly, from his writing, obviously unaware that early promotion was only a car's length from him.

'I could have done without that!' David Wallace settled back into his seat and exhaled noisily in an enormous sigh of relief.

'Steve will curse those coppers something rotten,' Dan Pengelly grinned. 'Old Taffy went over that sea-wall like a bat out of hell, and all for nothing. Wait 'til I see him!'

Wallace pursed his lips. 'What about the box we just planted beneath the Low Light?' he asked quietly. 'We needn't tell Steve exactly where it is, need we? He could get at it without our knowing.'

'Eh?' The driver took his eyes from the road momentarily to glance at his companion. 'Jesus, Dave, he'd go berserk if he thought for one minute we were holding out on him.'

'Well,' Wallace said in a matter of fact tone, 'think about it. If he does know exactly where to find that third container, then we can kiss it, and Steve, goodbye, when the row breaks over Ian and the one they'll find in the Feeder. Don't you see, Dan? Having got Ian, that detective, Cox, will know for sure it was an inside job. Steve is our danger man; he'll break and run under pressure, and take the third money box with him.'

Pengelly shrugged. 'I agree with you. I trust

Steve about as far as I can throw him, but if we push him too far he may try to use that bloody Luger of his again, so who is going to be first to refuse to tell him? That's going to be one mad Welshman when he finds out.'

They had reached the Queens Hotel and the corner of Pier Street.

'You can drop me off here,' Wallace instructed, 'then go on home. You can expect the CID men to be all over the place today, like a pack of demented ferrets, asking questions about Ian. We just have to sit tight and say nothing, and I hope to God that Steve can keep his mouth shut.'

'We don't have to worry on that score,' Pengelly said quietly. 'Whatever his faults may be, squealing isn't one of them.'

'No? Well, that's as maybe. Anyway, I'll keep watch on Steart Island while the tide is high tonight and tomorrow morning, then maybe you can take the next two watches, eh?'

'That's okay by me.'

'If you see Steve before I do, tell him to keep his wits about him when the detectives start asking questions.'

Pengelly stopped at the corner, and as he alighted Wallace was conscious of the fact that he was looking more than a little bedraggled. He hitched his wet clothing around him and smoothed his tangled hair into some resemblance of respectability, then crossed the road to the jetty, and allowed his eyes to

222

follow the line of the structure until he was looking out across the mouth of the Parrett. The tide was past its highest and was beginning to recede from Steart Island's northern summit in which the stolen fortune was now safely incarcerated. It was a good hiding place, Wallace thought; secure from predatory forays by any one member of the trio who might feel inclined to cheat the other two. He was sure of that now, as he gazed out over the ominous stretches of shining mud that were beginning to reappear.

He walked along the sea-front road until he reached his house. His black-roofed Avenger still sat alongside the driveway where he had parked it the previous night and he opened the door and quietly ran it straight into the garage. He noted that his neighbour's curtains were drawn back in the downstairs apartment, which meant that Mrs. Warren was up and about. The old lady usually liked to potter in the back garden when she awoke in the mornings, but it was probably too chilly for her to be out on this particular Sunday morning.

He was reaching up for the handle of the up-and-over garage door when, several hundred yards away, he saw a figure duck out of sight behind a fence, reappear, then sidle towards him. Ferret-like, Steve Williams' dark head bobbed up and down inquisitively, as if sniffing the air for the scent of trouble.

Eventually the little man stepped out into the open and scurried along the pavement until he reached the house, and as he walked up the drive towards Wallace, he scanned the taller man's face eagerly.

'Where is it?'

'You got your feet wet for nothing. That patrol car didn't want to know,' Wallace said evasively. He knew he was only postponing the inevitable and he began to wish Dan Pengelly was with him.

'Aye, aye, so I see,' Williams snapped impatiently. 'Where did you put the soddin' money?'

'Here, come inside where we can't be seen.'

David Wallace glanced both ways along the Esplanade before he stepped inside the garage and pulled the door closed after them. The bulk of the car took up most of the space inside the garage, so that they were crowded into unwelcome proximity.

'Well?'

'We had to dump it, Steve, in case the police were waiting for us.'

'Where did you dump it?'

'On the beach—in the sand dunes, that is.'

'Where in the sand dunes?'

Wallace began to get restive. 'By the Retreat,' he said irritably. The Retreat was a rambling caravan site which backed on to the beach near the Low Light. 'Don't worry, Steve,' he snapped, 'it's safe enough.'

'You and I had better take a walk along the beach together, and then you can show me the exact spot. Eh?'

'Don't be a bloody fool, man, for God's sake,' Wallace shouted. 'I'm dog-tired and soaked through. All I want to do now is lie in a hot bath and then crawl into bed and sleep for a week. We have to stay away from the money, in case the detectives start spying on Ian's workmates and friends. The cash is safe, that's all you need to know!' He hadn't meant to say the last sentence, or at least, had not meant to say it in such a condescending manner.

'So! It's safe, is it, lovely boy?'

'Yes.'

'And that's all I need to know, is it?'

Wallace bit his lip but made no reply.

'Sounds like the old heave-ho, to me.'

'You fool! We wouldn't cheat you—'

'That's the second time you've called me a fool within the last two minutes.'

Had Wallace's frayed temper not been at breaking point he would have treated Steve Williams with greater caution. A warning light seemed to flash in the depths of the little man's dark, Celtic eyes; he stepped backwards and as he did so his hand darted to the inside pocket of his jacket.

This time, Wallace was ready for him. As Williams moved back, the concrete wall of the garage brought him up short and threw him off balance so that he staggered slightly. That brief instant, while the other was off guard, gave Wallace enough time to act. He lunged for the smaller man, grasped Williams' gun-hand with both his own, and hung on for dear life, while using his greater weight to pinion the shorter man against the side of the car. Steve Williams struggled with ferocious violence so that their bodies rocked to and fro in the confined space and collided with car and wall with bruising force, but Wallace clung to him. Several times the shorter man tried to jerk his knee upwards into Wallace's genitals, but their straining bodies were locked together and they were too close for such savage trickery to succeed. Williams tried to punch at his antagonist's head with his free arm and he managed to land several hard blows before Wallace was able to hunch one shoulder so that the force of the half-swung punches were absorbed on his upper arm where they caused little damage. Williams had been viper-quick in reaching for his inside pocket and he had partly drawn the Luger from its hiding place before Wallace's heavier weight had trapped the weapon between their bodies, but now Wallace managed to force the other man's hand inwards so that the gun was pointed at Williams' own torso.

'Pull the trigger! Go on and pull it, damn you!' Wallace raged. 'Then you'll get another hole in that stupid belly of yours.' His face was inches from Williams' snarling features and he saw a look of pure hatred, that a trapped wild animal might show, in the dark, hooded eyes of his opponent.

There was no way of knowing how the battle would have ended had they not both heard the sound of the rear access door to the garage scraping on the concrete floor.

'Mr. Wallace?'

A thin, reedy voice reached them from the partly open door. The two men stopped struggling although Wallace still clung to Steve Williams' gun hand as tightly as he could. They looked towards the rear door.

'Mr. Wallace? Is that you?'

'It's the old girl!'

Wallace felt the shorter man relax under him and Steve Williams' face twisted into a sardonic grin. 'You'd better get off me, Dave, boy, otherwise the old lady will think you are making love to me.'

'Are you all right, Mr. Wallace?'

'Yes, it's only me, Mrs. Warren.'

'I thought I heard a noise—' The widow shuffled inside the doorway and peered inquisitively along the length of the garage to where the two men stood. She could not have seen the fracas but she obviously suspected that something was amiss.

'Everything is all right, Mrs. Warren. We were discussing some business.'

'I didn't want to interfere. It's just that I heard a noise, you see.'

Steve Williams pocketed the Luger. He grinned amicably at the old woman then rudely pushed his way past the impotent Wallace. 'It's nice to meet you, Mrs. Warren,' he said cheerfully as he smoothed his rumpled clothing, 'and just in time, too.'

'What?'

'Never mind, my dear.' He edged his way to the front of the garage, raised the up-and-over door, then turned in the entrance. 'I'll see you another time, Dave. There is no need to get emotional, I trust you implicitly,' he advised as he patted his breast pocket, 'and my friend here does too. I'm sure you wouldn't want to cross him, eh?' He turned and walked down the short drive. At the gate he turned again and gave a jaunty wave. ' 'Bye, Mrs. Warren,' he called, and with that he was gone.

Wallace stared after the disappearing figure until he became aware of the querulous voice of his downstairs neighbour.

'—but I hope you don't think that I was interfering, Mr. Wallace. I heard a noise, you see, while I was in the garden, and I thought some young hooligans might have broken in. You hear of such terrible things these days.'

He finally managed to soothe the old lady and take his leave of her. He climbed the outside stairs to his apartment, discarded his mud-caked clothing, then ran a piping hot bath and lay back in it, exhausted, his mind in a turmoil from all that had happened over the

228

past few days. The hot water had a soporific effect that enhanced his physical tiredness and he felt strange and unreal as he wallowed in the womb-like, warm water while his senses hovered on the verge of sleep. He finally forced himself to leave the bath and to pull on his pyjamas, then, after taking one last look through his telescope at Steart Island and at the Low Light, he fell into the unmade bed and slept until mid-afternoon. Even then it took the persistent ring of the telephone bell to awaken him.

'Hello, Dave.'

'Dan?'

'Yes. Are you okay?'

'I had some trouble with Steve after you left me this morning.'

'I know. He came around to my place and complained that you had refused to tell him where we buried the third container.'

'Did he also tell you that he pulled the Luger on me again?'

There was silence from the other end of the telephone.

Wallace said: 'Dan?'

'Yes, yes. What the hell happened?'

Wallace recounted the details of the skirmish and, as he spoke, he could hear Pengelly mouthing quiet obscenities.

'The crazy fool,' he said, 'he told me none of this.'

'How did you manage to avoid telling him

229

what he was after?'

'I said I'd take him to the beach tomorrow and show him. Don't worry, Dave, if he does get me there, I can point out any place and tell him that's where it is. He'll just have to take my word for it; he can't very well come back and call me a liar without having to own up that he dug for the money without us.'

'What if he does?'

'Call me a liar?'

'Yes.'

Dan Pengelly gave a short, hard laugh and muttered some crudity. 'Let's wait and see,' he advised. 'If that should happen then I reckon I would have to attend to our Welsh comrade. Believe me, I could do it, too.'

Wallace was of the same opinion. 'Have you heard anything about Ian?' he asked.

'Not a thing,' Pengelly replied, and he sounded worried. 'There's been not a word on the radio. I went for a walk with the wife on the beach this afternoon and I met plenty of lads from Forsters, but there was no gossip about Ian. Plenty of chat about the strike, but nothing about Ian. If news of his arrest had broken, then everyone would be talking about it; I'll get up the Berrow tonight for a drink and see what I can pick up.'

'It's sure to be on the news at six. I'll see you soon,' Wallace said, and he hung up.

But in the news programme there was only one minor reference to continuing police investigations into the original robbery, and that was only mentioned in connection with an industrial dispute at Forsters which had been building up for some time and had now developed into strike action.

From the front window of his apartment David Wallace had an uninterrupted view of the bay, and while the evening tide was high enough to allow a boat access to Steart Island, he kept vigil. His first-floor rooms gave a clear view of the island, although the exact spot where they had buried the two cash-boxes was just out of sight over its brow. If necessary, his telescope would allow him to study in detail anything that moved, either on Steart or near the Low Light where the third container now lay secreted. He watched until the tide turned and dropped its muddy waters away from Steart's lonely shores to leave it stranded and isolated once more.

It was later that evening that the telephone rang and he picked it up to find Rossiter, his Area Manager at Forsters, on the line.

'Did you hear about the strike being made official, Dave?'

'It was on the news tonight. Things went beyond the talking stage, then?'

'That's right. The industrial trades unions have withdrawn their labour and they've got pickets on the factory gates. It was a lightning walk out, they didn't give us much warning, but we managed to get most of the processes shut down in time. I did try to telephone you earlier in the day, to come in and help.'

'Hell, I'm sorry, but it is Sunday. I was out fishing.'

'Can't be helped. Anyway, only safety work is allowed, by agreement, so the instructions to management and supervisors are not to try to force their way past the picket line. Pass the word around, will you, Dave?'

Wallace frowned. Why did Rossiter make no mention of Myers being caught at the Feeder the previous night? God! It was an event of such importance that he would surely have said something about it had he known. What kind of cunning game were the police playing, Wallace wondered? He decided to probe a little further.

'Any trouble on my Section?' he queried.

'No, Dave. The shift crew managed to close everything down without much difficulty, though the steam supply went off a bit too soon and almost caught them unawares.'

'Nothing unusual, then?' He hesitated, wondering whether he had gone too far.

'How do you mean?'

'Well, anything—with the process, say, through shutting it down so quickly?'

'Oh, no. See you when this bloody nonsense is over.'

Wallace found himself in something of a quandary; now that the strike was on, neither he nor his partners in crime had any reason to return to work on Monday. Had they returned to work after the week-end they could have made some discreet enquiries in an endeavour to find out what had happened to the diver on that fateful Saturday night. But why hadn't Rossiter mentioned it?

It was unusual for David Wallace not to be at work on a Monday, and he passed the day restlessly, unable to learn any news of Myers, yet unable to ask about him in case his questions aroused suspicions. During the day he telephoned Dan Pengelly and arranged to meet him and Williams that evening in the lounge of the Berrow Inn. When he arrived his fellow-conspirators were already seated at the table by the fire. The room was quite full and he had to weave his way through several groups of early evening drinkers who were clustered around the bar before he could finally set his glass down on the polished table top and sit on a stool facing the two men.

'Still no word of Ian, then,' Wallace said grimly. There were people sitting several feet from them so he had to keep his voice low. 'Absolutely nothing! I can't understand it. Have either of you heard anything?'

'No, Dave. There are some lads from the plant in the other bar playing darts. Steve and I have been in there for half an hour before you arrived, but all they are talking about is the strike.' Dan Pengelly shuffled edgily in his seat. 'I went to see Ian's mother this afternoon; she hasn't seen him since Saturday, but she thinks he's just gone away on a diving job for the week-end and reckons he'll be back home in a couple of days. She's not worried—yet. What kind of game is that bastard Cox playing at?'

Steve Williams leaned forward. 'I was tellin' Dan, before you came in, Dave, the CID are like that; when they play it slow and easy they've got something up their sleeves, you mark my words. They are just keeping it all nice and quiet for the time being until it suits them to break the news that they've got poor old Ian safe and sound in the nick. They are trying to trick us, but it won't work, will it lads?'

He appeared to have forgotten the enmity of his previous encounter with David Wallace. He was conciliatory and friendly, so much so that Wallace began to wonder whether Pengelly had disclosed the hiding place of the third box to him.

'That may be, but what,' Wallace asked, 'is Cox hoping to gain by keeping quiet?' He took a long drink and emptied his glass. 'I'm not sure he can legally do it, anyway; keep a prisoner incommunicado, that is.' He put his glass down and studied the remnants of froth. 'I'm sure that Ian is allowed to see a solicitor, or make a 'phone call, or something. At least I'd have expected the reporters to have sniffed the story out by now. They were hopping about like fleas when we first pulled the job off.'

'Well, I don't know, I'm sure. I do know that we ought to sit tight and let them make the first move,' Williams said. He rose to his feet and reached for Wallace's empty glass. 'I'll get us another drink.'

As Steve Williams pushed his way to the bar, Wallace nudged Dan Pengelly. 'Steve seems very friendly tonight, considering what happened in my garage when we last met. Have you told him where we put that third container? Is that why he's so sociable?'

The tall man winked. 'Not exactly. I only told him enough to smooth him over.' Then Dan Pengelly grinned wickedly and added: 'I told him not to waste his time on you, that we ex-sergeant types must stick together against you pseudo-intellectuals. You ain't sergeant material, you see, Dave, you got no rapport. You leave young Steve to me!'

'As much as I possibly can,' Wallace promised.

A poker-faced Williams came elbowing his way back to the table with the drinks. 'Sit tight!' he warned as he set the glasses down, 'that Bristol detective has just walked in. He's standing at the far end of the bar and I think he's on his own.'

Wallace threw a quick glance through the groups of chatting people and caught sight of the now familiar, rumpled-suited figure of

Detective Inspector Cox at the bar.

'He must wear that damned pin stripe suit to bed. I've never seen him dressed in anything else,' Pengelly muttered.

The policeman paid for his drink and turned to survey the smoke-filled room. He stood, straddle-legged, in his 'captain of an old time sailing ship' pose, and cast an imperious gaze on those who dared brush against him. It was noticeable how, without moving, the man seemed to acquire space in the crowded area around him. There were a number of people present who worked at Forsters, and some of them gave the plain-clothes policeman a self-conscious nod of greeting while others chose to ignore him. The CID man seemed oblivious to the reactions his presence provoked as he stood with a pint glass clamped in one fist and gazed enigmatically about him.

'Do you think he's seen us?'

'He's seen us, all right! I'll bet he spotted everyone he knows within thirty seconds of coming in, the sly bastard,' Steve Williams muttered.

Wallace got to his feet. 'I'll be back,' he said.

Half a minute later he heard the door of the gents' toilet creak open behind him. There was a stainless-steel urinal along one wall and, as he stood at it, Cox came to stand alongside him.

'Good evening, Mr. Wallace.'

The Welshman looked sideways at the newcomer and affected surprise. 'Hello, Inspector,' he said. 'I didn't know you came to places like this.'

'Ah! We all enjoy a drink now and again, sir, even a poor policeman.' Cox studied the coffee-coloured tiles on the wall, twelve inches from his face. 'You lucky people at Forsters are on an enforced holiday, I believe?'

Wallace studied his own coffee-coloured tiles. 'I don't know about "lucky". This strike is nothing but a nuisance and it means a lot of extra work when the unions do decide to go back.'

'Sometimes I think I'm in the wrong job, Mr. Wallace, what with all this time off and the inflated salaries you get from your company. You must be a rich man, sir.'

Wallace looked down to avoid flinching visibly, then stood back. As he zipped up his fly, he glared at the back of Cox's ungroomed, dandruff-flecked, head.

'I think I might apply for a job at Forsters, when I find the culprits who robbed them, and the case is over.'

Wallace was ready to seize his chance; he had primed himself not to mention anything about Myers or the robbery unless Cox mentioned it first. The Inspector rested one hand on the chrome water pipe in front of him, and looked down.

'Have you had any luck yet?' Wallace asked.

'Luck?'

'You know, with the payroll theft from the plant. Have you made any progress yet?'

'These things take time, sir. We have to carry out a great deal of routine checking and cross-checking on people's past records.' The detective adopted a confidential manner and spoke in a lower tone. 'You'd be amazed if you knew just how many seemingly ordinary folk have a black spot somewhere in their past, folk who you and I would take for straight-forward, honest citizens, unless we knew better. It's a constant surprise to me, Mr. Wallace, I can tell you.'

Wallace noted with distaste that the policeman hadn't washed his hands as he followed him out of the men's room, then Cox came to a halt in the middle of the doorway and half turned. 'But make no mistake, eventually we'll get whoever pulled off the Forsters' job, we usually do where murder is involved.'

'Murder?' Wallace echoed. This time, not only was he startled, but he showed it. 'Who the hell has been murdered?'

Cox continued to block the doorway as he spoke, treating with ignorant indifference others who wanted to pass. 'Don't you remember the poor old messenger, Froggart, who died in the washroom of the administration building on the day of the robbery?'

'Of course I do. I thought you meant that someone else has died.'

'Why should you think that, sir?'

Wallace felt his pulses race. 'I don't know. It was just the way you said it, I think—'

'Well, no one else has been murdered, thank God! Though unless we catch the man who killed Mr. Froggart soon, he may kill again.'

'Do you think so?'

'When a man has killed once then it becomes easier for him to do so a second time. Believe me, this person wouldn't hesitate to murder again if he needs to.'

Cox finally relented and vacated the doorway to allow several fidgeting men to enter. Wallace walked back to his table and his white face must have shown how shaken he was.

'What did he have to say?' Steve Williams asked cautiously.

'About Ian, nothing. Not a word. He may just as well have vanished from the face of the earth.'

'Then at least old Myers hasn't squealed,' Williams said. He studied the faces of his companions, as if searching for their true feelings. 'That means we are safe, lads, but we mustn't allow that copper's trickery to make us do anything foolish. The boys in blue have got Ian in a lockup somewhere and they are keeping his whereabouts secret. The sly sods don't know a thing, but they are trying to prod someone into making a false move. Sit tight, I say.'

'And what do you say about Jack Froggart?' Wallace whispered bitterly. 'The Inspector mentioned him and he used the word "murder" again.'

Williams half rose to his feet and seemed about to rush from the room in a rage, but he managed to control himself with an obvious effort and subsided on to his seat. 'It's a trap, you fool, and you seem to be falling for it,' he snarled, his features mottled with anger. 'You are doing exactly what I've just been warning you not to.'

Wallace stuck it out for two more days until, early one morning, he drove to Dan Pengelly's house. He found him busily grubbing about in his tiny patch of a front garden, but he laid down his hoe and sat down on the low wall which fronted his plot, waiting for Wallace to join him.

Pengelly opened the conversation. 'I've been to see Ian's mother again, but she hasn't seen him nor heard from him since the night we raided the Feeder.'

'Jesus! What the hell do you think Cox is doing?'

Dan Pengelly shrugged. 'Like Steve said, it must be some kind of ploy to make us come out into the open. That's all I can think of.'

'Is there a chance that Steve is lying about

what happened to Ian?'

'Why should he lie? He would have wanted that fourth container out of the Feeder as much as anyone. He wouldn't have done anything to jeopardise its recovery.'

'Well, I can't simply sit and wait any longer. I'm going in to the plant to see if I can find out what actually happened on Saturday night. Anything will be better than just waiting, not knowing what's going on.'

'Wouldn't it only create suspicion if you go visiting the factory for no apparent reason when there are pickets on the gates?'

'I wouldn't force my way past them, but it's reasonable for a Section Manager to check the safety aspects of plant on standby. You can come in with me, that's okay,' Wallace reassured as the other raised his eyebrows, 'you are my Senior Process Foreman, after all.'

They drove along the A38, then turned off on the side-road and continued until they reached the main entrance gate of the complex. They recognised the Convenor of the Transport and General Workers Union among the group of arm-banded men who stood outside the gate, and Wallace wound down his window as the union man came alongside the car.

'This is an official strike, Mr. Wallace,' the Convenor reminded him, 'and higher management has agreed that there'll be no crossing the picket line while negotiations are proceeding.'

'But I need to run a check on a couple of things from a safety point of view.'

'I don't know about that.'

Dan Pengelly grinned at the man. 'Come off it, Fred,' he argued, 'you've agreed to safety checks, and that's all we want to do. It'll only take an hour.'

'Aw, well, I suppose it's in order,' the man nodded, and he stepped back and waved the Avenger through the gates.

One of Forsters' security guards came out of his office to greet them as they entered. 'What are you doing here? Can't you production people stay away when you get the chance?'

Wallace gave the man a mirthless grin in return. 'Apart from the strike, has there been any other excitement?' he asked, as casually as possible. 'No more robberies or gas leaks, I suppose?' He continued to smile as he spoke.

'Now, now, Mr. Wallace,' the guard chided, 'don't joke about such things, we don't want anything like that to happen again. The civil police gave our lads one hell of a time because of it, and thank God it didn't happen on my shift, that's all I can say. No, it's quiet as a churchyard, without your process men working. We get some of the engineers roaming about making safety checks, but nothing else. It's like guarding a morgue.'

'So things have been pretty quiet?'

'I'm on morning shift this week, and they've been deathly dull. No reports in the afternoon or night shift logs to the contrary, either. The CID men from Bristol still come in occasionally, though. Some of them are in this morning.'

'What for?'

'I'm not sure. They don't tell me their business, you know.'

Dan Pengelly shifting uneasily in his seat warned Wallace that he was going too far. They took their leave of the guard and drove towards Section Eight. 'You see, Dan,' Wallace said, 'it's just as if we never came to the Feeder that night. There's something funny going on, but what?'

'You shouldn't say too much to these guards, either,' Pengelly warned, 'you might let something drop accidentally. And what about the CID men being in this morning? Perhaps we should go home?'

'We have a valid reason for being here,' Wallace insisted. 'We can't very well drive out to the Feeder, but we can get a damned good view of it from the top of the Still House.'

He guided the Avenger on to the Section and parked under the towering bulk of the Still House. The Section was deserted and silent because of the strike, and the ringing noise their feet made as they stumped up the flights of iron steps, alongside the Iron Lady, echoed eerily around the galvanised-sheeted

243

walls of the building as they climbed to its summit. Once on the top floor they walked past the great, steel caps of the stills and stepped out on to the outside fire-escape. They were sixty feet above ground and David Wallace gripped the handrail in front of him very firmly. From their platform they had a panoramic view of the vast acreage occupied by the complex, and of the surrounding Somerset countryside. They had a clear view of the flat expanse of water that was Feeder Number One, though the service-gate they had used was hidden by the edge of the plateau in which the Feeder was sunk.

'I'm damned if I can see anything out of the ordinary.'

'You are right, there's nothing there,' Wallace said as he studied the place alongside the Feeder where, only a few days earlier, they had recovered three of the payroll boxes. 'My eyesight isn't perfect but I'm sure there's no sign of the equipment we left behind.'

'There wouldn't be, not after all this time. The police would have taken it away for forensic tests.'

'Maybe so.'

The two men looked at each other and the Welshman saw shadows of perplexity cloud his companion's clear eyes. There were too many questions which remained unanswered, too many doubts and uncertainties which could not be lightly brushed aside.

The silence was rudely broken by the sound of a heavy door slamming on the ground floor of the Still House.

'One of the engineers, do you think?'

'Could be.'

They stepped inside, off the fire-escape stairs, and walked to the top of the internal stairway. They stood and listened for sounds of further movement from below.

'I can't hear anything.' Dan Pengelly tried to peer down through the holes in the chequered steel plates from which the flights of stairs were constructed. 'Wait! What's that?'

At first all was quiet, then the unmistakable sounds of leather on steel reached their ears as someone slowly ascended from the first floor.

'If we go down the fire-escape we can avoid whoever it is,' Pengelly whispered.

'No, that might seem odd. My car is parked outside, so whoever is down there will know that I'm in the building. Let's go down.'

The two men began to descend and the sound of their footsteps echoed in synchronization with the sound of those ascending. When they reached the fourth floor, they stopped at the top of the flight of stairs that rose from the third level, and waited.

'Mr. Wallace? Are you there, sir?'

'My God!' Wallace looked at his companion. 'That's Cox's voice.'

245

'Are you there, Mr. Wallace? Ah! Got you— and Mr. Pengelly, too!' The detective's unkempt head came into view as he climbed the steps towards them. 'Oh, dear, dear,' he puffed breathlessly, 'you need a lift in this building,' and he rested awhile, with much blowing and panting, to recover his wind before climbing the few remaining steps. Then he said: 'I thought you were out because of the strike?'

'We production men are always on call, Inspector. Mr. Pengelly and I have to make sure that the maintenance engineers check the safety of the stills properly. It could be serious if they missed something.'

'Quite so, sir. Quite so.'

The detective was throwing too many 'sirs' into the conversation for Wallace's liking. Cox wore the crown of politeness about as comfortably as a bag of coal.

'You are lucky to have found us. It's a big plant.'

'I saw your car outside and I wondered whether you could show me over your ammonia storage tanks again. I'm not quite clear about one or two points.'

Wallace was glad he had not followed his foreman's suggestion to leave via the fire-stairs. 'There's not much more I can tell you that we haven't covered already,' he said, 'but if you like, then yes, of course. We'll make another tour of the storage compound right now.'

They had already escorted Cox and his men around Section Eight several times and had answered interminable questions, but once again they left the Still House and walked in single file until they reached the bund wall which surrounded the ammonia tanks.

'You know, it amazes me that, with all the experts on the staff of Forsters, no one has come up with the answer as to how ammonia gas got into the administration block.' Cox stared at the brick wall of the bund and rocked on his heels. He rummaged absentmindedly in his coat pocket, obviously searching for his smoking materials, then just as obviously remembered that they were in a no smoking area and gave up the search.

'If you want to go inside the bund we'll have to carry gas masks at the ready, Inspector,' Dan Pengelly said.

'Hm? No, no, that's not necessary. I was wondering, Mr. Wallace, whether the gas could, in some way, have seeped underground from a leaking pipe and surfaced inside the administration building. One hears of gas explosions in private houses caused in such a manner. Eh?'

The Welshman felt the palms of his hands go moist. My God! he thought, that's close. Too damned close for comfort. He noticed that Dan Pengelly had turned away under the pretext of checking a nearby pressure gauge. 'I don't think so,' Wallace answered slowly, as if taking time to consider the question carefully. 'No, that's not really a practical proposition I'm afraid, Inspector. Liquefied ammonia would vaporize far too quickly, you see, and filter up through the earth. Even the slightest ammonia leak is usually obvious by the smell of the stuff. In any case, we had no leaks on our Section at the time of the robbery. You were shown the stock sheets, if you remember, and the figures balanced.'

'Ah! Figures! Figures! I'm not very good with figures, I'm afraid. I leave all that to you more educated gentlemen, but I'm sure the figures did balance. They always do.' The sneer which accompanied his last remark showed that he had regained his abrasiveness. There was not a 'sir' to be heard.

David Wallace drove Pengelly home after they had taken their leave of Inspector Cox and Forsters.

'Never a word about Ian,' Pengelly said grimly as they swung off the A38 and headed towards Burnham-on-Sea. 'I wish to God we knew exactly what is going on in that detective's mind.'

EIGHT

Still no word of Myers! More than a week had passed since the night of their raid on the Feeder Pond, but although they listened eagerly to every news broadcast and scanned the daily newspapers, there was still no word of the diver.

Whenever Pengelly or Wallace questioned him about the details of Myers' capture on that fateful night, Williams would invariably lose his temper and accuse his companions of mistrust. That they did not trust him was obvious, but both men thought it unwise to push Williams into open conflict; their security was balanced on a knife edge, and they knew it. But where was Myers? Had he broken yet and told the whole story to Detective Inspector Cox? David Wallace found himself waiting in a state of dread anticipation for the knock on his door that would bring the entire nefarious escapade to an end.

The strike at Forsters was still in full swing, though there were signs of cracks in the determination of both sides in the dispute, and by the following Monday negotiations between Forsters and the union side had been resumed. The three conspirators had agreed to be seen together as little as possible; all they could do was to wait, and finally they

waited too long.

                *   *   *

It was early afternoon. Save for the solitary
figure slumped at one of the window tables,
the bar of the Queens Hotel had spewed forth
its bevy of bright-eyed lunch-time drinkers
into the chill air of a September day. Steve
Williams sat absolutely motionless as he
stared out through the window and over the
deserted Esplanade; an occasional overcoated
pedestrian hurried along the pavement of the
sea-front road and one or two cars drove by,
but apart from that, the place had every
appearance of a small seaside resort on a cold
autumn day. Only an occasional movement by
the girl behind the bar served to disturb his
brooding thoughts. Across the flat, oily waters
of a rising tide loomed the double hump-back
outline of Steart Island, to taunt him with the
knowledge of its hidden and untouchable
wealth.

'A bloody fortune!' Williams muttered
bitterly to himself. 'A bloody fortune! and it's
stuck out there in the soddin' mud.'

Faint wreaths of mist writhed out of a
leaden sky and knitted along the line of the
incoming tide. In the distance the Low Light,
clearly visible ten minutes earlier, had begun
to lose its sharp edges; became less and less
clearly defined even as he watched.

250

'A bloody fortune!'

He drained his pint pot and regarded the lager froth as it disintegrated and slid down the sides. Moodily, he got to his feet, glanced once more towards Steart Island, then moved to the bar.

'Another pint of Heineken, please, love.'

The thoughts of the absent-minded barmaid had been solely for her beau of the evening and whether his performance would live up to her expectations. Steve Williams had interrupted her very pleasant speculation.

'Sorry, sir. Time has been called,' she said abruptly.

'What?' He blinked at a clock on the wall above the bar. 'God damn! Just one, eh?'

'Sorry, sir.' The young woman watched him with old eyes.

'And one for yourself?'

'Well—' She relented swiftly. 'Oh, okay, then. I'll have a sherry.' She filled a schooner until the amber liquid trembled on the rim of the glass. 'Cheers!'

'Cheers!'

He carried his lager back to the window table, then reclined in the leather-upholstered chair as he sipped the clear, bitter liquid. Once again his gaze was drawn out through the pane of glass and over the mouth of the River Parrett to Steart Island.

'A bloody fortune,' he whispered.

Nine days had elapsed since they had

recovered the payroll from the Feeder, only to bury it in the ground again, to Williams' utter chagrin; nine days since, to Williams' way of thinking, Ian Myers had come close to ruining everything by his own stupidity. He had no conscience about the entombed body which lay pinned to the bed of Number One Feeder Pond. As far as Steve Williams was concerned, Myers had brought about his own downfall and only very quick thinking had saved Williams himself from retribution. There was no way in which the diver could float to the surface with a ton of steel on his back, so there was no danger to Williams in that respect, but nevertheless, the continuing absence of any reports on Myers' capture had roused Wallace and Pengelly to harangue him continually about Myers' well-being. He had managed to parry their doubts and half accusations so far, but he knew it was only a matter of time before something, or someone, broke.

He sipped at his lager as he surveyed the foreshore. The mist had really closed in, and along the beach the stilted Low Light was barely visible. To the south-west, the Quantock Hills and the block-like structure of Hinkley Point atomic power station were obliterated from view by a silver blanket, and only by concentrating hard could Steve Williams discern detail on Steart Island itself. On the sands, across the Esplanade and in front of the hotel, a lone boatman leaned over his beached dinghy while, squirrel-like, he sorted and stored his nautical paraphernalia, to make it safe against the quickly rising tide.

To the man from Blaina, opportunist leader of front-line combat patrols in war-torn France and Germany, the idea came as quickly as the gathering mist.

'Hell—yes!' he exclaimed. He slowly sat upright and placed his drink on the table. His stomach knotted with a sudden excitement. 'Why not?'

The question was not concerned with moral issues but with practical problems. He uttered the words half aloud so that the barmaid looked up from her task of washing glasses, but her curious stare went unheeded. That was it! The rapidly thickening mist would soon completely cover Steart, the beach, and the intervening stretch of water. He could row out, get the money and be long gone before the other two had realised anything was amiss. His mind raced. Come to that, he needn't run until he was ready to decamp for good, since Wallace and Pengelly would be unaware that the containers were gone from their hiding place on the island.

'Serve the bastards right!'

The Welshman slammed his fist hard on the table causing the empty glasses on it to jump and rattle and his eyes gleamed as he peered at the vague outline of his goal. The tide was coming in fast; a nice peaceful tide; everything fitted. He must seize this golden opportunity which his Celtic Gods of War offered.

'Here—you feelin' okay, dear?' The blonde barmaid eyed him warily.

'Me? Oh, yes,' Williams reassured her and he grinned. 'Just a sudden thought, you know.'

'Gawd! I thought you was going to smash all me glasses—and you been talkin' to yourself.' Her eyes narrowed. 'Not having a funny turn on me, are you, dear?' she asked.

Steve Williams thought furiously. He had to keep this stupid bitch happy and not show any odd behaviour which she might remember should anyone ask awkward questions in the future. 'Not me, darling,' he said. He carried his empty glass to her and set it down on the bar. 'Maybe I'll see you again,' he suggested, and he made some bawdy small talk until he had assuaged her suspicions and could safely take his leave of her.

He walked from the hotel with swift, decisive steps until he reached his car, which he had parked in Pier Street on the south side of the building. Satisfied that no one was watching, he unlocked and opened his car door on the passenger's side and leaned in to finger the catch of the glove box. The door of the compartment snapped open; black metal gleamed briefly in the subdued daylight as he took out the Luger, checked its magazine, and slipped the weapon into his pocket. He patted the bulge it made in the side of his coat. He felt safer now. Much safer.

He closed the glove compartment and relocked the car, then crossed the Esplanade and walked down the jetty. Several small boats lay askew on the soft sand, drawn up above tide level for safe-keeping, and amongst them the lone boatman, whom Steve Williams had seen through the windows of the Queens Hotel, was still working on his dinghy.

'Hell of a mist,' the little Celt said conversationally. He stood on the jetty at a point where it rose only four feet above the level of the sand, and gazed down on the boatman.

' 'Tis,' the boatman agreed in a slow, steady Somerset accent. ' 'Er'll be here thick'n heavy in another five minutes, I reckon.'

'I don't suppose we'll be able to see Steart Island soon?' As he spoke, Williams reached into his trouser pocket and produced a packet of Dunhill. He thumbed open its lid then jumped down on to the firm sand and held the packet out at arm's length. The Welshman nodded his encouragement with an easy air of camaraderie. 'Smoke?'

'Aye, thanks.' The middle-aged man with the boat took the proffered cigarette.

'Light?' Williams took a cigarette for himself then flicked a match into flame with his thumbnail before cupping the burning sliver of pinewood in both hands.

The boatman leaned close to the wavering

flame, puffed at his cigarette, then exhaled smoke slowly before turning to regard the island. He raised his face to the sky and sniffed at the closing mist with an air of wisdom. 'No, we shan't see much more of Steart today,' he vouched. 'With this mist coming down, 'er'll be out of sight in less than ten minutes; best be off home by the fireside in this sort of weather.'

As the man at his side lipped his cigarette, Steve Williams looked thoughtfully towards the faint outline of the island. 'Any chance of borrowing your boat for half an hour, friend?' he suggested casually.

'Eh?' The man looked dubious. 'What's on, then?'

'For a couple of pounds?'

'Well, now—'

'A fiver, then. It would be worth five pounds to me,' the Welshman pleaded. 'You'd be doing me one hell of a favour and I'd only need it for half an hour or so. What about it, eh?'

Across the flooding waters of the bay the last, dim outline of Steart Island became obliterated by rolling vapour. Fast-encroaching water streamed in from the Bristol Channel, crawled up the beach and lapped at the disintegrating wall of the old boating lake. With rapidly growing impatience Williams turned to scan the Esplanade for signs of surveillance but by this time the sea-fog had so reduced visibility that only the nearest hundred yards of the sea-front road could be seen from where the dinghy lay on the beach. Both beach and road were deserted, save for Williams and his companion, and only the chance that a passerby might suddenly appear held Williams from taking the boat by force. As it was, he gripped the Luger in his pocket with ready fingers.

'Where on earth would you want to go, with this mist coming down?' the man asked. 'You could easily get yourself lost in these waters. It's a tricky tide, you know.'

'It's like this, friend. My mate borrowed some fishing tackle from me the other day, and then the fool went and left it out on the island,' Williams explained. 'He was afraid to go back for it then because it was getting dark, but it cost me over forty quid. I can't afford to throw money away like that.'

The Welshman had the gift of plausibility. He could fabricate a story at will, but it was as much his manner as the words he used that persuaded the gullible, and so it was with the boatman.

'I suppose—' The boatman hesitated and peered into the gathering clouds of vapour.

'Just let me borrow it for half an hour. The sea looks dead calm,' Williams reasoned. Inwardly he raged with impatience at this delay to his instantly-fostered plans. When the stakes were high he always acted with quicksilver speed and any opposition to his plans was apt to bring forth a swift and violent reaction.

'Come on, then, but I'll have to take you myself,' decided the boatman. 'Unless you know Burnham waters they can be dangerous, however calm they may seem.' He gripped the gunwale of his dinghy and began to drag it down the beach towards the rising tide. 'Give us a hand then, mate,' he said.

'Good lad,' Steve Williams grinned. 'Let's go!' He relaxed his grip on the gun in his pocket and laid his hands on the boat. He was used to dealing with emergency situations; the devil take this cretin and his goddamned boat afterwards, should any difficulties arise. The main thing was to get possession of the money, then deal with any problems when, and if, they arose.

Together, the two men half-carried, half-dragged the clinker-built dinghy the three hundred yards to the water's edge. After they had cleared the two-hundred yard wide strip of clean sand, they ran into thick, jellied mud which sucked at the keel of the small craft, and they only managed to keep clear of the mud themselves by walking along the jetty, which was only a foot above beach level at this point, dragging the boat alongside them. With one final heave they jerked it clear of the mud's embrace, embarked, and floated out over the cloudy waters that spilled into the mouth of the River Parrett. With a steady rhythm the boatman plied the oars against the remorseless pressure of the incoming current, as the second-highest tide-rise in the world surged in from the Bristol Channel to sweep the Parrett's suspension of soil and sewage back upriver.

'You are doing well, friend.'

Williams slewed around on his seat in the stern of the dinghy and squinted back along the way they had come, in the direction of the town. He could see nothing. The row of houses and hotels along the sea-front were blocked from view by an impervious silver blanket, and even the sea-wall had disappeared from sight. He looked to the front and found that he could see no trace of Steart Island, even though they must be more than a third of the way across.

'Right, Wallace,' the little Welshman muttered. 'Now we'll see, boy.'

'What's that?'

'Huh?'

'I thought you said something?'

'Oh—no, no. I was talking to myself. Can I give you a hand?'

The oarsman shook his head. 'Not to worry,' he said. 'I may as well earn my five pounds.' The blades of his oars dipped and rose in quiet unison to thrust them towards the distant spit of land.

'I can see it,' Steve Williams exclaimed. 'I can see Steart Island!'

' 'Er's still there, then,' the oarsman said with a heavy humour. He glanced briefly over his shoulder without missing a stroke. 'I was beginning to think that maybe we had missed it, and were heading for Cardiff.'

Low-lying, seen dimly through the writhing mist, the mile-long sliver that was their island goal assumed an eerie and menacing aspect. No sound could be heard, save for the lap of wavelets on unseen banks, the slow 'dip-dip' of oar blades and the rower's even breathing. An occasional chuckle from restive sea-fowl also pierced the enveloping cloud which cocooned them in its clammy sheath.

As they approached the island it became obvious that a landing would not be easy. The incoming tide had not yet covered the sloping banks of greasy mud which moated the entire strip of land; some twenty yards, or more, of the treacly, treacherous mixture would have to be negotiated before clean shingle could be reached. The action of sea and surf had, in fact, sculpted the mud which lined the approaches to Steart Island into a series of waist-high ridges which ran, end on, from sea to shore. The boatman took a final, strong pull on both oars, then shipped them and allowed the craft to nose its way between two ridges of mud. They heard a squelching sound and at the same time felt the underbelly of the dinghy ground itself in the repulsive slime.

'Whereabouts is your tackle?' the rower asked. He looked askance at his passenger's shoes. 'How are you getting ashore?'

Williams had not bargained on this difficulty and he frowned at the band of mud that separated him from a fortune. 'How long will it be before the tide covers this stuff?' he queried. He indicated the unwelcome barrier and said: 'Maybe we can wait until the water reaches firm ground, eh?'

The boatman shook his head and spat on to the offending shore. 'It's not a very high tide today and it'll be top of the tide soon, there's slack water already. Maybe the tide will be high enough, maybe not. My tide tables say that we would have to wait here for another hour or more to find out, and I don't fancy that, not for ten quid!'

'I'll chance it,' Steve Williams said, and he stood up in the boat. 'Perhaps the mud isn't too deep?' he suggested hopefully. He gripped the gunwale of the dinghy for support and gingerly lowered one foot over the side. Immediately his shoe sank into the soggy, black morass and he felt the cold chill of it rise up his leg as he transferred his weight on to that foot. The mud gave way, divided, and flowed around his limb as if to swallow it whole. There was no support to be had from the stuff, and a nauseous odour of rotting sewage and decomposing marine life rose to his nostrils from the disturbed ooze as he plunged into it. 'Bloody hell!' He lifted his other leg over the gunwale, leaning heavily on the side of the boat as he did so in order to reduce his downward pressure. Nevertheless, he was up to his thighs in the mixture before he stopped sinking.

'For God's sake, be careful,' the boatman cried anxiously. 'There are patches of quicksand in Bridgwater Bay and you'll sink a mile if you strike one of those.'

'What a soddin' awful mess—' Steve Williams tried to lift his right leg but it was stuck firmly in the quagmire. He threw his weight to one side and strained and heaved until he managed to pull the foot up and forwards, without clearing the surface of the mud, and the hole from which he drew his foot collapsed in on itself with a loud, sucking implosion.

'Come back another time,' the man in the boat urged. 'You'll ruin your clothes; the fishing gear will still be there.'

Williams cursed continuously as he fought his way towards a solid footing, swaying and stumbling as he went. He floundered and overbalanced several times during his progression and had to plunge hands and forearms into the all-pervading slime in order to prevent himself from falling on his face. Finally, leg-weary, he felt his feet strike firm ground beneath the layer of ooze, and he felt an enormous sense of relief as he forced himself through the last few yards of mud to reach clean shingle. Having done so, he subsided to his knees and crouched with hanging head like some exhausted sea-creature while he sucked great gasps of air into his heaving lungs.

'Are you all right, mate?' the oarsman called. 'Are you all right?' His honest face reflected genuine concern.

'Aye,' the muddied Welshman panted. He raised his head and managed a grin. 'Aye, I'm okay,' he reassured as he pressed an elbow to his aching ribs. 'Got one hell of a stitch, though.' As he waited to recover his breath, he jerked his hands and flung his fingers wide in order to dislodge the larger lumps of mud which clung between them. A mass of the thick and glutinous muck was glued to his arms and to his legs; he had lost one shoe, lost it irretrievably, deep under the surface.

'It's never worth it.'

Williams stood upright and surveyed his caked legs. 'In a bit of a mess,' he agreed, but at the same time he thought to himself: 'If you only knew, boy.' He said: 'I won't be long,' then turned on his heel and plunged into the mist to disappear from view before the other could object.

He headed directly for the central hump of this northern end of the dumb-bell-shaped islet as the mist rolled ponderously overhead to bind everything in its damp embrace; it had thickened and had become extremely dense, so that he could only see for a distance of some ten to fifteen feet ahead of him. He pressed on, up the slight incline towards the apex of the little knoll, while swathes of grey cloud churned and eddied past him like the wake of a ship at sea as he made for the cache. He found it easily enough. His one fear had been that he might overlook the bare, pebble-strewn patch in which they had buried the containers, that a wind assisted tide might have erased the distinguishing features of the spot, but he found it easily enough. Excitement mounted within him as he dropped on all fours and started to scrape at the packed scree, and as he worked he began to pant with effort and expectation. He looked for all the world like a bedraggled terrier retrieving a long-lost bone. The digging was hard on his hands; he had overlooked the need for some kind of digging implement with which to scrape the covering of shingle and pebbles from the buried cash-boxes; impulsive action had left no time in which to remember details.

'Damn!'

One of his fingernails broke off, painfully short, but he tore it away impatiently in his eagerness to resume digging. Small pinks of blood stained his fingers where sharp flints lacerated the skin.

The boxes were heavier than he remembered. When the lid of the uppermost container lay revealed, he unearthed one of its braided handles and hauled on it with all his strength, but it took a long, sustained effort for him to drag the box from its hiding place and the leaden grip of wet sand. With a grunted curse he finally eased it from its bed and then knelt alongside his prize. His sharply-exhaled gasps of breath churned the curdling fog as he worried at the metal catches of the payroll container with fingers numb from exposure and ill use.

'Iesu Mawr!'

He flung back the flat lid of the box to disclose the rows of neatly packed banknotes it contained. A thin stream of liquid mud ran from one of his sleeves to solidify in a twisting trail across the serried notes. It was his second sighting of the regained wealth, and it transformed the kneeling Welshman; made him forget his physical discomfort. Elation and excitement rose inside him and produced a sob of emotion in his throat. The money was his!

'Hel—lo! Taff- ee!'

The mist-muted cry floated over the shrouded island, making Steve Williams look up nervously. The acoustics were so warped by the wall of fog which surrounded him that the shout could have come from any direction, though he knew it must be the boatman calling. He straightened up and peered into the vaporous cloud without success, but he reassured himself with the thought that the hail could only have come from the boatman. He was getting edgy, he thought, and he patted the comforting bulk of the Luger in his pocket.

'Keep cool, now, Stevie boy—'

He began to mutter aloud to himself, through mud-speckled lips, but nevertheless his pulses raced as he reclosed the lid of the container. One of its clasps jammed and refused to slip home as he fumbled at it with numbed fingers.

'Better leave it—get the other box out—'

The enshrouding mist gave him an overwhelming sense of isolation; cut him off from sight and sound as surely as if he had been blinded and deafened. He was not a loner by his very nature, he was the archetypal Celt, gregarious, a lover of company, not solitude.

The second box was, if anything, even more difficult to extricate, and by the time he had manoeuvred it alongside the other, the Welshman was perspiring profusely. The dull ache of a stitch thumped painfully in his side as, with his body bent double, he began to drag both containers slowly along a tortuous path towards the waiting dinghy. He could not see the dinghy, had not seen it for—how long? How long, he wondered, had he taken to recover the buried hoard? He had lost all track of time and the mud-encrusted watch strapped to his wrist was now useless as a timepiece. A sudden, horrifying thought struck him. What if the boatman had thought him lost when he did not answer the call? If the man had gone for help and a search party was organised, then things could become extremely awkward, to say the least. Loose shingle gave way to clumps of marram grass, and the containers slid more easily over them as Williams scrabbled through the sparse growth. Suddenly he stopped. Which direction should he take? Oh, God! He must not get lost. Not now. Dense clouds swirled around him and obliterated any sign of the route he should take.

'Taff—ee! Taff—ee!' The high pitched call emerged from the mist to his left.

'Hang on, boy, you keep callin'. I'm coming!' A grateful Steve Williams lunged towards the disembodied voice which wafted at him out of the mist. His feet stumbled in soft sand, and then he saw his own footprints heading towards him.

'Hel-lo-ee!'

The source of the call was closer now, and then Williams caught sight of the prow of the dinghy and the hunched figure of the boatman who patiently awaited his return.

'Here I am, safe and sound.'

The boatman stared, open-mouthed, as the

mud-covered figure skied the two containers down the incline to the perimeter of the clean sand.

'Gawd! Look at your clothes! You are in one hell of a state, Taffy. I'm glad to see you back, though, I thought you'd wandered off and got yourself drowned.'

'Better late than never, eh?'

That was the worst part over, Williams thought to himself. It only remained to coax this oaf into offloading him and the payroll containers on the mainland at some place away from the Esplanade where his partners, or rather his ex-partners, might be spying. Then life would be one long holiday. One long, rich holiday.

'What's all this?' the boatman queried. His face wore a puzzled frown.

The Welshman kept smiling. 'Give me a hand,' he suggested, 'and I'll tell you about it later.'

The tide had risen a little and in so doing had floated the dinghy closer to firm ground, though several yards of the glutinous mud remained uncovered by water.

''Ere! Are you sure this is on the up and up?' The boatman was clearly suspicious and he leaned over the side of his small craft to inspect the containers more closely.

Steve Williams ignored the man's question. Instead he slid the first container out across the slimy surface of the mud which still separated them. He found that the comparatively large base area of the box prevented it from subsiding more than a few inches, so long as he maintained its forward momentum.

'Quick, friend, give us a hand.'

As the heavy, metal box progressed over the morass, Williams sank steadily. As he treadmilled a path to the boat, his legs plunged deeper than ever from the exertion of keeping the precious cargo on the move. Even so, the box tilted ominously at its leading end.

'Quick! For Christ's sake!'

The thought of losing a fortune in this stinking bog drove him to greater effort, only to find himself sinking deeper as a result, and he felt the odious ooze gulp over his thighs and surge up under his crotch. Finally, though, the leading handle of the cash-box was within reaching distance of the dinghy.

'Steady now, I think I can manage it,' the boatman grunted, and he bent over the gunwale and grappled for the slippery metal box with strong fingers. His gnarled, weatherbeaten fist closed over the braided steel handle and he pivoted his weight away from the box to prevent it sinking further. 'Right, I've got hold of it. Let me take the weight.'

'Well done!' Steve Williams gasped with relief and his chest heaved as his lungs sucked in oxygen from the dank, moisture-laden air.

He leaned for support on his prize, safe now in the firm grip of his helpmate, and managed an infectious grin. 'That was bloody heavy, boy. Phew! For a minute there I thought I'd— thought I'd lost it.' After every few words he had to stop speaking in order to regain his breath. He coughed excess phlegm from the back of his throat and spat it on to the barrier of mud.

'I thought you said you was after fishing tackle?'

'Eh?' Willliams played for time as he slowly lifted his gaze to meet the enquiring frown on the face of the boatman.

'I thought you said you was looking for fishing tackle?' the man repeated.

'Fishing tackle?' Again Williams bargained for time until his eyes cleared and his breath came more evenly.

'What's on, mate? This is no fishing tackle. I don't know if I like this business.'

The Welshman brushed back his matted hair with one filthy hand, and his mind worked furiously as he invented and embellished a suitably glib explanation to meet the current situation. 'Hey, come on!' he chided, 'I'm no smuggler. Do you think I've got brandy from Swansea in those boxes, to cheat the Burnham customs men? Eh? Well, this is some sailing gear that a friend of mine had to leave out here, that's all. I couldn't find my fishing tackle but I thought I may as well recover this stuff for my friend, and if I get it back to town for him it might be worth a couple of pints. Don't you worry about your fiver, you've earned that.' Williams grinned ruefully and made coarse jokes about his condition. With comic gestures and words he eased doubt from the other's mind.

'I suppose it is your own business.'

'Come on, boy, help me to get the boxes ashore and I'll treat you to a drink in the Berrow tonight.'

Together they heaved, and the man in the boat managed to tug the leading end of the container free from the sucking mud while Williams struggled to lift its other end. He sank a little further with each movement that he made and soon the morass rose to his waist and he felt it inch over his belt to crawl clammily on to his shirt. They had managed to prise the container free from the pudding-like mess and had coaxed it to a forty-five degree angle with its leading edge resting on the gunwale of the dinghy. Then it happened! With a loud, metallic 'click' the clasps of the cash-box flew open and its lid sprang back to expose its contents.

' 'Ere! What the hell—?'

The boatman gawped, open-mouthed, at a hundred thousand pounds worth of banknotes which lay before him in neat bundles. He sat down heavily, and stayed immobile with astonishment as he stared at the fortune, then comprehension slowly dawned and a sense of outrage began to replace his initial feeling of shock. But he was much too slow. Amost as the lid flew open, Steve Williams realised what had happened. This must be the first box he had dug out, the one he had opened, and he remembered, now, that its clasp had not resealed tightly and, in the confusion of his return to the boat, he had forgotten that vital omission.

'I'm off out of this. I reckon the police will want to know about this little lot.' The boatman reached for his oars.

'Well, now, lovely—' Steve Williams' reflexes were faster and more deadly than those of his companion. He wiped his right hand on his shirt front and reached casually into his coat pocket.

'What in hell's name—?'

'You really ought not to have seen that.'

The sing-song, lilting Welsh voice held menacing overtones. Williams' hand withdrew from his pocket with something hard and black in its grasp.

'A gun! What's the game? Here—you wouldn't!'

The boatman came to his feet as he found himself looking down the obscene, black barrel of the Luger; snake-like, it hypnotised him, slowed his frantic tongue and held his wide-eyed gaze with a lethal fascination.

'I'm afraid I would.'

Steve Williams smiled gently, then, taking aim, he carefully shot the man through the heart. The man's eyes widened. The Welshman liked to watch their eyes; the old, sadistic thrill twisted in his belly and spurred his groin. With a quiet sigh his victim buckled to his knees, and died. An almost noiseless splash rippled the water as he spilled tiredly from his small boat into the contaminated waters of the Parrett. And there, under the dark lee of Steart Island, he sank to pastures green.

'So long, lovely.'

The killing was over in seconds. That was how Williams liked it, clean and easy, with the corpse disposed of with little fuss or bother. The smile stayed on his lips at the thought of another problem solved.

His alertness to danger was momentarily dulled by his appetite for a slaying and he did not realise, as quickly as he should have done, that the tumbling body had eased the dinghy from its berth in the mud and had given the craft sufficient impetus to free it from its tenuous anchorage. As the boat inched sideways, the raised end of the open money container slipped from the gunwale and landed with a splash to spill its contents before the slowly rising tide. Released from this extra weight, the dinghy jerked up, and gained momentum from the vectoring thrust of the falling box.

'Oh, God!'

The horrified Welshman saw the boat glide silently from him. He struggled violently to free himself, to try to reach the boat before it was too late, but the all-embracing mud held his weary legs in its adhesive clasp as they threshed and treadmilled, ever more slowly, to no avail.

'Oh, God!'

With a herculean effort he threw himself flat on the viscous surface. One leg came partly free, then sank again, as he writhed and twisted to release the other limb. Around him, in an ever-increasing circle, hundreds of banknotes spilled from the open container, to dot the mud and lapping tide, and as Steve Williams lunged this way and that, his wildly beating arms scattered the circle wider still. It was hopeless. As he sobbed into the evil-smelling gel, he saw the tiny craft tremble as its stern caught the main current of the channel. The dinghy began to spin, slowly at first, in a last, mocking gesture of farewell, and then it slipped away into the swirling mist, up river, towards Bridgwater.

The Welshman lay back, exhausted. He felt the slap of the first, tiny wavelet to reach him as it nudged into his cold, numb body. Wearily, he raised his head; the tide was still rising! How long before it turned, he wondered. He rubbed at the useless watch on his wrist with bleeding, mud-caked fingers as he tried to school his thoughts. He could not remember exactly what the fool had said about tide tables. Was high tide at four o'clock—or was it at five? He tried desperately to clear his mind. What if it were five o'clock? Then the creeping water must surely rise above his prison.

The thought of this calm, filthy liquid washing over him, blotting him out, frightened Steve Williams more than anything had done before in his life. The accursed mud had him fast in its grip; held him chest-high. He swore and he cried and he beat at the stuff with flailing arms. He could no longer move his legs, they were locked deep in an inexorable embrace. Slowly, ever so slowly, the water rose up his chest. Floating banknotes swilled around him, rolled on the tide and were swept away into mid-stream.

'Help! Help me!'

His scream echoed back at him from the wall of mist.

'He-lp! He-lp me!'

'Spang!' The staccato bark of the Luger pistol cracked as he jerked its trigger, and the sound rang out across the River Parrett in signal of his plight.

'Help! Please help!'

He was demented now. Very slowly the encroaching water circled his neck; reached for his upturned face.

'Spang—spang—spang!' The Luger barked

275

in rapid succession as he fired in futile rage at the mist, at the mud, and at the awful water. As if deciding to be merciful, the flooding water of the Bristol Channel surged a little, to slop its muddy suspension into the man's mouth, to block his nose, to fill his ears.

'Mam! Ahhh! God—Mam!'

It was Steve Williams' last, choking scream on earth, at a death he could not face. It was his ultimate cry for a help that could not be. One last retort echoed out over the deserted Burnham beach and rolled eerily on the blanketing fog.

NINE

Dan Pengelly and David Wallace had arranged a comprehensive schedule of surveillance to ensure that Steve Williams kept away from Steart Island and the fortune they had secreted on its northern extremity. They each had a tide-table and Wallace had drawn up a rota system so that one of them would always keep a close watch on Steart and its approaches during those hours around high water which allowed a landing on its treacherous banks. It was Pengelly's turn to keep watch, though because it was a period of low tides which only just reached the island's shores, prolonged surveillance was not necessary.

David Wallace's sleep, when it came, was fitful and so disturbed by wild dreams that often he finally found oblivion in a stupor of exhaustion. It was not his habit to drink at home but lately he found himself downing several whiskies at night which left him woolly headed on awakening. So it was on that Tuesday morning. He slept on, blissfully unware of his fellow Welshman's final act of savagery and of the drama that was to follow. Only later, when Dan Pengelly, white-faced with fury and trepidation, recounted the events of the morning which led to his rude awakening, did Wallace begin to realise just how tightly the mesh was being woven around them by Detective Inspector Cox.

*　　　*　　　*

By early morning the sea-mist of the previous day had almost cleared.

At the jetty end of the beach a number of people stood in small, inquisitive groups. Two police Panda cars, whose radios crackled to empty seats, rested imperiously on the double yellow, traffic-restricting lines of the Esplanade while a dark-blue police van was parked at an angle on the jetty itself, all of which indicated some considerable activity unusual for such an early hour.

The morning tide was half an hour from its

highest reach. At the extreme end of the jetty a knot of half a dozen men stood precariously close to the single, rusting, safety chain which separated them from deep water and an early grave. Urgent discussion seemed to be in hand and occasionally one of the men would point towards Steart Island on which their attention was apparently focused. They were obviously estimating the tide rip and the height of water in the narrow, dangerous channel; frequently they consulted their wrist-watches.

*   *   *

Dan Pengelly let himself out through his front door and quietly eased it shut behind him. Upstairs in the small, neat house, his wife and daughter were asleep and he smiled to himself as he thought of them. Soon they would get the best of everything that money could buy.

It was too early for many of his neighbours to be up and about, but one or two of the nearby houses had their bedroom curtains drawn back. He left the housing estate where he and his family lived, and walked along Berrow Road. At the edge of town he turned into Saint Andrew's churchyard, strolled past the ancient church, then stepped out on to Burnham's North Esplanade. He wore a wind-cheater over his long-sleeved pullover, since there was an autumnal chill in the air, but he felt comfortable and relaxed in the freshness of the morning. He had patrolled the beach and Esplanade the previous day, as arranged, for an hour around the time of high tide, but it had been a waste of time. A clammy, chill mist had covered Burnham like a blanket, but he knew from experience that even at its highest reach the tide had been too low to completely cover the mud which surrounded the shrouded island.

He crossed the road and rested his elbows on the metal railing which lined the Esplanade at that point. There were no boats out yet, so far as he could see; the island was too far away for him to be able to distinguish detail, but certainly no craft lay beached on its shore. The river was much too low as yet, anyway, for a crossing to be accomplished. He looked to his left, along the beach-bordered road and in the direction of the Queens Hotel. A cabin-like, sea-front shelter some twenty feet from where he stood, and the bulk of the squat pier-cum-amusement arcade further along the Esplanade, shielded the activity on the jetty from his view. Reassured, Pengelly sauntered along the wide pavement with its patchwork of chequered, high-tide release grilles. He felt good in the rays of a new sun as he strolled along the Esplanade.

'Christ!'

He stopped, frozen in mid-stride, as ahead of him he suddenly saw the police vehicles parked at the head of the jetty. His startled gaze traversed seawards and followed the horizontal line of the stone structure down to the river's edge where the tiny knot of men stood looking out to Steart.

'Oh, Christ!'

Wait, he thought, maybe it had nothing to do with the payroll containers. Some accident, possibly a drowning; there were a hundred and one reasons why the police should be on the jetty, but what the hell were they looking at so intently? He hurried on until he had an uninterrupted view. He stared out to sea to scan the island, then lowered his gaze and studied the half-submerged sand-banks which lay between island and mainland shore, but he could see nothing unusual. His eyes were not as keen as they used to be, but there was nothing to get alarmed about. Nothing moved out there and there were no small craft beached on Steart's rim.

Wait—what was that blob on the buttressing mud of the islet, close by the green-painted Steart Beacon marker post? Too small to be a man, it looked about the size of a seal. Dan Pengelly almost giggled with relief; that must be it, a seal, or some animal, stranded on the mud which surrounded Steart Island and they must be trying to save it, the fools. It would free itself at the height of the tide and swim to freedom of its own accord. This kind of thing happened once or twice a year; a seal, or a dog, or even a child would get itself stuck in the infamous Burnham mud and then get itself rescued. Such incidents usually made a front-page story for the local newspaper, the Burnham Gazette and Highbridge Express. He walked a few, short steps to where a gleaming white, sea-front telescope stood, and thumbed a coin into the smooth, concave slot of the machine before aligning the telescope's sight with the unknown object trapped out there in the slimy filth. The machine clicked. Gears whirred. The blank eyepiece cleared.

Magnified, grotesque, the legless torso of Steve Williams filled Pengelly's vision. His fingers whitened in their grip on the whining instrument as the crouching man stared with stunned disbelief at the grisly apparition. The carcass of the Welshman stood in an upright position, gripped to its chest by mud. Sightless eyes stared back from a face distorted with fear at the manner of its dying. Most of the lower jaw had been shot away in a last, desperate attempt to die quickly, an attempt which had failed, leaving the little Celt to die slowly and in agony. The telescope clicked briefly, then went blank. A shiver passed through Pengelly's spare frame as he slowly straightened himself to his full height.

'God! What a mess,' he breathed. 'What a bloody, pig-stinking mess!'

During the last few seconds of the instrument's function, Pengelly had seen one empty wages container lying on the glass-smooth mud alongside the body. Seen too, the second box which lay higher up Steart's shore. For a short time he lost control and cursed in a wild, blind rage at Steve Williams, at Steart, at the whole futile escapade.

'Here—are you all right?'

Pengelly spun on his heel at the sound of the voice. A man walking his dog had come up behind him and was eyeing him curiously.

'What? Oh, yes,' Pengelly snapped brusquely. 'Forget it!' He turned again, to stare at the unspeakable blob that had been Steve Williams. 'You bloody fool, Taff,' he whispered. 'You just had to try for it, didn't you? You bloody, bloody fool!'

As soon as the first, awful shock had passed, he began to realise the full import of the situation and he started to walk with ever-quickening footsteps in the direction of the South Esplanade. A rising wave of fear and apprehension knotted in his belly as he neared the head of the jetty, but he had to pass that way in order to reach his destination. As he approached the police cars he forced himself to slow his rapid stride to a normal pace; it would be natural in the circumstances to pause and gaze at the activity on the jetty, he thought, and since there were not too many sightseers gathered yet, any odd behaviour might attract the curiosity of the police.

'Panda Five. Panda Five. No helicopter assistance necessary. I say again, no helicopter assistance necessary.' The young constable seated in the first car addressed a whistling microphone. He looked up as Pengelly passed, but took no further interest in the new arrival.

Dan Pengelly slowed his step and paused just where the Esplanade opened on to the sloping jetty. He recognised some members of the group at the water's edge on the far end of the stone salient, there were several uniformed officers from Burnham police station and also one or two members of the local yacht club, talking to one of the local pilots.

'Good morning, Mr. Pengelly.'

The ex-army sergeant knew exactly who the owner of that voice was, even before he turned to meet the level gaze of Detective Inspector Cox.

'It is Mr. Pengelly? From Forsters, yes?'

'That's right, Inspector—'

'Sorry if I startled you, sir.' The policeman eyed Pengelly with mild concern and smiled in apology.

'No, not at all.' Pengelly cursed inwardly at his own hesitancy.

'Let me see, now. You are Mr. Wallace's senior foreman. Number—um, I seem to have forgotten what number Section that is.'

Around the two men the gathering of onlookers grew larger as new arrivals joined those already watching developments at the far end of the jetty. No one took any notice of

283

the two men who stood amongst the crowd, but Dan Pengelly felt isolated and lonely as his tormentor turned bland features to gaze out towards Steart Island.

'Number Eight Section. You've been to see us several times on the plant.'

'Ah, yes, I remember now. How forgetful of me. Section Eight, the one that uses ammonia.'

The Inspector did not speak again. He appeared to have forgotten the presence of his companion as he delved into his coat-pocket and produced a pipe and tobacco. Dan Pengelly stood awkwardly at the man's side. He almost blurted out a reminder to Cox that Section Eight was not the only section in the complex which used ammonia, and yet felt restrained from doing so; the time to make some rejoinder seemed, somehow, to have passed, but wouldn't it be natural to say something? God damn the man! Their conversation seemed to be at an end, yet the policeman made no move to leave. Instead he slowly filled the bowl of his pipe with curls of tobacco and pressed them down into the coke-encrusted implement with one grimy thumb. Pengelly felt compelled to speak. He wondered, frantically, whether he had behaved normally so far, then suddenly realised he should have made some enquiry about the police presence.

'What's going on?' he asked, as casually as

possible.

'Out there?' Cox nodded vaguely in the direction of Steart as he sucked noisily on the stained mouthpiece of his briar. He struck a second match and puffed at the smouldering weed without looking up. When he had completed the operation he raised his eyes to meet those of his victim. 'On Steart Island, Mr. Pengelly?'

The tall man turned his face away from the other's searching gaze. He looked at Steart and at the shapeless thing which stared back from its resting place near Steart Beacon. 'Yes,' he insisted with a mirthless grin. His voice wavered as he kept up the pretence but he managed to add: 'Your lads are out and about early this morning.'

'I suppose they are.'

Both men stood in silence and watched the men grouped at the extremity of the jetty. Each waited for the other to speak until at last the Inspector removed the pipe from his mouth and exhaled a cloud of smoke which expanded and rose in a bluish haze on the clean, morning air.

'Do you know what that is out there, sir?' the policeman asked. His badly-shaven, pock-marked face was devoid of expression.

'No.' Dan Pengelly bit his lip. Was his reply too quick? Too sharp? His mind worked furiously as he searched for the right answer. Was his reaction that of a normal person? He avoided meeting the other man's calculating stare but instead screwed up his eyes and made a pretence of deciphering the scene on Steart. 'Well—it looks like a body,' he said hesitantly. 'I heard someone in the crowd say it was a drowned man you were trying to reach.'

'It is a body, sir,' Cox said in the same conversational tone, 'but do you know whose body?'

Dan Pengelly felt his stomach muscles tighten as he suffered the sharp edge of inquisition. 'Me?' he queried with a forced laugh. 'Not me. How could I?' At that precise moment Pengelly realised that his inquisitor was testing him, playing with him, like a cat with claws as yet unsheathed. He also realised that he could never hope to match the Inspector in the thrust and parry of verbal exchange.

'It's the body of the Welshman, Steve Williams.'

'Who?' Pengelly stammered. He forced himself to meet Cox's eyes and could only hope that the mixture of astonishment and concern he displayed was realistic. 'Who did you say it is?'

'Your colleague, Steve Williams.'

'Steve—God! Is he dead?' The ex-sergeant was thankful that he could at last release some portion of his pent up emotion in a show of disbelief.

'With half a face and at least two hours submerged beneath a tide?' Detective Inspector Cox shrugged. 'Yes, he most certainly is dead.' He indicated a pair of binoculars perched on the back seat of one of the Panda cars. 'Want a look?'

Dan Pengelly knew that the man was scrutinising him closely, noting and analysing his every minute reaction to the skilled interrogation. Perspiration broke out freely across his chest and he felt it trickle down towards his waistband. Christ! How he wished he were out of this.

'You knew him quite well, I believe? Drinking companions and all that?' Cox said as he nodded in the direction of the corpse. The policeman puffed vigorously on his pipe several times and then, as if suddenly remembering his offer, he marched to the police car and retrieved the binoculars. 'Here,' he said as he held them out, 'you will also see what look extraordinarily like two of the payroll containers which were stolen during the raid on Forsters. It looks as if we are getting somewhere with that case at last, though I'm sorry another man had to die for it. When will people learn, Mr. Pengelly? When will they ever learn?'

'Inspector! Inspector Cox!'

A call from the jetty made the policeman cease the slow shake of his head with which he accompanied his remarks, and look up to greet the caller. One of the civilians, the Trinity House pilot from the group at the end of the jetty, scurried up the slope towards the two men and shouldered his way through the onlookers.

'Yes?'

Pengelly heaved an inward sigh of relief as the detective swivelled to meet the pilot.

'I'll be able to get my launch out in another half an hour. Would you want to come with us, sir?' The pilot looked doubtfully at the detective's scuffed shoes. 'I can probably find a pair of waders for you to use in the mud.'

'Thank you, yes.'

Detective Inspector Cox issued a few brief instructions to an attentive uniformed police sergeant who had joined the trio. Cox seemed oblivious to Dan Pengelly's presence; it was as if he had completely forgotten their conversation of a few moments past and he still clutched the binoculars to him as he turned away without a glance in the other's direction.

'Come on, lads,' the police sergeant bellowed to the group at the end of the jetty, then he followed the Inspector who clambered into one of the police cars.

Dan Pengelly stood still, awkwardly uncertain whether to leave or to remain where the abruptly-ended verbal intercourse had left him stranded. He felt people push past him through the gathering crowd as the policemen made their way towards the little two-coloured Panda cars. Car doors slammed as the vehicles pulled into tight U-turns across the road before they raced along the South Esplanade to head for the River Brue, a tributary of the Parrett, where the pilot's launch lay at anchor.

'Excuse me.'

Pengelly shouldered a path through the rapidly-increasing throng of sightseers. With worried, quick footsteps he half-walked, half-ran along the route the cars had taken, until he reached the house with the large, bay windows.

*   *   *

David Wallace balanced precariously on the wall of the old boating lake on Burnham's beach, a wall which was somehow high as a cliff and the stones of which crumbled to dust beneath his feet as he treadmilled to retain his position. He looked down on the rushing tide race of the River Parrett, far below, and saw the colour of its murky waters turn a venous red. Wave after wave of floating bank notes swept past him, while anglers seated on the wall laughed amongst themselves as they reeled in note after note of money that was his. He scrabbled along the wall and screamed soundlessly at each man who unhooked pound notes from his line, and each of the multitude of fishermen who ignored his pleas had the face of Steve Williams.

Wallace awoke from his nightmare to the persistent ringing of his front door bell. He was drenched with perspiration and it took some moments for him to come to his senses, while all the time that damned bell called and called. He had taken two Mogadon tablets during the night to make him sleep, and although they had done the trick, they also left him feeling slightly unreal as he rolled from his bed and grunted himself awake.

'I'm coming, for God's sake, I'm coming,' he grumbled as he stumbled towards the door of his first-floor rooms. He was halfway there when he caught sight of the tall, urgent figure outlined through the distorting scales of the frosted glass panels of the door, and he paused and leaned weakly against the wall at his side, for it was Dan Pengelly who thumbed the door bell with such impatience! Wallace felt a sickness born of panic rise in his gut.

'Dave! Dave! Come on, man, open the bloody door!' Pengelly cried.

David Wallace could see the tall man's lips moving as he pressed his face close against the glass in an effort to see inside. He realised that the caller must already have detected some movement through the shadowy panes. 'Wait! Wait!' he shouted as he fumbled with the lock. He had the door partly open when it was flung back in his face as Dan Pengelly surged through.

'It's Steve—the bastard! He's really done it this time!' There was no mistaking the look of fear on the face of the newcomer.

'My God, what is it? What's happened?'

'Look at the island! Take a look at Steart! The game's up, Dave, it's all over!'

As the tall man leapt over the threshold he clutched the startled Wallace's arm and his voice cracked as he literally trembled with rage.

'Shut up! People can hear you.' David Wallace shook off the grasping hand and slammed the door shut.

'But, you don't understand—'

'Not here,' Wallace cautioned with a finger to his lips. 'Come through to the lounge. We won't be overheard there.' His voice demanded discipline though his stomach heaved with apprehension as he followed his visitor into the main room of the apartment.

'Now then, tell me what's happened.'

Pengelly seemed to steady himself. He began to recount the avalanche of disaster which had overwhelmed him in such a short space of time that morning, and when he had done so, Wallace knew that even the strongest of men might have given way temporarily under such pressure.

'It's Steve! The bloody, crazy fool! He must have gone out after the payroll yesterday in the fog.' Pengelly strode to the front window of the lounge and swept back the curtains.

'Look for yourself. What's left of him is stuck out there in the mud.'

Bright, morning sunlight flooded the room, causing Wallace to wince and raise one hand to shield his bleary eyes. He hitched his pyjamas together and followed his companion to the window, but he was totally unprepared for the scene which greeted him. To his right, a large crowd of people clustered around the head of the jetty and scattered groups of sightseers strung out down the beach to the water's edge. A police car rushed along the road beneath his window and the sound of a siren moaned its clarion call as an ambulance cruised on to the Esplanade from Pier Street.

'All these people!' Wallace whispered in dismay.

'I know. It's like carnival night down there.'

'Where is he?'

Dan Pengelly stabbed a forefinger towards Steart Island. 'There! Look just to the right of Steart Beacon. Can you see that lump sticking out of the mud? Yes? Well, that's Steve.'

Wallace followed the line of the tall man's finger with his eyes until they reached the thing that lay bloating in the morning sun. He reached for the telescope which stood permanently on its tripod in the bay window, and swung it into focus. For several long minutes he stared at the transfixed caricature of Steve Williams.

'Is that—is that Steve?' he finally asked,

unable to tear his gaze from the eyepiece, yet unwilling to believe the horrific truth.

'Yes,' Dan rasped, 'and can you see the two cash-boxes alongside him? That's as far as he got with them.'

'But how on earth did he get out to the island?' Wallace scanned the shore-line. 'I can't see a boat of any kind.'

'God knows, Dave.'

'Did you check the beach at high-tide yesterday?'

'Of course I did!' The tall man's voice rose in indignation and he slammed a fist into the palm of his hand in emphasis. 'Yesterday's tide was too low for anyone to cross to the island, but even so, I went out in the mist for the hour around top of the tide. There was no sign of life on the water that I could see, and the tide was so low that it didn't cover the mud on the Burnham shore. A landing on Steart Island would have been impossible.'

The Welshman stood back, aghast, and released his hold on the telescope. 'Then that's what happened,' he said. He nodded towards Steart Island. 'He went when it was impossible.'

'Oh, Christ!'

The words were not blasphemous this time, but merely a forlorn cry of despair. Then the room was filled with the sound of wild, obscene curses as Dan Pengelly gave vent to his feelings and railed incoherently against their lot. When at last he quietened the two men stared at each other in open dismay.

'Should we run for it?'

'Wait a minute, now,' Wallace said. He sat on the nearest chair and forced himself to speak calmly. He wanted time to collect his scattered thoughts. 'This needn't involve us. Steve being found with the cash-boxes doesn't implicate us. The police can have no proof that we took part in the robbery,' he reasoned hopefully, 'so why should they suspect us any more than any other employee of Forsters?'

Even as he argued his case he remembered those conversations at the plant he had had with Cox, and the endless, seemingly trivial questions the policeman had asked about those who worked on Section Eight and about the technicalities of handling ammonia in bulk. Above all he remembered the extreme incisiveness of the man, and he felt a cold chill of doubt sweep through him at the memory.

Dan told him, then, how the events of the morning culminated in his meeting with the detective at the head of the jetty and of the probing interrogation to which he had been subjected.

Wallace froze and he felt his scalp creep in a warning signal to his whirling senses. 'Did he see you come here?' He knew that the voice that shouted the question was his own. 'Did Cox see you come to this house?'

'I don't think anyone was watching me,'

Dan Pengelly stuttered. 'They all went off in the police cars, but I just don't know with that bastard of a detective.' He spread his hands wide in a gesture which meant that anything was possible.

The sudden, shrill jangle of the telephone bell made both men jump. The instrument stood on the sill of the bay window and Wallace walked to it and lifted the receiver with quick, adrenalin-promoted movements before giving himself time to think.

'Hello?'

'Good morning, sir. It's a nice morning.'

The Welshman stared at the mouthpiece. 'Who is that?'

'I'm sorry, Mr. Wallace. That's one of my failings, you know, I often forget the formalities when I'm dealing with members of the public. It'll get me into trouble one of these days. This is Cox; Detective Inspector Cox of the Bristol Criminal Investigation Department, to give you my full title. I must have one of those boards made, like you managers have on your office doors in Forsters, with my name and rank on it. But then, I couldn't add any letters after my name like you more educated gentlemen can. I'm not clever enough for that, sir.'

The voice broke off with a chuckle but the sound reproduction was loud enough for Dan Pengelly to overhear what was said. As David Wallace stood there, barefoot and pyjama-clad, he felt weak and vulnerable.

'What do you want?'

'Sorry to call you so early, Mr. Wallace. I suppose I woke you?'

'Well, yes. You did, actually—' His mind was still befuddled with drug-induced sleep and by his sudden, rude awakening and so the Welshman did not see the trap until it was too late.

'I suppose Mr. Pengelly has already told you the bad news?'

'Bad news?'

Immediately, Wallace knew that was the wrong reaction. Within the space of a few sentences the policeman had trapped him into lying on two counts. Cox knew he was awake before telephoning, and Cox was also aware that Dan Pengelly was with him in his apartment and would obviously have told him of Steve Williams' demise.

'Yes, sir. Come along! About the death of Mr. Williams? Surely you are aware of all that's going on outside your window?'

David Wallace knew without doubt, then, that he and his companion were being watched. He clutched the telephone to his chest and turned to look through the bay window to his right, along the South Esplanade. He spotted the man at once, which was not difficult since the uniformed police constable made no attempt to conceal himself but stood in full view, quite brazenly, on the roof of the Queens Hotel. Wallace could see that he held something to his eyes before the morning sunlight glinted on the glass of binoculars. The Queens Hotel was a large Victorian structure which sat further along the Esplanade but on the same side of the road as the house which contained Wallace's apartment. From his vantage point on the roof the constable could see directly into the apartment and must have been watching for some time, ever since Pengelly yanked the curtains open. Wallace thought he could see the man's lips move but it took a few more seconds for him to realise that the Peeping Tom was relaying his observations by means of his two-way radio to some unseen person, and that unseen person must be none other than the caller who taunted him on the telephone.

'Are you still there, sir?'

David Wallace knew that he must now contradict his initial answers and he also knew, with ice-cold certainty, that the man on the other end of the telephone must be sure of his prey. He motioned Dan Pengelly away from the window, but was himself forced to remain at the end of the wire like a dog on a leash. He turned his back to the spy on the roof and forced himself to speak into the mouthpiece.

'Yes, I'm still here.'

'Ah.'

'What is it you want with me?'

'I was asking if you had heard the bad news, about the accident?' There it was again, the polite, deadpan question, 'About the accident?' but volunteering no details. Deadly in the extreme, and forcing hesitancy where an innocent man might talk freely.

'Yes, yes, of course—you mean about Steve. I'm sorry if I'm a little slow. It's the shock, you see, and Dan Pengelly has only this moment told me.'

'Of course, Mr. Wallace. It's a bad business all round.' The abrasive, disembodied voice which reached out from the plastic earpiece was capable of tearing guilty nerves to shreds.

'And then there's Myers.'

'Myers?'

The Welshman held his breath expectantly. Ever since he and the veterans had recovered the three boxes from the Feeder, every single day since the police had taken Ian Myers, he had waited for some news of his capture. Cox must now be about to close the trap by divulging the diver's confession.

'I'm somewhat concerned. You see, he's been reported as a missing person.

'Missing—?'

'Have you any idea of his whereabouts, Mr. Wallace?'

Like a replay of an old, silent movie, pictures of their flight from Feeder Number One flickered through Wallace's mind. Steve

Williams had insisted on locking the service-gate and had even gone back to do so, despite alleged discovery and chase! He stared into Pengelly's eyes in incredulous horror.

'Oh, my God!'

'Sorry, sir?'

The Inspector's voice sounded a requiem for Myers. The police did not have him. He must yet lie in that lonely, awful pond.

Without quite knowing how, Wallace managed in some fashion to stumble through the remainder of the conversation, all the while having to parry the exquisitely-laid verbal snares of the detective. As he replaced the telephone on its cradle he caught a glimpse of the uniformed constable out of the corner of his eye, as the man turned and disappeared down behind the leading parapet of the roof of the hotel.

'What do you reckon, Dave?'

Wallace looked at his companion. 'You were right,' he whispered brokenly. 'He has done for us. Why in hell doesn't he come and get it over with?'

'I told you!' He grabbed Wallace's arm and pulled him away from the window. 'But we can still make a run for it. Let's grab the rest of the money and get out while we can.'

'What about your family?' Despair left Wallace weak. Tragedy was about to disrupt the lives of innocents once again.

'We'll get abroad, Dave. I know some great

places in the sun where no one will ever find us, and I can send for the girls later. They'll be all right until you and I are settled. Come on, now, we must move!'

David Wallace scrambled into the clothes that his companion threw at him; as if in a dream he could hear Pengelly's voice urging him on. His car was locked in the garage at the side of the house and the drive from the garage opened directly on to the sea-front road.

'We can't use the Avenger, Dan. If we try to drive out on to the Esplanade we would just run straight into their arms.

'Then we'll make it on foot,' Pengelly decided. 'Over the back wall and away through the houses to the Catholic Church. We can cut down Oxford Street, pick up my car and then drive along the beach to the Low Light.'

When Wallace was dressed he hurriedly rifled his bureau for what valuables and cash he could scramble together. As he pocketed his passport he took a last look around the apartment, then followed Dan Pengelly down the stairway and out into the garden at the rear of the house. He guessed that Mrs. Warren would be watching all the happenings on the Esplanade from her front window and so would not see them leave. The house had no access road to the rear and they were forced to scramble over the wall of the garden to reach Steart Drive, but they managed it without being spotted by any of the inhabitants of the surrounding bungalows. Steart Drive was a road which led off at right angles from the Esplanade and so took them directly away from the hideous climax being enacted on the foreshore.

'I can't keep this up,' the Welshman gasped and he slowed his run to a walk. They had run as fast as they could across the gardens and then along the back-road, but he was not fit enough to run any distance and his leg muscles trembled from their unaccustomed use. 'You'll have to go on without me and I'll catch up with you.'

'We stick together,' Dan Pengelly insisted. He kept looking over his shoulder for signs of pursuit. 'We'll walk for a while until you get your breath back, then you can try to run again.'

They left Steart Drive and walked quickly along Steart Avenue, travelling all the time towards the east side of town and away from the beach. They had to cross a hundred yards or so of rough ground in order to reach the circular-shaped Catholic church, but at least they were moving further away from the police activity with each step.

When they reached the rear of the church, David Wallace stopped in his tracks and raised his eyes heavenwards, as if in search of an explanation.

'Keep moving, Dave,' his companion

pleaded. 'You can rest when we get to my car.'

'Ian is dead, Dan.'

'What?'

'The police don't have him. Steve lied about that.'

'Then where is he?'

'Something must have gone wrong when he made his dive that night. Horribly wrong.'

'But Ian —?'

'The Feeder, Dan. He must be in the Feeder.'

The circular bulk of the Church of Our Lady and the English Martyrs towered above their heads as Dan Pengelly clenched his fists in frustrated rage. 'God curse you to hell, Steve!' he roared insanely.

They ran, then, from that place and panted their way through the back roads of town until they reached Pengelly's house. He ran straight to his garage door, unlocked it, and swung it up. 'There's a spade in the back of the garage,' he instructed. 'You find it and put it in the car. I'll be with you in a couple of minutes,' and with that he pushed his way between the car and the wall of the garage and disappeared through an internal door into the house.

David Wallace delved amongst a pile of accumulated junk at the rear of the garage until he found the spade, and also a garden fork. He hardly had time to stow them on the back seat of the Jaguar when the door at the rear of the garage burst open and Pengelly reappeared. His face was thunderous and he looked more distraught then ever as, without saying a word, he leapt into the driving seat, jerked the engine into life and accelerated out of the garage and on to the road.

Wallace did not know what the veteran had said to his wife by way of explanation, or whether he had managed to explain anything in such a short space of time, but as they roared down the short drive he caught a glimpse of a pale, frightened face as the curtains over one of the bedroom windows parted briefly.

'Are they all right, Dan?' Wallace asked softly.

'No, they are not all right. How could they be?' The voice that answered sounded lost and forlorn.

He drove fast and hard, on to Berrow Road, then off it again to swing into Maddocks Slade. This was a short stretch of road which passed several houses before disgorging itself down a ramp and on to the beach. The driver channelled the Jaguar out on to the surface of the sand and the tyres crunched over bunches of dried seaweed and piled jetsam until they reached the clear beach. They paused briefly, and to their left, some two miles distant, could see the pilot's launch nosing its way across the mouth of the River Parrett.

'There they go,' Wallace said as he pointed towards the launch. 'Let's hope Cox is on

303

board. It'll take them an hour or more to reach Steart Island and return. They'll have the mud to contend with; today's tides are still not high enough to cover it.'

'Let's hope the damned boat sinks and takes that bastard to the bottom with it,' Pengelly snapped.

Wallace caught a glimpse of his companion's face in the rear view mirror as he spoke, and he saw that Pengelly's eyes were staring and his face was drawn into a feral snarl. Then Wallace saw his own features reflected in facsimile. They turned right and drove in a tail-wagging sprint to the north where the stilted lighthouse beckoned, half a mile away. The white-painted body of the Low Light gleamed as it reflected the rising sun, and Pengelly drove swiftly along the strip of virgin sand until they reached the wooden structure.

'Thank God the tide is right for us!'

Wallace nodded. The tides at present were so low that the incoming sea was still some fifteen yards from the base of the nine-legged lighthouse. 'Park on the far side, Dan,' he suggested, 'then we'll be hidden from sight of the town. You are right about the tide, the water won't reach us; we have plenty of time to dig the box out and be long gone.'

Pengelly swung the car in a tight circle around the Low Light and they slithered to a halt at the foot of the flight of wooden steps that climbed the inland side of the structure. They grabbed the spade and the fork and fell from their seats in their eagerness to recover the remainder of the payroll and flee.

'Keep an eye open for trouble,' Dan Pengelly warned, 'though it looks as if we've given them the slip. They seem to be more interested in what's left of Steve at the moment; they probably think we are still trapped in your apartment, waiting to be picked up.' He plunged the spade deep into wet sand. 'In that case they've got a surprise coming, eh?'

Through the great timber legs of the forty-foot high lighthouse, the two could see that the pilot's boat had almost reached Steart Beacon, but appeared to be having some difficulty in achieving a landing. Although it was a long way from them, they could also see that the jetty and its immediate surrounds were the centre of attention of a large crowd of sightseers. The north end of the beach was deserted, and two men digging, apparently for bait, in the worm-cast strewn sand was not an unusual sight. Steel flashed in the sunlight as they dug great chunks of hard, wet sand from the spot where they had secreted the container, alongside the concrete raft on which the Low Light stood.

'The damn thing is deeper than we buried it,' Dan Pengelly cursed. 'It's sunk through the mud.'

They had dug down past the top layer of clean sand and were now delving in a shifting mixture of sand and black, sticky mud. The Welshman stood back to catch his breath. He was unused to such muscle-searing work and that, combined with the frantic mental and physical exertions of the morning, was beginning to take its toll.

'You keep watch, then, Dave. Leave the digging to me.' Dan Pengelly continued to swing the spade with unabated vigour, though the bottom of the hole had now become filled with liquid mud which seemed to regenerate itself almost as fast as he removed it.

Wallace glanced quickly along the line of sand-dunes which lined the beach at that point, but could see no sign of life.

'Where will we make for, Dan?'

'Bristol!' Pengelly swung the spade with easy movements, though he had become a little breathless. 'There'll be plenty of ships out of Bristol or Avonmouth. With a hundred thousand quid we shouldn't meet much trouble coaxing some skipper to smuggle us out of the country.'

Wallace peered into the quagmire in the hole. 'Jesus! You don't think it could have sunk out of reach, do you?' he queried anxiously.

At that moment the blade of the spade struck something hard beneath the liquid surface.

'Got it!'

They both dropped to their knees and began to scoop the morass from the hole with cupped hands. They scraped away feverishly until at last they managed to uncover part of the payroll container.

'One end of it has sunk lower than the other. It's almost standing on end.'

They leaned into the hole and clawed for one of the metal handles, then together they dragged the heavy container from its impromptu hiding place and laid it on the beach.

'That's the first step on the road to a life of plenty,' Dan Pengelly said triumphantly. 'Now to load up.'

And then Wallace saw him! He had just straightened up from the task of lifting the payroll box when, out of the corner of one eye, he caught sight of a dark figure perched on the balcony at the top of the hundred-foot-tall High Light. From his position at the foot of the Low Light, Wallace could see the top half of the white, tower-like, inland lighthouse, neatly framed in a gap in the sand dunes through which an arrow-straight path passed from the beach. The figure on the balcony stood out in stark relief against the white face of the High Light, and the red-coloured stripe painted down the full length of that structure seemed to point like some giant indicator to the lone man on the balcony. A thrill of horror shook Wallace as he realised that from his vantage point at the summit of the High Light, the watching man could also see them with equal clarity, framed in the same gap in the dunes like two marionettes who danced on a stage.

'What is it, Dave?' Dan Pengelly cried as he suddenly became aware of the other's immobility. He spun on his heel and screwed up his eyes, as if in pain, as he tried to identify the focus of his companion's attention.

Wallace flung an outstretched arm in the direction of the dark figure, half a mile distant. 'Look at the High Light!' he screamed. 'There! On the balcony—it's that detective. It's Cox!'

Even at that distance there was no mistaking the identity of the dark-suited figure who stood in his eyrie and watched their every move. The veteran raised one fist and shook it at their tormentor. It was a futile gesture, a primeval display of hatred by the hunted for the hunter.

'Damn your black soul!' Dan Pengelly cursed, and foul, terrible blasphemies poured from his lips in a torrent of abuse for the man who stalked them. As the veteran turned to Wallace his eyes rolled like those of a wild stallion. 'Quick! Into the car,' he cried, and he leapt for the payroll container and lifted it bodily from the wet sand.

'It's no use,' David Wallace yelled, and even

as he spoke, the ominous, sleek shape of a police patrol car slid on to the beach from the jetty and headed towards them. Then another police car with siren wailing hurtled off the slipway from Maddocks Slade.

'Christ!'

Pengelly dropped the metal box at his feet and ran for the open door of the Jaguar. 'Dave! Dave! Come on,' he called as he dived inside and gunned the engine into life.

The big Welshman stood as though transfixed. The shrill blast of a whistle sounded in signal, and instantaneously a line of several dozen walking, uniformed policemen broke cover to appear over the sand dunes in a wide, disjointed yet encircling line which closed inexorably on the Low Light. Wallace could only stare numbly into the fear-crazed eyes of Dan Pengelly. The man seemed to be saying something, words of exhortation mingled with curses, but Wallace could not hear him clearly and he could not distinguish appeal from curse.

'It's no good, Dan!' It seemed to Wallace that some other person shouted but used his throat and voice to utter the bitter exclamation. 'It's hopeless!' he screamed, but his words were drowned by the roar of the Jaguar's engine as Pengelly ripped at the gear lever. Wallace's shoulders slumped in a gesture of submission. They were trapped. Trapped against the encroaching tide.

'Go to hell, then!'

A snarl of defiance burst from the veteran's lips and he spun the car beneath him in a tight, wheel-spinning curve. Twin sprays of flying sand spewed from the rear of the vehicle as the thrust of its threshing engine was suddenly transmitted to protesting tyres and the Jaguar seemed almost to take off as it accelerated over the hard, compact sand and gathered speed to head north, away from the pursuing police cars and along the seven-mile strip of sand that stretched from the town to Brean Down.

Suddenly, suspended in that indeterminate division between beach and sky, fully two miles distant, two pin points of blue, speckling light appeared which grew rapidly in size like exploding nebulae. At first distorted in a wavering haze of rising heat, the points of light continued to grow until their twinkling, star-like appearance dissolved into an urgent, harmonic blink. More police cars! They had run along the coast-road until they reached Brean, and there lanced out on to the beach before turning back towards Burnham, to complete the trap. The onrushing patrol cars grew in size and took shape as they raced, pack like, towards the victim at bay.

The tail lights of the Jaguar reddened briefly as Pengelly saw the danger and braked so savagely that his car jack-knifed from side to side as it slewed to a halt. The Jaguar turned in its tracks, hesitated for a moment, then sped back the way it had come, towards the Low Light and the line of walking policemen. As the car thundered down on them it became obvious that Dan Pengelly was driving, like a madman, straight for the uniformed figures, and the thin line broke in confusion as men flung themselves from its path.

'Stop, Dan, for God's sake stop!' Wallace heard himself shout, and his heart seemed to stop beating as those vulnerable bodies scattered and ran for cover. He could only watch in horror as one man, slower than his colleagues, slipped and fell sprawling on the jetsam which lined the high-water mark, and a single, piercing yell rent the air as the offside wheels of the heavy automobile rolled over the man's pelvis.

Along this section of the beach a row of oddly-shaped concrete blocks lay partly buried in the sand. The blocks had once been part of the country's coastal defences during the war years and had later been set where they now lay in an attempt to stabilise shifting sands. Now they jutted from the surface of the beach like gigantic broken teeth.

Pengelly did not see the blocks until it was too late, and his tall figure bowed over in his seat as he heaved on the handbrake in a frantic effort to regain control. The roaring Jaguar struck one of the projections embedded at an angle so that it stuck out like a ramp from the surface. Wallace saw Dan Pengelly's face clearly through the windscreen, saw too that the driver still mouthed obscenities of rage as he lost his grip on the spinning steering wheel. The car leapt into the air, fully a man's height clear of the beach, then lunged forwards as if to attack the leading police car which had raced up from the town. The crash of tortured metal echoed out over the incoming tide as the Jaguar ripped away one side of the patrol car as if it were a toy from which blue-clad rag dolls were flung. Then, as the car writhed a path over the hard sand, like some badly wounded creature, it tilted on to its nose and balanced there for a moment as if performing one last trick for the approbation of the onlookers. It fell on to its back with a sickening crunch, crushing the driver into his seat as the roof collapsed. A flicker of flame ran the length of the overturned vehicle; the muffled 'whump' of a vapour explosion rent the air.

Pengelly did not lose consciousness immediately. Wallace saw him move! Saw his eyes open in a face and body which were compressed to one-fifth his normal size, and the eyes that blinked at Wallace, blinked from the features of an upturned dwarf. The man still clung to life as he sucked air past shattered teeth, and one last mad grimace of total agony swept the caricature of Dan

Pengelly as his raw nerve-endings fried in a wash of burning petrol. A merciful surge of fire engulfed him. Black smoke rose into the fresh morning sky to mark the funeral pyre of the passing man.

The dark-suited figure of Detective Inspector Cox left his refuge in the high, grass-topped sand-dunes beyond the flaming car, and walked slowly across the beach towards the Low Light. About him, as he walked, men screamed and shouted, all was chaos, but the detective continued to walk purposefully through the milling throng towards the spot where Wallace stood.

The Welshman could not move. He averted his eyes from the flames and from the horror of the roasting man. The stench of incinerating flesh filled the air as he stared at the last of the payroll containers which lay unopened at his feet. He felt a sudden tiredness sweep over him so that he could hardly stand, and as his legs gave way he sank, exhausted, to his knees. Slowly he lifted his head to meet the expressionless gaze of the approaching policeman.

Detective Inspector Cox stopped some ten feet from the kneeling man, and looked about him at the carnage. Then he turned back to Wallace, and spoke softly.

'Was it worth all this?'

Wallace thought of Dan Pengelly, whose body still burned, of Ian Myers who lay in dark waters, and of Steve Williams whose remains were even at that moment being eased from the relentless mud. He thought of the innocents who had suffered. Wraiths of smoke wafted between him and the waiting detective.

There was nothing he could say.